FALSE
FLAG

RACHEL CHURCHER

To Chris + Cordelia,
Time to be strong...

False Flag (Battle Ground #2)

First published by Taller Books, 2019

Text copyright © Rachel Churcher 2019

ISBN 9781088467046

Cover design by Medina Karic:
www.fiverr.com/milandra

WWW.TALLERBOOKS.COM

Notes

Leominster is a town in Herefordshire, UK. It is pronounced 'Lem-ster'.

KETTY

AUGUST

Prologue

Trapped. Cornered. And all I can feel is the pain. The bullet against my knee.

I crawl between the trees, into the darkness, fighting to get away from the voices on the path.

Survive, Ketty. Live through this. Get out of sight, and away from the guns. Away from the tiny fighters.

I crawl, clenching my teeth against the pain, while the children behind me argue about putting a bullet in my back.

Discipline, determination, backbone. Keep quiet, and keep moving.

Let them go. Protect yourself.

Get through this.

KETTY

JUNE

(TWO MONTHS EARLIER)

Newbies

They've been marching for days, these kids. They're scruffy and smelly and dirty. No one's taught them how to march, and they look as if they've never taken a shower or seen a washing machine. Would it kill them to use soap? Or a hairbrush?

They file into the camp, dead on their feet. Have they done any exercise in their lives? The newbies usually look exhausted, but these are beyond that. They're a disgrace.

Commander Bracken sent Jackson and Miller to meet them, and parade them in along the bypass. If it had been up to me, I'd have hidden them away and brought them in the back way, along the lanes. But it's not up to me, and here we are. I'm sure the good citizens of Leominster feel much safer, now that they've seen the urchins who are supposed to be protecting them.

There are some posh kids in this group, from some expensive boarding school up north. Kids with expectations that the world will be kind to them, and bow to their needs. It will be a pleasure to teach them the truth.

Jackson leaves the new arrivals with the camp staff and walks back to the Senior Dorm. He finds me at my table next to the window, finishing the commander's paperwork for this evening. He sits down opposite me.

"Did you see that?"

I sit back in my chair, arms folded. "I did. You two just marched that crowd of grubby civilian children past all the cars on the bypass. Feeling proud, are you?"

He ignores my grin.

"They're going to be tough to train, these kids. They didn't sign up. They don't know what's coming."

"Neither do the volunteers."

"No, but these recruits are soft. They don't want to be here. It's going to be hard, getting them up to fighting standard. Bracken isn't going to cut us any slack. We're the ones who'll need to put the pressure on, and we're the ones who'll get the blame when the kids can't handle the training."

He's right. I can mock them, and I can entertain myself with their incompetence, but I'm the one who needs to impress the commander. I need them to shape up fast, or it's my promotion that goes to someone else.

"No mercy, then. Whatever it takes to get them trained and ready, we do. Right?"

"Right", says Jackson, a wicked grin creeping across his face. "I won't report you, if you don't report me. Iron fists and steel toe caps. Deal?"

"Deal." Sounds good to me.

*****

After dinner, we head to the new recruits' dorm, and hang around outside the dining room. The camp staff are setting up their uniform distribution tables, and Commander Bracken is giving his usual speech. Jackson and I can do it by heart.

"Things I do not wish to see: dirty uniforms; torn uniforms; damaged uniforms; disrespected uniforms!"

We keep our voices down, sing-songing along with him, and watching the recruits we can see from the corridor.

They are pitiful. They are struggling to even stay awake. One hot meal and they think it's time for bed. Are they expecting a cup of warm milk and a bedtime story?

And then it happens. One of the recruits falls asleep at his table. We're watching from the corridor, and it is delicious. He's tiny, this kid. Hair all over the place, scuffed shoes, dangling shoelaces. His head drops, and he actually starts snoring! Snoring, while the commander is talking.

Jackson and I are smothering our laughter, making sure we're not overheard. We should walk away, but we're not missing this for anything.

Commander Bracken stops his speech, and looks at Assistant Woods. There's the flicker of a smile on Woods' face, and he walks over to the sleeping recruit and crashes his clipboard down on the table. I think the recruit is going to hit the ceiling. He wakes up in a hurry, and gets a fearsome earful from Woods.

I'm biting my knuckles so as not to make a noise, but this is the best entertainment we've had in weeks. Jackson is actually doubled over, gasping for breath, and now I'm laughing at both of them.

The commander picks up his speech again. The sleeping kid is shaking, and the others have a new look of terror on their faces. Good. They're going to need that.

The commander is reaching the end of his speech, and the kids are going to start leaving with their uniforms. We need to get out of the corridor.

As we're walking away, the commander addresses the sleeping kid.

"Saunders!"

"Sir!"

"You will stand where you are until the other recruits have their uniforms. When the last of your colleagues has left, then you may collect your uniform."

Jackson and I look at each other.

"So Saunders is the new whipping boy?"

He nods. "Saunders is the new whipping boy. Let's see how long it takes to put him in the hospital, as an example to the others."

I smile. "I'm going to enjoy this."

*****

When we arrived at camp, we all wanted to be here. We were fit, we were clean, we were eager to get started. We were fighters, and we wanted to be trained. We wanted to get better.

I signed up as soon as they'd let me. It was a ticket out of a dead-end job, and a ticket out of home as well. At the camp, life was simple. Do as you're told, keep fit, don't let them see you breaking the rules – and things would go well for you. You could earn promotions, special treatment, new opportunities. Screw up, get lazy, do something stupid, and expect punishment.

Justice.

It made a change from being punished because your Dad was drunk, or because he'd gambled away the housekeeping money. It made a change from apology gifts that he couldn't afford, and the anger that followed. At camp, there would always be enough food. Clothes to wear. Enough hot water in the pipes. And protection from the fists and boots of the person who was supposed to be your protector.

I have no idea what he's doing now. He's probably been evicted from the house. Without the income I kept hidden, he won't have been paying the rent. Too bad. You need discipline and determination and backbone to get anywhere in life, and he had none of those things. If he's on the street, he deserves it.

And I'm here. I'm doing fine without him. I'm going to get my promotion, and I'm getting out of here, too. If training these disastrous recruits is the price, bring it on. I'm ready.

Disappointment

This is going to be harder than we imagined.

These kids are hopeless. Miller took them out for a run, and they've come back looking like the last people left alive after some terrible disaster. They're still standing, but their eyes are begging for the chance to rest and cuddle a blankie. It's the morning run! They need to do this every day. They have no idea what the weeks ahead have in store for them.

Day one, and they're already getting their hands on the guns. Command must be desperate. And I'm the one who gets to introduce them to weapons they are nowhere near being able to use.

Miller lines them up, and leaves me to run their first training session. I walk out in front of them, holding up the gorgeous rifle. There's no way they should be touching these yet, but here we are.

"Can anyone tell me what this is?"

Absolute silence.

"Come on. Anybody."

No one says a word. They're all trying to look invisible. Standing up straight and fading into the group. I look them over.

And there he is. Saunders, the whipping boy. In the front row, begging the universe to make me look the other way. He's out of luck.

"Saunders! Mr Sleepy himself. Can you tell me what this is?"

"A gun, Sir." His voice is shaking, and it's practically a whisper. Some people make such easy targets.

"Louder, Saunders!"

There's a pause, while he takes a deep breath. "A gun, Sir!"

"Thank you, Saunders." That's confused him. He's braced for more, but I turn away to address the group. Keep him guessing what's coming next.

"This is a gun. But this is not any gun. This is a prototype next-gen power-assisted rifle, firing armour-piercing bullets."

And you don't deserve to be playing with it.

"Under normal conditions, you lot wouldn't get to see one of these until you'd been training for years, if ever. You'd have to pass tests, and show that you're big enough to use one of these. But these aren't normal circumstances. This is war, and this is war on our home territory, and the decision makers have decided to let you worms loose with their favourite toys."

Several of the recruits wince at being called worms. At least they're listening.

"You'll be starting off with training bullets. We'll see how good you are, and whether you deserve to progress to armour-piercing rounds. Don't be fooled – training bullets will still kill you, so don't be stupid."

And don't get in my way.

"Make no mistake. You are getting your paws on these because the government wants to see them in use. The people in charge, they want you out there, waving these around to show Joe Public that we're protecting him."

And lucky me – I'm the one who has to train you to impress Joe Public.

"This isn't about you. This is about public confidence. About stopping panic and protecting people from themselves. While they can see you, and your guns, they'll be happy to get on with their lives and leave us to get on with ours."

If I can train you up in time.

I can't see any of these kids inspiring confidence, with or without deadly weapons.

"You are not fighting this war. We have a real army for that. You are showing the people that the war is being fought. You are the government's action figures. The front-line dolls. And public-facing dolls get the best weapons."

They don't like being called dolls. There are several scowls on the faces in front of me. I make a mental note to make sure they are clear on this point.

I switch my attention back to the whipping boy. His eyes widen as he realises that this isn't over.

"Saunders! Step out here."

He slouches out from the line of recruits, still willing the universe to ignore him. He's making it so easy for me to get them all quaking in their shiny new boots.

"Stand up straight, Saunders!"

He twitches his backbone a little. His shoulders still sag, and he looks as if he'd like the ground to swallow him up.

"Straighter! You're the line between life and messy death for those civilians out there. Try looking as if you could protect them from a bomber."

He straightens his shoulders, and I realise that he really is trying. This is honestly the best that he can do. I roll my eyes and shake my head. We have some long, torturous months ahead of us.

"It's like working with fluffy kittens. Grow some backbone, recruits!"

"Sir!"

He gives it his best shot, and it's a big improvement.

"Better. Now, Saunders. At ease. I'm going to hand you the gun. Show me how you'll be holding it when you're on patrol."

He stands clumsily at ease, and puts his hands out to take the gun. He looks terrified. His grip is hopeless, and he moves his hands along the barrel, trying to figure out how to hold it. I'm about to grab his hands and put them in the right places, when he seems to get it. He grasps the pistol grip firmly, and cradles the barrel with the other hand. His sudden confidence takes me by surprise.

"Not bad, recruit. Not bad."

I take his hands and correct his grip, just enough to make him doubt his own ability. His fingers are ink-stained, and his fingernails are chewed. He watches everything I do, making sure he knows how to get it right next time. His quick, shallow breathing is close to panic.

I take his shoulders and turn him round to face the group. He really is tiny, compared to the rest of them. Tiny, and fragile.

"This is a good grip. Watch and learn!"

Miller and Jackson and the other Senior Recruits are waiting as I split the kids into teams. I assign each team a Senior Recruit and a gun, and take the last team myself. The fluffy kittens follow every move as I show them how to take the rifle apart, clean it, maintain it and rebuild it.

As I work, I teach them the mantra.

"Safety on. Unclip the magazine, put it down. Unclip the pistol grip. Slide the handguard off the barrel, unscrew the barrel from the gun. Slide the stock up and away from the central section. Slide and unclip the elements of the central section. Lay them out neatly on the table."

I demonstrate several times, taking the gun apart, laying out the individual pieces, putting them back together. Some of the kids are whispering the mantra, desperate to memorise the actions.

I let them have a go. And it's all I can do not to laugh.

There's the kid who gets everything in the wrong order. There's the kid who knows the mantra, but can't make his hands stop shaking to take the gun apart. There's the smart kid who thinks she knows what she's doing, but forgets to clip the stock back into the gun before she attaches the pistol grip.

It's like watching a troupe of clowns.

Every time they get something wrong, I shout a little louder. By the end of the session, they're all shaking, and they all know how much they have to learn.

The whistle sounds for lunch. I call the recruits back into lines, and make sure they know how disappointed I am.

"That was pathetic! None of you is capable of handling a gun. None of you is competent enough to maintain a gun. None of you should be anywhere near a gun."

And if I had anything to do with it, you wouldn't be.

"But the commander wants you out there, looking competent and scary. And to be scary, you need guns. We will train, and train, and practice, and practice until every last one of you can handle a gun. Maintain, clean, hold, and use a gun. Look after your own gun, and look as if you know what you're doing with it.

"We are a very long way from that point. You have a lot of work to do."

I can see their shoulders sagging. The despair kicking in.

"Dismissed!"

And they slouch off to the dining room like injured puppies.

*****

I left school when I turned 16, as soon as they'd let me out of the doors. I went straight to the indoor market and found a job, cleaning and doing the filthiest tasks at the butcher's shop. Ken, the butcher, told me I wouldn't last a day. All the other girls he'd hired walked out after an hour. But I'm not other girls.

After a month of mopping blood and breaking bones and scooping chicken guts into bags, I demanded a pay rise. He was so shocked, he agreed – but it wasn't enough to leave home. Dad still thought I was at school. Where he thought I was going at five in the morning is anyone's guess. He probably never noticed.

I worked, all the days I could. After work, I ran. I had a circuit of the park I could do in the dark, in the rain, in the snow, and it kept me sane. I'd end the run with a takeaway on a park bench with the other school drop-outs, and when I went home to get some sleep I'd leave them there, drinking cheap lager and picking fights.

I got into a few fights to start with, with boys who thought they could take advantage, and girls who didn't like how I was keeping myself fit and holding down a job. We'd wind each other up, but most of the time we'd laugh it off, play-fight, and see who could swear the loudest to shock the passers-by. It was good to let go, and let off steam occasionally, but I would always be at work on time the next day. No point letting Ken down and losing my job.

The others seemed happy with this life. No ambition. No running, either. Most of them couldn't run for the bus, let alone keep up with me on a lap of the park. And I'd creep home at night, and hope that Dad was out, or already drunk enough not to care where I'd been. I'd had 16 years of practice, avoiding his shouting and his fists, but every night was a gamble. He could still hurt me if he wanted to.

I paid the rent, and kept us in the house. Who he thought was paying it, I don't know. Maybe he assumed he'd paid it himself.

And then the bombings got worse, and the government advertised for new soldiers. Good pay, proper training, and a chance at a real career. Plus they didn't care what exams you'd passed – they just wanted volunteers to fight their war. On my 18th birthday, I quit my job and signed up.

Ken nearly cried. He'd got used to me turning up and doing everything he asked me to do, every working day for two years. He kept saying that he wouldn't be able to find another helper like me, and asking what he was supposed to do now. I told him about the dropouts and their takeaways, and sent him to the park bench to find someone new. I don't know who got my job, but good luck to them.

I made the mistake of telling Dad I was leaving. I've never seen him so angry, and so afraid. We shouted and screamed at each other – 18 years of resentment and failure makes for a good fight. When he threatened me with a kitchen knife, I locked myself in my room and methodically packed my bag. I could hear him shouting and raging downstairs, but I knew how to stay calm, and concentrate on making sure I could carry everything I would need.

When I came downstairs to leave, he'd dropped the knife. He was sitting at the kitchen table, his head in his hands, weeping like a small child.

He begged me not go. He called me his 'little girl'. He said sorry, more times that I could count.

It wasn't enough. I walked out, caught the bus, and never looked back.

Assault

We have a recruit with a mother complex.

One of the posh kids thinks she's here to look after everyone else. Wipe their noses, tie their shoelaces, cheer them through the assault course as if they're in kindergarten.

We need to train these newbies into a proper fighting force. The Recruit Training Service exists to turn kids into soldiers who can take their guns into high streets and shopping centres and hospitals and schools, and command respect. This is my shot at a real promotion, and I'm stuck with Mr Sleepy and Mummy Ellman.

Give me strength.

Jackson's not happy either. We're putting the recruits through the assault course together, and most them can't climb the wall, can't run, and can't figure out what they're supposed to do next. They're all flailing arms and legs and no sense of balance.

Jackson's putting the fear into them every time they fall, or give up on an obstacle. I'm making sure they get to the end, and making sure they know that we're watching.

The third team sets off, and I see that Jackson is sending me a gift. Mr Sleepy and Mummy Ellman are running together, alongside two more hopeless recruits. I jog back from the finish line to watch their progress.

This is the worst team yet. Sleepy and Ellman manage to get past the cargo net and the water, and get each other onto the wall, but then they turn round and help the other two up. They don't seem to understand that this is a timed exercise. That their performance matters.

Jackson shouts at them to hurry up, and Ellman's off, getting herself across the rope line, jumping straight onto the zip wire, and crawling under the barbed wire. She's actually not bad, and not too slow, but her team is struggling behind her.

Jackson tracks her through the obstacles, jogging alongside the course, so he's on hand when she realises she's left her friends behind. She's about to run through the last obstacle when she turns instead, and starts shouting encouragement. She even starts moving back towards her team, shouting at them that they can do it, that they just need to keep going.

She doesn't seem to hear Jackson's whistle as he charges over to where she's standing. She's still walking back towards the others, still shouting at them. Her shock when she's suddenly face to face with Jackson is comical. She jumps, and her whole body stiffens.

"Turn around, recruit!" He bellows in his best parade-ground voice. "Turn around and get yourself to the end of the course! There's no time for teamwork here. You are responsible for your own safety. Turn around and clear the course. Now, recruit!"

That should be enough. That should give her a clue that her behaviour is not appropriate. She should turn around and run towards me, and towards the finish. But she doesn't. She plants her feet, squarely in front of Jackson, and yells at her friends over his shoulder. I can't help putting my head in my hands for a second. I know Jackson too well to think that he's going to put up with this.

His reaction is quick. He aims a swift kick at her shin, catches her just below her knee, and down she goes into the mud. She looks up at him, indignant, while he screams at her to get up.

This is it. This is where we need to take the fight out of her. Go on. Give him a reason to hurt you, Ellman.

But she stands up, turns round, and jogs through the last obstacle towards me, favouring her leg where Jackson's kick landed. She reaches the line, and turns back to watch the rest of the team planting their faces in the mud under the barbed wire. I expect her to shout, to encourage them again, but she's silent. She's shivering, and she wraps her arms around herself as she waits for them to finish. Her clothes are soaked from the water obstacle, and she's covered in mud. She looks pathetic, just standing there.

Does she get it? Is that all it took? It can't be that easy. She stands a chance of being good at this, if we can pull her away from this need to mother everyone else. I need to reinforce Jackson's lesson, let her know that her friends aren't worth the effort.

I walk up behind her and keep my voice low. She jumps as she feels my breath on her neck.

"Save your effort for where it matters, recruit. Leave the losers to lose."

She doesn't react, and waits there, shivering, until the others have crossed the line.

*****

"I don't want to hear this, Ketty. You know that."

"Yes, Sir."

"We need these recruits to be independent. Autonomous. Concerned about the TV cameras and the civilians they're on show for. I do not need to hear about good recruits throwing their skills away to help the ones who won't even try."

Commander Bracken sits back from the desk in his private office. I'm standing at ease in the middle of the small room, listening to a lecture I've heard a hundred times before. I've just delivered my report on the new arrivals, as requested, but the commander doesn't like my conclusions.

"It's your job to sort this out. I'm relying on you to get these kids trained and ready for front-line work. I don't want to hear about kids who aren't up to standard. Get them there. I don't want to hear about kids who would rather be nurses, or nannies to the others. Make them understand. I don't want teams, Ketty. I don't want Kumbaya round the camp fire, and hugs, and BFFs. We're not making happy memories here. I need individuals who can go on patrol with anyone, look out for anyone, and behave professionally for the cameras."

I've heard all this before, but I've also learned that it pays to keep the commander in the loop, even if he thinks he doesn't want to know what goes on here. It pays to make sure he knows how hard this job is. It pays to make him see how hard we're working.

I try to remind him every week that training clueless recruits is tough, and challenging – and that I'm up to the job. It was bad enough when the trainees wanted to be here, but the new kids are so much harder to motivate.

"Prove that you can get me trained, interchangeable robots, and I'll move you up the chain of command. Get these kids in shape, and I'll recommend you for promotion. Fail, and I'll happily leave you here to run assault courses and shout at incompetent recruits forever.

"Don't bring your problems to me. Sort them out. I don't have time for every bruised knee and every sticking plaster. If you've got kids who want to be kind and helpful, make sure they know that's not what they're here for."

"Yes, Sir."

"Dismissed." He waves his hand towards the door, and I spin on my heel and leave him to his work. I'm smiling as I leave his office. That promotion is within reach, even working with these schoolchildren. I just need Jackson to back me up.

Iron fists and steel toe caps. We make a good team.

*****

Jackson rocked into camp the same day as me, totally sure of himself. Expensive jeans, expensive trainers, and an attitude that earned him a reprimand before the commander had even finished his introductory briefing.

After dinner on the first night, he found me in the corridor. He slammed my shoulder into the wall and tried to steal a kiss. He got the benefit of 18 years of my learning to defend myself, from my knee and my fists. I left him lying in the corridor, and went to bed with a clear conscience.

The next day, after breakfast, he found me again. I was ready for another fight, but instead he held out his hand.

"I'm Jackson. And I'm sorry. Can we start over?"

"Ketty", I said, bracing for another attack. I didn't shake his hand.

He looked uncomfortable, and stuffed his hands in his pockets.

"Do you have something to say?" I looked him in the eyes, challenging him to answer. By the look of his face, I'd given him a black eye the night before.

He couldn't meet my eyes.

"Yeah. I'm ... sorry. I shouldn't have done that last night."

"You're right. You shouldn't."

"I'm not used to ..."

"To what? Treating people like human beings? Being civil? Asking permission?"

"... to girls who know what they want."

Girls?

"Women, Jackson. Women. There are no girls here. And yes, if we're here, we know what we want. We've signed up to train and fight. You want another black eye? Then lay a finger on me again. Are we clear?"

He nodded, looking at his feet, and brushed his fingertips over his bruised face.

"Yeah. We're clear."

"And don't let me catch you hassling anyone else, either. No one needs your creepy, entitled attitude. We'll all need to fight together, when the training's done. Don't be the guy we leave behind."

He nodded again.

"Yeah. Yeah."

I turned to walk away, but turned back when I realised what he'd said.

"And a girl who doesn't know what she wants? That's fine. But trust me – you really don't know what she wants. So keep your hands to yourself."

"Okay, okay!" He lifted his head and finally looked at me, his velvet brown eyes meeting mine, hands out of his pockets and held up in mock surrender. "You're something else, you know that? I've never met anyone like you." He touched his face again. "I think I'm going to enjoy training with you. I think you're going to make this place interesting."

He held out his hand again, and this time, I shook it. His grip was firm and businesslike. Respectful. He nodded, dropped my hand, and walked away towards his dorm room, glancing back over his shoulder and smiling as he went.

Test

One week into training the new recruits, and there's a change to the briefing session. The commander's been sent a video file for the recruits to watch, and they want everyone to pass a test on it afterwards. I don't know what happens to any recruits who fail, but that's not my problem. I'm just running the briefing.

The recruits are all waiting in the dining room when I walk in and switch on the TV. Sleepy and Ellman have formed their own little crew, and they're sitting together, as usual. The others seem more flexible about who they sit with, but everyone's paired up, or grouped together at their tables. We need to train them out of this habit.

I introduce the video. The commander and I were both surprised by the level of detail in the film. It seems to be much more than these kids need, and a waste of time that could be used to develop their public interaction skills. But I'm not making the decisions here.

"Today the government has decided to educate you all about the various weapons that you'll see in use when you're on patrol. Some, you might get to handle. Others, they want you to know that you must not touch. Those toys are not yours. Those are for the real soldiers. But don't worry, tiny fighters – you get some toys of your own."

They squirm at 'tiny fighters'. Some of them still think they're the big soldiers. Some of them really can't get their heads round their role, as the distraction that lets the army get their hands dirty behind the scenes, while everyone's watching the brave young people on patrol.

"After the informative video, you'll have five minutes to complete the questionnaires in front of you. Don't screw this up. Identify the weapons, and identify whether they are for you to use, or for the grown-ups.

This isn't rocket science, recruits, but it is important, so pay attention."

I hope they can hear the sarcasm, and the boredom. I think this is a waste of time, but here I am – so they can shut up and get on with the learning experience.

I play the video, switch out the lights, and grab an empty chair with the group of recruits who came in last. They look terrified to have me sitting at their table. Maybe they'll actually pay attention.

The video shows all the government-issued weapons and equipment that our tiny fighters need to know about. The kids I can see from my seat are all paying attention, drinking up this exciting grown-up knowledge.

I let my attention drift. Dan Pearce is sitting opposite Ellman, staring intently at the screen. He's rolled his shirt sleeves up to his elbows, as he always does when he's not on the training field. He's another of the posh kids, and he's got that posh-shabby-gorgeous thing going on. He manages to be effortlessly good looking, even when his hair's a mess and his clothes are crumpled. Unlike some of the other kids, it's as if his clothes really fit. As if, subconsciously, he knows how to wear them.

In another place, I'd be checking him out, even though he's only – what? 16? 17? He seems older than the others, more sure of himself, but without the defensive attitude of someone like Jackson. It must be nice to feel so at home in the world, and so certain about your life.

The video recaps the information they'll need for the test, and I send the recruit sitting next to me to switch the lights on while I switch off the TV. I wait for everyone to move their chairs back to their tables, and then shout into the silence.

"Grab a questionnaire. Grab an answer sheet. Grab a pen. Show me that you can watch a short video without falling asleep. No conferring. Five minutes. Go!"

I pace up and down the room while the recruits scribble on their answer sheets. I keep an eye on the tables in the corners of the room, but I don't see anyone conferring. I honestly don't care what they do, but the commander cares, and I'll be in trouble if he thinks I can't control a briefing session.

Dan and Ellman are intent on their questionnaires. Heads down, determined. Some of the other recruits are less focused, taking longer to think about their answers. I roll my eyes. There might have been plenty of new information, but it wasn't hard to understand, and there was a recap, in case they missed something the first time.

I check my watch, and the clock on the wall. I pace some more. I stop, and look over some shoulders, watch the kids panic when they realise I'm standing behind them.

"Time's up! Pens down."

I move round the room, collecting the answer sheets from the tables, and hand over to Jackson to run the rest of the session.

*****

I head to the Senior Dorm and claim a table where I can sit and mark the papers. I work my way through, and I'm genuinely amazed that most of them pass. Even Sleepy scrapes a passing mark, and most of the posh kids get every question right.

I put the papers in a file for Commander Bracken to look at, and pull out a large sheet of paper. I'm drawing up a pass/fail list using the scores from the test, when Jackson walks in, ready for dinner. He sits at my table.

"So – how many fails?"

"Not many."

"Not even Sleepy?"

"Nope. He passed."

"Huh. I guess he's found something to be good at."

I finish writing up the list, and lean back in my chair.

"Right! Your gun training. How was your extra lunchtime tutoring?"

Jackson rolls his eyes.

"I don't know how Sleepy gets anything done. I don't know how he gets dressed in the morning. I don't know how he ties his own shoelaces."

"He doesn't, usually."

"True. Well, he can't fit his gun into the armour, either."

"A lot of them had trouble – it is their first day in their shiny new armour. I had to personally dress most of the girls in it today, like some sort of babysitter. They're so distracted by how cool they look wearing it that they're not paying attention to the things they need to learn. Attaching their helmets, or clipping and unclipping a gun from their backs when they need it. Things that could save their lives."

"Sleepy couldn't find his back with a map."

"Did shouting at him for the whole of lunchtime help?" I can't help smirking.

"He managed it in the end. And then I made him repeat it, and repeat it. I think he was actually feeling proud of himself by the time I let him go."

"Wait – you're not feeling sorry for him, are you? Whipping boy, remember?"

"He tried really hard …"

"And he's still useless. And not yet in the hospital, I can't help noticing."

"Also true."

"Iron fists, steel toe caps."

"Yeah."

But he looks as if I've just tried to shoot his favourite puppy.

Come on, Jackson – I need you. We need to work together on these kids.

*****

It took three weeks to attract Commander Bracken's attention. Three weeks of being the first in line for breakfast every morning, the first in line for every activity, and the first to volunteer at the briefings. Consistently being the fastest female recruit on the morning run and the assault course helped, too.

He called me to his office after dinner, while everyone else was playing cards and chilling out. My file was open on his desk, and he invited me to sit down.

"Katrina Smith," he began, and I couldn't help correcting him.

"It's Ketty, Sir."

He raised his eyebrows at the interruption.

"Ketty?"

"No one's ever called me Katrina, Sir. It's always been Ketty. Sir."

I knew that wasn't true, but the commander didn't need to know. Dad said that Mum used to call me Kat, before she left, but I don't remember that. I don't remember her. Dad said that Ketty is what I called myself, before I could say 'Katrina'. As far as I could remember, I'd always been Ketty.

He made a note on the file. I hoped I hadn't messed up whatever good impression he had of me. I needed him to notice my abilities. I needed him to be my ticket out of here.

"You've made an impression here, Ketty."

"I hope so, Sir."

He looked at me, inspecting my face, as if he hadn't expected a reply. He paused, then consulted the file again.

"Your fitness is excellent. Your enthusiasm is excellent. You've never been late, never unprepared. Your uniform is always neat and clean. You always take part in the briefings." He looked up. "You are an excellent recruit."

I tried to hide my smile.

"How do you see yourself progressing through our training programme? What do you want to achieve?"

I paused, surprised by the question.

"I want a career, Sir." I said, eventually. "I want to be the best, and I want to be promoted. I'm willing to work hard, and do what I need to do."

"So do you want us to put you through some courses? Get you some qualifications?"

I thought about it, and shook my head.

"Only if I need the qualification to do my job. I'm not interested in certificates. I'm not interested in studying unless it's something I need to know. I want to be out there, getting good at the job. Working hard."

He nodded, as if he'd been expecting me to say that, then picked up a pen and made a note in my file.

"We'll start with the Emergency Response course, and some vehicle training. Driving skills are always useful."

Then he put the pen down and leaned forward, elbows on the desk, hands clasped in front of him.

"I have a proposal for you.

"I need an assistant. Not an official assistant, like Woods. I need someone on the inside of camp life. Someone who can keep an eye on the other recruits for me. Solve problems before they reach my office. Keep everyone in line, without me having to bring rank into the equation.

"Think you can do that?"

I tried to bring the excitement in my voice under control.

"What exactly are you expecting me to do, Sir?"

He waved his hand.

"Whatever you think will work. You know these recruits. You've been training with them from day one. Just keep them in line. Make sure they know it's in their interests to do as they're told. Stop issues from turning into problems that I'll need to deal with."

I nodded. "I think I can do that, Sir."

He smiled.

"I think you can, too. I gather you taught Jackson a lesson on your first night here. That's the sort of situation management we need."

I stared at him, wondering how he knew about my encounter with Jackson. I almost forgot to nod.

"Just – not so many black eyes from now on. Okay? Keep it subtle, keep it low-key, and keep teenage antics out of my office."

"Yes, Sir."

I waited to be dismissed, but he looked at me, appraisingly, for an uncomfortable moment.

"You've got discipline, Ketty. You've got determination. I think you understand what we're doing here. Show me that you can do this, and I'll make sure it is worth the trouble."

"Thank you, Sir."

"Dismissed."

And I walked out of his office, glowing with pride. Of all the recruits, he'd chosen me. He'd noticed me. I wasn't going to let him down.

JULY

Lessons

We've been training the hopeless puppies in their armour for weeks. They can run in armour now, and most of them can get their guns in and out of their clips when they need to.

It's my week to lead the morning run, so we set out across the bypass and the railway, and take the route through town to show off the kids to the citizens of Leominster. Hopefully they're telling their friends about the wonderful, brave young people stationed in their town.

It's a gorgeous morning, sunshine with the occasional bright cloud, and we're making good time. I stop the traffic when we cross the bypass again to come back to camp, and I'm catching up with the group when I notice Sleepy, running at the back with some of Ellman's little fan club. He's still clumsy in his armour, and he's obviously exhausted and dragging his feet. As usual, his boot laces are untied. I should probably tell him, but looking ahead I can see an opportunity to break up Ellman's happy family, and maybe teach them to run with the others. They're not the only kids on site, and they need to work with everyone.

Good luck, Whipping boy. Learn the hard way that your laces won't tie themselves.

I run past Sleepy to where Ellman and Pearce are running together. Inseparable, these two. I push between them, and challenge Pearce to a sprint. He's up for it, and we sprint together along the path through the woods. Mummy Ellman can learn to run by herself, without Dan to hold her hand.

We run past the other recruits, and make it back to the gate ahead of the group. I thank Dan for the sprint, send him on to Jackson's gun training session, and wait for the others to arrive. It's clouding over as I wait for the runners. It looks as if it might rain.

One by one, group by group, they run through the gate, following my shouted orders to line up on the field with Jackson. There's a pause, when there's no one in sight along the path. I've counted everyone in, and we're missing four recruits.

And then Brown and Taylor are running round the final corner, out of breath. I shout to them to get to the field, but they stop, pointing back along the path.

"It's Saunders! He's busted his ankle!"

Saunders. Mr Sleepy. That'll teach him to tie his shoelaces.

"Bex is helping him. They'll be here as quickly as they can."

"Thank you, recruits. Get yourselves to Jackson's session. I'll deal with this."

They walk away towards the field, glancing back at the gate. I wait until they're out of sight round the corner of the closest dorm, and then tell the gate guards to close the gates. One of them clips his gun and runs to pull the gates closed. The other wants to know why we can't wait for the recruits.

"They're late, and they know that we close the gates after the run. If they can't get themselves back here on time, let them wait until I'm ready to let them in."

"So you want us to keep them here."

I smile. "Yes, I do. I'm ordering you not to let anyone else in. I need to be somewhere else. I can't verify their identities. Who knows what might have happened on the run? We lost sight of the recruits. They could be terrorists in stolen uniforms."

The guard nods, and the second guard returns my smile.

"No problem. We can keep them here. No sense in taking any risks, eh?"

"None. I can trust you on this, right? No one comes through without my permission."

They're both grinning now.

"No one. We'll make sure of it."

So I leave them to do their jobs. I have better things to do than wait for Mummy Ellman and her invalid.

*****

Jackson is busy on the field with the gun training, and I have paperwork to do for the commander. I sit at my usual table in the senior dining room, and get to work – glancing out of the window every so often to see what happens at the gate.

And it is glorious.

She's practically carrying him. He's leaning on her, hopping his pathetic way beside her in painful slow motion. She leads him up to the gates, and shouts something at the guards, who don't let me down.

One of them stares straight ahead, as if these two sad recruits are invisible. The other lifts his gun to a combat-ready position.

But does she back off? Does she put her hands up and wait? This is Ellman, and Ellman with a wounded buddy. Of course she doesn't. She shouts back at them, guns or no guns. This kid really needs to learn some self-preservation skills.

The guards ignore her, and she stands there, disbelief on her face. The guards continue to ignore her. I'm laughing under my breath.

Life isn't fair, Ellman. Just because you've been a nice person today, that doesn't let you get round the rules.

Eventually, she gets the message, and walks Sleepy over to the grass verge, swings him down so he's sitting on the ground. I wait for her to sit down as well, but instead she walks back to the gate. I've forgotten my paperwork now. This is all about Ellman.

She walks right up to the gate, grabs the chicken wire with both hands, and starts shouting at the guards.

And the guards raise their guns.

I punch the air. I owe these guys a drink. This is perfect.

How's that mother complex treating you now, Ellman? Should have left him on the path.

But she doesn't back down. Not until the guards step towards her, guns pointing at her head. She lifts her hands and steps away from the gate – but she's *still* talking!

I'm standing at the window now, in the shadows. I can't believe she's picking a fight with armed guards. One of them heads back to the guard hut, and my radio crackles to life.

"Gatehouse to Ketty? We could use some backup here."

"On my way."

How the hell is one little girl freaking out my guards? This shouldn't be a challenge, leaving two late, slow, unarmed recruits outside the gate until I say they can come in. I hurry to the gate, before the commander notices what's going on. I'm authorised to solve my own problems, but if one of the guards gets twitchy and calls the commander, I'll have some inconvenient explaining to do.

Don't you dare get me into trouble, kid. I've got more invested here than you know, and I need the commander on my side. Sit down, and shut up, until I decide you're coming back in.

Sleepy looks utterly pathetic, sitting on the ground, trying not to cry. Ellman is still on her feet, so I ignore her pleas and head directly for the guards.

"They're late." I say, loudly, for Ellman's benefit. "Leave them out there."

I'm walking away, when one of the guards asks how long they should wait.

"I'll let you know."

When I've had enough of teaching these kids a lesson about authority, and rules, and looking after themselves.

I walk quickly back to the dining room, and go back to my paperwork.

*****

I'd been at the camp for nearly a year before Commander Bracken named me Lead Recruit. For eleven months I'd been his in-camp enforcer. I kept the other recruits in line, reporting back any matters of concern to the commander, and dealing with everything else myself. Breaking up fights. Breaking up couples (no favourites allowed, here). Keeping dorms tidy and training running smoothly. It helped that there were witnesses to my first night encounter with Jackson, and that he had become one of my most loyal helpers.

After a year of intense training, we were ready to train new recruits ourselves. Most of the volunteers who joined with me were sent to other camps to train the growing numbers of young recruits. They had started advertising for more 16-year-olds to sign up, so there were plenty of kids fresh out of school to shape and train.

Jackson and I stayed on at Camp Bishop, along with eight other recruits. We were made Senior Recruits, and given the responsibility of running the training for the newbies – as well as keeping ourselves fit and combat-ready. It was a challenge, but it was also straightforward. Run the schedule. Pass on the skills. Keep the kids on their toes. Practice, practice, practice.

I had weekly meetings with the commander, passing on anything he needed to know about, and keeping things he didn't need to hear about to myself. At one of these meetings, he offered me the promotion I'd been hoping for.

"I've been given permission to hire an official assistant." He waved his hand, dismissively. "Not Woods – he's part of the chain of command, and he reports back to HQ. Someone from inside the camp."

I sat up straighter in my chair. If this was going where I hoped it was going, it would put me one step closer to a promotion out of the camp.

"You've impressed me this year, Ketty. You've kept everyone in line, you've kept time-wasting incidents from my door – and you've made it look easy.

"The recruits respect you. They also know that you're right there, training with them. If they screw up, you'll see it. If they step out of line, you'll see it. They behave better, because they know that you're standing beside them."

I allowed myself a smile. This was what I'd been waiting to hear.

"So. I have a new position to fill. A promotion. A pay rise. A stepping stone to greater things.

"There's a lot more work involved. You'll be supporting me directly with paperwork, planning, reports for HQ. You'll be spending more time working, but I expect you to keep up with your training, and the training of the new recruits. This isn't an easy way out of responsibilities at camp – this is extra work on top of everything you do now.

"You'll also be given security clearance to take part in HQ briefings, and to work on classified documents. You'll be closer to the top, closer to the decision-makers, and your name will be on their promotion lists.

"I'd like to offer you the opportunity to be Camp Bishop's Lead Recruit. I know I can count on you to work hard and fit in everything you need to achieve. I don't think we've found the limits of your abilities yet, and I'd like to have you officially working for me.

"What do you think? Will you be our new Lead Recruit?"

I felt dizzy, and my chest felt like an expanding balloon. This was exactly what I'd been waiting for. Recognition by Commander Bracken, and a promotion to working with him. I couldn't have hidden my broad smile, even if I'd wanted to.

"Absolutely, Commander. It would be an honour."

He smiled, and reached out to shake my hand.

"Welcome to the RTS inner circle, Lead Recruit."

I thought I might burst with pride.

Falling

The whistle sounds for lunchtime, and the first spots of rain start to tap against the windows. I check the gate, and Ellman and Sleepy are still out there, looking miserable. I'm about to go and tell the guards to open the gates, when the commander walks in to the dining room.

"Recruit Smith!"

He's shouting, he's angry, and he never uses my surname in private. I kick the chair in frustration as I stand to attention.

"Sir!"

"There is an injured recruit locked outside my gates. Do you know anything about this, Recruit Smith?"

I was in control of this situation, but I can feel that power slipping away. I try to keep my voice strong and my body language confident.

"Yes, Sir."

"Is he out there on your orders?"

"Yes, Sir."

He pauses, shakes his head, and then addresses me like a toddler. As if he's trying to patiently teach me the right thing to do. He speaks slowly and clearly, and I realise that he's using this as a way to control his anger.

"Recruit Smith. Get yourself to the medical centre. Get me a medic and a stretcher. Meet me at the gate."

And he turns and leaves the room before I have a chance to respond.

I aim a hard kick at the table, which skids across the floor, scattering paperwork, and slams into the wall. I punch my fist into a tabletop, take a deep breath, and start to walk briskly towards the medical centre. I've gone too far, and I need to win back the commander's respect.

At the medical centre I open the door wide enough to shout through, and call for a medic and a stretcher. Doctor Webb comes running, and we carry the stretcher between us to the gate, catching up with Commander Bracken on the path. The rain is heavy, now, and I'm not dressed for it.

"Open up!"

The Commander's shout brings the two guards running to open the gates. One of them flashes me a look and a quick shrug, but I ignore him. I'm here to hold the stretcher, and to get this situation under control.

Ellman helps Sleepy onto the stretcher, and the commander sends her to get ready for the assault course.

No lunch break for you, Mummy. Enjoy the assault course on an empty stomach.

The doctor and I lift the stretcher and carry it back to the medical centre.

We hold the stretcher next to a bed. A nurse helps Sleepy to move across, and tucks a pillow under his injured foot. His hair is plastered to his head by the rain, and his face is a grimace of pain. He can't even look at me. The nurse starts to remove his armour, and the medic thanks me for my help. I take the stretcher back to the nurses' station, and head back out in the rain.

When I walk into the dining room, I'm surprised to find the commander there before me, his back to the door. I stop, and wait for him to speak.

"Attention, Recruit Smith!" He shouts, before turning round and fixing me with a needle-like stare. I stand to attention, waiting for him to speak. He makes me wait a very long time.

"I don't understand what I've just seen, Recruit Smith." His voice is calm and controlled, but far from friendly. I open my mouth to explain, but he holds up a hand.

"I did not give you permission to speak." I close my mouth, and look straight ahead, fighting the urge to defend myself.

"I was crossing the field at lunchtime today, and I noticed two guards at the gate who seemed entirely unaware that there were two of my recruits sitting on the ground, in their armour, with their names on, outside the camp. What's more, the gates were locked. And I wondered – who was on duty for this morning's run? Who managed to lose two recruits, and then lock the gates with those two recruits still outside? And who managed to convince the guards that these recruits, however much they begged to be let in, should be left to sit on the floor in the rain?"

I bite my tongue.

"Imagine my surprise when I discover that this act of either gross incompetence, or gross cruelty, is down to my lead recruit. Katrina Smith. My eyes and ears. My trusted assistant. The person with authority to stop screw-ups like this from bothering me."

When he calls me Katrina, it's like a stab in the gut.

"So, Recruit Smith …"

He's about to continue, when Jackson crashes through the door, shouting at me to watch out, because the commander is looking for me.

Thanks for that, genius, because I'm not in enough trouble here already.

He stops as if he's hit a wall when he sees the scene in the dining room. The commander turns towards him.

"Recruit Jackson! Attention!"

"Sir!" Jackson stands up straight, looking ahead.

"I think you can stay for this. I have questions for you as well." And he turns back to me.

"Recruit Smith. What do you have to say for yourself? Can you explain to me, in very small words, what happened out there today?"

I swallow. My mouth is suddenly dry and my throat is tight.

"Sir. The recruits were late back from the run. They've been told that the gates will be closed before the next session begins, and they know not to be late."

"So you locked the gates."

"Yes, Sir."

"And you told the guards not to let them in."

"Yes, Sir."

"How long were you going to make them wait, Recruit Smith?"

"I was heading down to the gate when you came in …"

"So you were happy to make them wait for an hour or two, in the rain?"

"Sir, I -…"

"Yes or no, Recruit."

"Yes, Sir."

He nods.

"And you, Recruit Jackson."

"Sir."

"You ran your gun training, short two recruits, and you didn't think to come looking for them?"

"No, Sir."

"Why is that?"

Jackson glances at me, then back at the commander.

"I knew Ketty had them, Sir."

The Commander nods again.

"So, knowing that *Katrina* had your recruits, when they were supposed to be with you, you let it slide. Is that because you knew about her plans to teach them some sort of lesson?"

Neither of us speaks. The silence stretches uncomfortably between us. The commander begins to pace across the room, ignoring the scattered paperwork, and the table thrown against the wall.

"I am extremely disappointed in you, Recruit Smith. You have been trusted with keeping the peace in my camp. You have been given access to information that no one else has been given. You have been trusted to keep the recruits disciplined, but you have also been trusted to keep them safe.

"Today, instead of keeping an injured recruit safe, you left him outside the camp with the only person who bothered to help him. Ellman missed a training session, thanks to your incompetence, and Saunders' injury may well be worse because he was forced to wait for treatment.

"I know that one of the aims of our training here is to separate the recruits from their friends, and to instil a sense of independence. We need them to be confident for the cameras, and we need them to rescue civilians before they pick up their fellow recruits. I agree with this. I demand it.

"But what I do not demand …" he crashes his fist into a tabletop, and Jackson and I both jump. "What I do not demand is gratuitous cruelty."

He turns and looks out of the window. Jackson and I exchange a panicked look.

"Recruit Smith. As of now, you are stripped of the title of Lead Recruit. I shall find another assistant – one who can tell the difference between a learning experience and a dangerous, petty power game."

He turns to face us again. I clench my jaw and keep the expression on my face neutral as he continues. I don't trust myself to speak.

"Recruit Jackson. You are no longer in the running for becoming Lead Recruit. Don't let me find you aiding and abetting your friend here in any more stupid games. You are capable of thinking for yourself – please do so from now on."

"Sir." Jackson's voice is surprisingly steady.

"Now get out. Dismissed, Jackson."

Jackson is out of the room, and out of the dorm, before the commander can change his mind.

"Recruit Smith. Clean up this mess." He indicates the table, and the scattered papers. "I want the paperwork filed and on my desk in fifteen minutes. You are no longer authorised to work on it."

He walks to the door.

"You can do better than this, Katrina," he says from behind me. "Don't let me down again. Dismissed."

And he leaves me alone with the mess I've made.

*****

We partied, Jackson and I, the night I made Lead Recruit. We went to the kitchen, where the camp staff let their hair down every night, and for once we joined them.

They weren't impressed, at first. Two RTS soldiers gatecrashing their private party. But then Jackson pulled out the bottles of vodka he'd picked up on a rare visit to town, and you'd think we'd all been friends forever.

We turned up the music, mixed drinks and danced. I must have danced with everyone – boys and girls, I didn't care. I'd got my promotion. I'd got security clearance. I'd be noticed at HQ. I was one step closer to getting out of the camp and getting an important job – maybe even a job in London. Dad couldn't stop me. Dropping out of school couldn't stop me. I'd proved myself, and I'd done it on my terms. Commander Bracken, all chiselled jaw and film star good looks, had noticed me. I was unstoppable.

I remember dancing with Jackson on a table, everyone cheering us on. I remember one of the kitchen girls pulling a lipstick from her pocket and drawing war paint stripes on my cheek bones. I grabbed the lipstick and gave Jackson stripes of his own, and soon everyone was painting their faces, and whooping, and dancing on the tables.

It was my one night of crazy celebration before I had to prove myself to the commander all over again. And this time the stakes were much higher. I could screw up, or I could get myself out of there. Get myself a real job – not crowd control for teenagers, but a promotion to the grown-up world. My choice, my responsibility.

Jackson got his kiss that night, but no more. No couples allowed at Camp Bishop, and that would have been be a pathetic way to lose my promotion. Besides, I needed Jackson where he'd always been – happy to work with the commander's enforcer, but at a respectful distance. I needed to be able to count on him, with no complications. I needed him on my team.

Revenge

I'm sitting on the floor at the end of my bed. I can't believe what I've done. That I've thrown away my chance of getting out of here. I punch the wall so hard that I make a hole in the plasterboard, and my knuckles are bleeding, but I don't care. I'm shouting all the swear words I can think of, over and over again, but none of this is making me feel better. Nothing is helping.

I'm furious with myself, and I'm furious with Ellman. Why can't she stick to the rules? Why can't she keep it simple, train herself, get herself ready for being on the front line? Why doesn't she get it?

I aim a kick at the metal bedframe, and it scrapes across the floor, the sound painful and satisfying.

She'd be a great recruit, if only she concentrated on her own training. Why does she have to look after everyone else? Why does she think she's everyone's mother? And her little gang. Two posh kids and three losers. What's the attraction? What does smart, gorgeous Dan see in the rest of them? Brown, Taylor, and Sleepy – they follow her and they follow Dan like a line of ducklings. It's as if they don't know the rest of us are here.

We need to change this. We need to split them up. We need to show them what happens when they don't do what we need them to do.

Someone knocks on the door, and when I don't respond, Jackson opens it puts his head round. He's not allowed in the female dorms, but I'm guessing he's looked for me everywhere else.

"Can I come in?"

I sit, looking at the floor, suddenly exhausted. I shrug.

"Yeah. Whatever."

He steps inside, closes the door, leans back against it.

"I'm so sorry, Ketty. I …" He stops. There's nothing else to say. He's sorry. I shrug again.

He walks into the room, pushes my bed back into place and sits down. He notices the wall, my hand. My bleeding knuckles.

He tries to take my hand, but I snatch it away.

"Ketty …"

He's trying to be nice. He's trying to be sympathetic, and I can't handle this. He's going to make me cry.

"Jackson. Shut up. There's nothing you can do." I stare straight ahead, teeth gritted. I will not cry in front of Jackson. I will not be weak.

He looks genuinely upset. Let him. He can cry, if he wants to. Self-indulgent snowflake. This is my loss. Not his.

We sit in silence for a while. I channel my disappointment into clear-thinking anger.

"We need to teach them a lesson."

Jackson looks up, surprised.

"Who?"

"Bex Ellman. Dan Pearce. Their little group of losers."

He thinks for a moment.

"We've finally put Sleepy in the hospital."

"That's true." That does make me feel better. "What about the rest of them? What about Mummy Ellman?"

Jackson checks his watch.

"Ellman's in the medical centre, visiting Sleepy."

I look up, and Jackson continues. "She's always taking walks after dinner. We could take her on a detour. No one will miss her."

I can feel my anger building into something constructive. There is something we can do.

"Iron fists and steel toe caps?" I ask.

He grins.

48

*****

It's getting dark as we walk out onto the field. There's no one around, and there are lights on in all the buildings. The staff dorm is noisy, as usual, but everywhere else is quiet.

We walk, quickly and quietly to the medical centre, and wait in the shadows outside. The lights are on in Commander Bracken's office, which means he's busy, so we're safe out here for now.

The door to the medical centre slams shut, and a figure in fatigues and a thin raincoat walks down the steps. She turns her head, and we can see that it's Ellman. She walks away, towards the staff dorm, and we follow, treading softly on the wet grass.

She's ambling along, hands in her pockets, looking up at the cloudy sky. It's as if today hadn't happened. She looks smug and happy and content.

We step up behind her. Jackson grabs her arms, and at the same time I throw my hand over her mouth, and brace it with the other hand behind her head. We pull her backwards, so she loses her footing, and we half drag, half carry her across the field to the fence.

She tries everything. She tries to shout, she tries to kick. She even relaxes her whole body, and we nearly lose her, but we grab her again, and drag her dead weight between the trees to the gap under the fence.

I need to let go of her, but she'll be able to shout. I glance around the field, but there's no one in sight. We're a long way from any of the buildings, and it's getting dark, so I take a chance.

"Don't make a sound," I hiss in her ear, before releasing my grip on her head.

And of course she shouts. Jackson's holding her arms with one hand, and he smacks her cheek with the other, hard enough to snap her head to the side.

"Not her face!" I can't believe I need to explain this to him. The commander cannot find out about this. This is between me and Ellman.

I stand up, and go to the fence. There's a line of security lights on the fence posts, and that's a public footpath on the other side. I check up and down the path, but there's no sign of anyone walking past. "All clear."

Jackson drags Ellman to the fence, and crawls underneath while I hold up the bent mesh. There's a deep puddle on the ground where the fence curls up, and Jackson drags her through it. I drop the mesh as he makes it through, and watch the sharp edges catch on her raincoat and trousers.

I hope that hurts.

She shouts and kicks as she's pulled through the puddle, but I'm sure that no one can hear us out here. I make a final check of the field behind us, then crawl through after them.

Jackson lets go for a second, and as she pulls her arms out from behind her back, I grip them again and pin her to the floor.

"You're in trouble, Ellman." I keep my voice down, my face close to her ear.

"We keep telling you, Ellman", says Jackson, his voice quiet. "Save yourself. Don't be a martyr. Don't go helping the useless kids who can't make the grade. But what do you do? You make friends. You carry them home. You patch them up." He kneels down, straddling her legs, one knee on each side in the mud, pinning her down.

"You get us into trouble." It's all I can do not to laugh. We could do anything to her now, and we'd get away with it. She's outside the camp. That's strictly against the rules – and who's to say she didn't drag herself out here, under the fence, for one of her evening walks?

"We don't like trouble, Ellman. We like things to run smoothly. We like recruits who do as they're told."

"You need to learn to do what we tell you." This is absurd. The speech before the beating. It's like a gangster movie.

And it feels great.

I nod to Jackson, and he pulls back his fist. He flashes me a grin, then punches Ellman, hard, in the ribs. She flinches, and I nearly lose my grip on her arms. I lean over and pull them up, over her head, before she can react. I plant my knees on her elbows, and lean my hands against her shoulders, using my weight to push her down. Jackson nods, approvingly, and starts raining down with his fists as if she's a punch bag in the gym.

"Not her face!" He's out of control. I can't have the bruises showing. He nods, flexes his fingers and clenches his fists again, aiming for her torso instead.

She's stopped crying out. Jackson's winding her with every hit, but she's not shouting any more. She seems to relax, to decide to let this happen.

Good. That's the first step to accepting the rules.

Every hit is a revenge. Every hit makes me feel elated. I can feel her moving under my hands, flinching from Jackson's fists. This is exactly what I needed to do. We rain down justice on our disobedient recruit, and it feels utterly amazing – like touching a live wire. Like winning a game. We're holding her life in our hands.

Jackson stops, rubbing his knuckles. We look at each other. She's lying very still, and very quiet. I wonder how long we've been out here. He nods. I nod back, and stand up. Ellman doesn't move.

She needs to know how lucky she's been. How close she's come to really screwing up.

"You do this again, Ellman – you get us into trouble, and you won't be walking home."

I step away, take Jackson's arm, and lead the way back under the fence.

We're half way across the field when he turns to me, a mischievous grin on his face.

"Better?"

"Much better." I've done something with my anger, and I've made Ellman understand the limits of my tolerance. I feel calm. I feel powerful. I grin back at him. "Thank you, Jackson. I'm glad you're on my side."

And I give him a kiss, on the cheek.

I need to keep him on my side, after all.

*****

Becoming the commander's Lead Recruit was the gateway to a new world of information and access.

For the first time, I was seeing a clear picture of the people we were supposed to be fighting. There had been bombings and terror attacks for as long as I could remember, but they were always things that happened to someone else, somewhere a long way from me. I'd never needed to care.

But this was different. This concerned me, and my recruits. And the commander. This was important.

The terrorists wanted to overthrow the government. In report after classified report, I saw descriptions of their targets, their methods – even the confessions at their trials. I saw that there were more attacks all the time. That the government wanted more to be done to protect the population.

I saw some of the history, too. How the government had suspended elections after the Crossrail bombing. How the King had given them indefinite powers to run the country and beat the terrorists. How they'd taken down the mobile phone networks and the civilian Internet, and started executing terror suspects.

Even our TV had changed. They'd shut down all the independent news channels and created the Public Information Network, so everyone was getting the same news, and not rumours spread by the terrorists. There were lists of banned films, banned TV shows – even banned books. All the newspapers had government-appointed members of staff checking their stories for accuracy and language.

I'd signed up to fight, as much as I'd signed up for a safe place to sleep and a good career. Working for Commander Bracken showed me what I was fighting for, and what I was fighting against. Defending the rights of innocent, hard-working people against the terrorists who wanted to take everything away. Keeping the country running and stopping the attacks. Defending my career against people who wanted everything to fall apart.

I knew you needed discipline and backbone to get by in life. People needed rules and boundaries, not handouts and hugs. Society worked when everyone worked hard and took care of themselves.

And that's what I tried to instill in the recruits.

Secrets

Sunday morning, and the tiny fighters are heading out for their first patrol. There's some outdoor concert in Birmingham that needs security, and it's Camp Bishop's turn to test a new group of recruits. They'll walk around in their armour, show off their guns and skills to the TV cameras, and they'll make the music-lovers of the Midlands feel safe and warm and cared for.

I'm watching from the senior dorm as they run around, getting ready, bringing their armour out to the coaches. Jackson steps up beside me, on his way to join them on the coach.

"It's like watching your babies going off for their first day at school. Poor Mummy, left here on her own!"

I shove him hard, in the shoulder, and he laughs.

"What will you do on your own here all day, Mummy? Will you drink gin and be sad?"

"Shut up, Jackson. Go and babysit for them."

He crosses his arms in mock offence.

"Hey! Running all the communications for the day is hardly babysitting. You're just saying that because you've got something *mysterious* and *important* to do while we're away. You're just jealous that you won't be there to watch them screw up."

"Sitting at a desk, listening to their conversations, solving their problems, telling them what to do? And you've got Sleepy as your special helper. Which part of that doesn't sound like babysitting?"

"The part where I control everything that happens?"

I nudge him again, more gently. "Go on. They need someone to give them hell. I hereby give you that responsibility."

"Accepted!" He says, and grins.

*****

54

The coaches pull away, Commander Bracken and the other Senior Recruits on board. Miller and I are the only people in uniform left on site, guarding the gate while we wait for HQ to pick us up. Our fatigues are clean and ironed, our boots polished. Like the kids, we'll be on show today.

Everyone but the medical staff and the kitchen staff is going to Birmingham for the concert, but we've been excused. We're being drafted in as local liaison for a weapons deployment exercise. It's top secret, and even Commander Bracken couldn't tell us what we'd be doing. Jackson was right – I'd rather be in Birmingham.

"What do you think we'll be doing today?" Miller sounds nervous.

"No idea. Sharing our extensive local knowledge?"

Or proving to the Commander that I can be trusted as Lead Recruit again.

Miller is tall and boring, but he's good at the techie stuff. He's the one who fixes our radios and sorts out problems with guns and armour. I'm not looking forward to a day with him for company, but if they want Miller, we should at least be doing something interesting.

A soldier arrives in a camouflaged Land Rover to pick us up, and drops off three guards to take our place. The guards bring crates of equipment with them – armour, guns, and other supplies. Gate guards don't normally need armour. Is this standard procedure for guarding a camp with no trained backup? I wonder what they're planning to do today.

The driver takes us to a field south of town. It looks as if the circus has arrived – there are so many vehicles parked on the grass. The ground is soft under our feet as we climb down from the cab.

Our driver takes us to a large, white trailer, and knocks on the door. Another soldier opens it and beckons us inside. We climb the steps into a briefing room. There's a single, long table in the centre of the space, with chairs along both sides, all occupied. A man in fatigues is addressing the team, referring to images on a screen behind him, at the far end of the room. He pauses and signals to us to join the group.

"You must be our local liaisons. Take a seat at the table – we've just started the briefing. I'm Commander Holden. You must be ..." He consults a sheet of paper in a file on the table. "Miller and Smith." He looks up, expecting an answer.

"Yes, Sir!" We both respond. He nods, and waits for us to join the briefing. The soldier who let us in pulls two chairs over to the end of the table, and we sit down.

"As I was saying, the object of today's exercise is a proof-of-concept test of a large-scale weapons system."

An aerial view of Leominster appears on the screen.

"We'll be delivering the payloads to pre-identified locations in town, and observing the response of the local population."

A series of red circles appears on the screen. Tens, maybe hundreds of locations, in a rough grid across the town.

"We'll be dropping these in by drone at around midday. The drone team is setting up in their Ops trailer, and we'll have one of them here in a few minutes," he checks his watch, "to explain their role in this exercise."

A diagram of a cone-shaped object appears on the screen.

"This is what we're testing. Most of you will recognise the latest, slimmed-down model of the City Killer Urban Attack System, or CKUAS. We've shaved off some weight, and some bulk, and these can now be transported and placed by heavy-duty drones. No need for us to have boots on the ground in potentially dangerous situations."

I recognise the device. I've seen them in Commander Bracken's paperwork, and in the video we had the recruits watch in their briefing session, weeks ago. This is interesting. I lean forward and rest my elbows on the table, and I notice Miller doing the same.

"This is as much a test of our systems here as it is of the weapons in town. You will each be issued with an NBC suit, and required to wear it for the duration of the test. The trailers will be locked down for the duration of the test. You will be required to behave as if this was a full deployment. You will be expected to report back on your experiences after the test."

There's knock at the trailer door, and the soldier behind us opens it.

"Anderson. Come in."

A tall man in camouflage trousers and a black T-shirt walks up to the table, and Holden beckons him to the front of the room.

"This is Captain Anderson, our lead technician in the Drone Team. Ben – can you give us a run-down of your plans for the day?"

Anderson reaches the front of the room, and Holden moves to one side to allow him to address the group.

"Drone deployment is at the heart of the CKUAS system. Our job today is to demonstrate that these units," he indicates the diagram on the screen behind him, "can be delivered safely and efficiently to their desired locations on the ground. Delivery takes a few hours, so we'll be busy for most of the afternoon.

"In a real deployment, we'd most likely be positioned further away from the target, but that may not always be possible. Given our proximity to the deployment locations, and the opportunity to test a line-of-sight target, we will be observing NBC protocol on site at all times.

"Our job is to deliver the units, and to confirm delivery. That's where the local knowledge comes in. I'll need the local liaisons on hand to answer questions and check our deployment locations."

He looks at Holden, who stands, and thanks him.

"Today's operation will be controlled from this briefing room. Local liaisons and drone operators will be in the drone trailer. Weapons technicians will be outside, mounting weapons onto drones and monitoring our progress. All personnel will be issued with radios, and all commands will be issued by radio. NBC suits must be worn at all times, and gas masks kept within reach. We will order you to wear them as you would during a real deployment. Do not ignore these commands, as we need to test our readiness and our ability to protect our personnel.

"Brigadier Lee is the official observer from HQ for this test. He will be observing the operation from here." Holden waves a hand at an older man in a khaki service uniform, a row of medals on his chest. His face is distinguished and attractive under his greying hair, and his eyes sparkle as he watches Holden. "Brigadier Lee has full clearance to inspect all aspects of today's test. If he asks you a question concerning your activities, I expect you to offer him your full cooperation."

Brigadier Lee nods to Holden and looks round the table. "I'll be staying out of your way. Commander Holden has filled me in on your skills and training. I'm excited to be working with you, and I'm expecting a smooth ride.

"I don't need to remind you all that this is a classified weapons deployment test, and as such is not to be discussed with anyone. Whatever you see, or think you see, today – we have permission from the government to do everything we need to do to test the new CKUAS."

"Thank you, Sir," says Holden, turning his attention back to us. "At the end of this briefing, make your way to the equipment store, where you will be issued with your suit, mask, and radio. Advisory panel and research assistants – in here with me. Drone operators and local liaison – assemble in the drone trailer. Everyone else – meet at the equipment store.

"Questions?"

No one moves.

"Dismissed."

Miller

We follow the group from the briefing to an olive green marquee, and join a queue to pick up our equipment. A technician hands us each a white Nuclear-Biological-Chemical jumpsuit, a gas mask, and a radio, which clips to the waistband of the suit.

As we walk out of the tent, Anderson waves us over to another trailer in the line of identical vehicles.

"Smith and Miller?"

"Yes, Sir."

"You're with me." He turns and leads us up the steps into a small hallway. "Welcome to the nerve centre," he says, smiling.

He opens a door to a larger room, and gestures us to follow him inside.

It's dark inside, the only light spilling from banks of monitors around the walls. There are workstations in front of each monitor, with keyboards, joysticks and other controls. Men and women in black T-shirts and camouflage trousers sit in front of the screens, headphones on. Most of them are watching views of the field outside, but a couple are actively steering drones over the town. I watch as one follows the route of the morning run from the bypass into the industrial estate.

Anderson claps his hands, loudly.

"Listen up, people. These are your local liaison officers: Recruit Smith and Recruit Miller. Ask them questions. Run things by them. Make use of their local knowledge. They are here to help you."

He turns back to us, and indicates a table in the corner of the room, and two office chairs.

"This is you. Keep quiet and don't disturb the work. Be on hand in case anyone needs you. If someone asks for your help, you may leave your table and stand with them at their station. By all means talk quietly between yourselves, but be aware of the work, and be ready to help. When we begin, there will be no leaving the trailer. Everything will be sealed against NBC attack. There's a bathroom across the hall." He points back the way we came in. "Don't open the external door."

He checks his watch, and turns again to the room.

"This operation is officially underway. NBC suits on, radios on, gas masks within reach."

He turns back.

"That includes you two. Get ready, get sitting down, and get waiting." He gives us a smile.

We all stand up and pull on the white jumpsuits over our uniforms. The small room suddenly feels crowded, with everyone moving around at once. I pull the zip up to my throat, smooth down the Velcro seal over the top, and clip the radio to my waist.

We sit down and wait for questions.

*****

"So where were you, before Camp Bishop?"

Miller looks up from inspecting his gas mask.

"Before signing up?"

"Yeah. What did you do before you were Bracken's techie genius?"

"I was at school."

Of course the techie genius stayed at school.

"Don't tell me. A-levels in all the sciences?"

"Maths, further maths, physics, chemistry."

"You passed?"

He looks offended.

"Oh – you did well?"

He nods.

"So what are you doing here?"

"They were advertising for technical roles, so I signed up."

"Too cool for uni?"

"It's much more interesting to fix things that need fixing. I like working under pressure, and doing things that other people can't do."

I think about my own choices. He's right – I'd rather be here, learning on my feet and proving myself every day than passing a bunch of exams.

"I get that."

"So what about you?"

I tell him about the butcher's shop. Gutting chickens, chopping muscle and gristle and bone, washing floors. He nods, and goes back to playing with his gas mask.

We sit in silence for a while. I glance around the room, but no one seems to need our advice.

"Bracken told me he's looking for a new Lead Recruit."

Miller has put down his gas mask. I'm surprised by his comment, and by his sudden focus on me.

"He did?"

"Yeah. But I thought that was you."

Great. This is what we're going to talk about?

I nod. "It was."

"So what did you do? Why doesn't he need you any more?"

He does, I want to say. *He'll realise it soon enough. I just need to remind him what I'm good at.*

"It's complicated."

"Oh."

"I stepped over a line. I did something he didn't like."

Miller says nothing, but stares at me.

"I upset a couple of the baby recruits."

"What did you do?"

I really don't want to be thinking about this now, but there's nothing else to do.

"I tried to teach someone a lesson. The commander didn't like how I did it."

"But that's your job."

"It was. But it turns out that the commander has rules – rules I didn't know about. And I broke one of them."

"So he dumped you?"

That was brutal, Miller. Dumped me? Really?

I shrug, fighting an urge to shout, thump the table, kick something.

"Yeah. He dumped me."

"But you did so many jobs for him."

Can't we leave this alone?

"Yes, Miller. Yes I did. I did them really well, too." I hiss at him to avoid shouting. I'm so close to losing my temper.

Thanks for rubbing it in.

There's shout from the other end of the room. Someone wants to ask us a question. I nod to Miller, and let him go this time. I don't think I can be professional at the moment.

I stare at the wall and take some deep breaths. I need to be calm if I'm going to make a good impression today. The last thing I need is Miller needling me about the Lead Recruit job.

He spends a few minutes with the drone operator, then sits back down at the table.

"What did they want to know?" I tip my head towards the far end of the room.

"Whether there are any tall structures near one of the drop points."

"OK." That sounds like a question I could answer without shouting.

Good.

Miller is looking at me again.

"So why did you want to be Lead Recruit? It looks like a lot of extra work, just to be in Commander Bracken's good books."

We're doing this, are we? Dissecting my life choices? Fine.

I roll my eyes.

"It's a way out, Miller. It's a way up. If I can impress Bracken, maybe he'll recommend me for promotion. Maybe he'll take me with him when he gets promoted. Maybe it was my ticket to a job in London."

Was.

"You get a lot more power over the recruits, don't you?"

"I get a lot more responsibility, if that's what you mean. It's up to me to sort out trouble before it reaches the commander. He trusts … trusted me to find out what was going on at camp, and to keep it under control."

"You certainly have more influence than the rest of us. If the kids won't listen to us, all we have to do is threaten to tell you, and they sort themselves out pretty fast."

Do they? Interesting. I didn't know that my name was being used as a threat.

I flash Miller a grin.

"That's good to know. I'll bear that in mind." That electric feeling of power is back, and it feels good. If I can convince Bracken to take me back, I'll have that power again.

"So how do you do it? Make them afraid of you?"

I do things you wouldn't dare.

He wants to understand what it takes to scare the recruits. Maybe I can demonstrate it for him. I lean slowly across the table and put my face close to Miller's. He looks uncomfortable, but he waits for me to answer.

"I make it personal," I keep my voice quiet, so he has to stay close and listen. "I remember who they are. I remember what they've done, and I follow through with my threats. I never let them forget who's in charge, and I never pull my punches."

He raises his eyebrows, clearly thinking about what I'm saying, but he doesn't move away.

"But most of all? I enjoy it. And they know I do. They know they can't beg me to let them off, because they know I'm not looking for a loophole. I *want* to punish them. They know they have nowhere to hide."

I watch his reaction as I lean back, slowly. He stares at me, a look of horror creeping over his face.

And now I understand. And I can't help laughing.

"You want the job, don't you, Miller? You want to be Lead Recruit?"

"I … maybe …"

"What did Bracken offer you? Did he say he would consider you for the promotion?"

I can't keep the laughter out of my voice. Miller looks at the floor and his face flushes red with embarrassment.

"He said I was in the running," he says, quietly.

I should stop. I should leave him alone, but this is too easy.

"He did? Okay. What did he think that you … *you* … could bring to the role?"

Miller stays quiet, shaking his head.

"Let me think. Did he promise you power and respect? Extra authority to use against the kids?"

Miller sits very still, eyes downcast. I lean towards him again.

"Here's the thing, Miller. Bracken can't give you that authority. He can't decide who the kids respect. You have to earn that. If you can't crush them with a word, they'll eat you alive. They know when you're weak, and they know what they can get away with. If you want to control them, you need to give them a reason to do what you tell them. You need them to be properly afraid of you.

"Can you do that, Miller? Can you make them afraid? Because if you can't, you're not the Lead Recruit, whatever Bracken says."

Miller shakes his head, slowly.

"I can't believe it's that cruel," he says, so quietly I have to strain to hear him over the noise of the computers and operators behind me.

"You think you can run Camp Bishop with hugs and campfire songs? You think you can get the kids to push themselves and throw themselves at the assault course and the morning run day after day with *kind words*? We're not a holiday camp. We're not a babysitting service. We have soldiers to train and send out onto the streets, and we have an insanely short time to get them ready.

"We can't just scare them occasionally. We have to make sure they internalise the fear. They have to want to push themselves, because if they don't, they have to deal with me.

"If I don't scare them enough to train themselves, and push themselves, and keep themselves ahead of the pack, I'm not doing my job. They'll be scared enough when they get out in public. If all they've had from us is encouragement, they won't stand a chance against the terrorists."

Plus the role is no fun if you try to be everyone's mother. Let Ellman do that job. See where it gets her.

There's a shout from behind us. Someone else needs our local knowledge. I leave Miller to think about what I've said, and walk over to help the drone operator.

Internalise some fear of your own, Miller. Understand that you can't replace me. You don't have the backbone.

Drones

We spend the next few hours going from operator to operator, guiding their placement of the drones and explaining the conditions on the ground at each of their target sites. The weapons need to be on hard, level surfaces, and this isn't always possible at the predetermined sites, so we are asked to find suitable locations nearby.

One of the aims of the test is to see how local people react to the weapons. The town isn't too busy, but there are people on the streets, and there are witnesses to the drone placements.

"Why aren't they freaking out?" I ask the woman I'm helping. "How come they're just watching?"

"They've been told there's a test today. They just haven't been told what it is. This way we can see how disruptive the deployment is, without having to worry about people calling it in as an attack."

I watch the people under the drone, staring up, shopping bags in their hands, as the weapon drops slowly to the ground in front of them. They watch, and point at it, and when it lands they walk round it and keep walking, as if this happens every day. The operator places the weapon on the ground, and disconnects it from the drone. She sends her drone back into the air, the view pulling out until we're over the rooftops, and we can see other streets and other drones and other weapons.

*****

By three o'clock the weapons have all been placed. Anderson congratulates the drone operators, and explains that their role is now one of monitoring and filming the next stage of the test. The images will be seen in the command trailer, so they need to stay in the air over the town and follow what happens next.

"Remember. Everything you see here is classified, and everything we do today is done with permission."

His radio crackles, and Commander Holden's voice commands everyone on site to put their gas masks on.

"You heard the commander. Gas masks on!" There's a rustling, as everyone in the trailer follows the command. I pick my mask up and pull it down over my head, adjusting my ponytail to make sure it fits. Miller and I look at each other, and he shrugs. There's not much talking to be done with our voices blocked by the gas filters. We sit in silence and watch the screens.

*****

Nothing happens to begin with. The drone operators station their drones over the town, and we watch as people walk past the weapons, as cars drive along the roads, as people go about their Sunday lives.

Then there's some action on one of the screens at the edge of town. An army truck driving along a road into town suddenly pulls what looks like a U-turn, and parks itself across both lanes. Six, seven soldiers jump out, and block the road completely, guns trained on the oncoming traffic. No one is allowed in, and no one is allowed to leave. The cars start to build up behind the truck, and the soldiers turn them back, one at a time.

I check the other screens, and this is happening on all the roads in and out of town. Trucks pull up, block the road, and soldiers in armour jump out. Within minutes, all the roads are blocked. Cars heading out of town are being sent back in, and cars heading in are being sent away.

Twenty minutes later, we're watching the screens and suddenly buildings start to crumble. Trees wobble until they fall. Streetlamps draw white lines across pavements and roads. Cars run into each other.

I'm trying to be professional, but I can't help raising an eyebrow under my gas mask.

What exactly do you have permission to do here, Holden?

And there are soldiers, in armour. More soldiers than I've ever seen in one place, running from building to building and vehicle to vehicle, rounding people up and evacuating them. The people seem happy to follow them, running along, keeping away from buildings that are tumbling into the streets, or collapsing into their own footprints.

People stumble, but the soldiers help them to their feet, and keep them moving. I'm watching several screens, and the drones are showing lines and crowds of people being led away by the soldiers. From where I'm sitting, I can't see where they go.

So we're testing an evacuation. Useful to know how long it takes to clear a town.

I focus on the screen closest to our table. It shows the industrial estate where we take the recruits every day on their run. The buildings are caving in, and the trees are lying on the floor. I can see two of the weapons, in the car parks of the buildings. I can't see any more people, or any more soldiers.

The outline of the closest weapon starts to look hazy. Before long, a plume of smoke is blowing from the weapon across the car park and the buildings. The same thing happens to the second weapon, and the smoke begins to spread.

Testing the chemical delivery system. Good idea.

I wonder what they're using to simulate the toxic gas. Something we can see clearly on the screens.

As we watch, a blanket of smoke drifts across the buildings. Within ten minutes, all the screens I can see from my seat show a blanket of fog. Zero visibility.

It takes nearly an hour for the smoke to clear. The view slowly returns, and we're looking once again at broken buildings and fallen trees. The room is quiet.

Anderson's radio crackles again.

"Congratulations, everyone. That's a successful test. Drone operators, please return your drones to HQ. Drone technicians, please be ready to receive them. Maintain NBC protocols – suits and gas masks on – until I give the all-clear."

"You heard Holden!" Shouts Anderson through his mask. "Bring the drones home."

The view on the screens I can see starts to draw back, as the drones move away from their monitoring locations and make their way across the town and the fields towards us.

After that, there's nothing for us to do but sit and wait. We can't take our masks off, so we can't talk. We can't go outside. The drone cameras are switched off one by one as they arrive back in the field outside. Miller plays with the Velcro seal of his suit.

I don't know how long we sit there. It seems like hours, sweating in our masks and suits. Eventually Holden sounds the all-clear, and I pull my mask off and take deep gulps of the stale air in the trailer. I stand up and peel off my suit, along with everyone else, and almost forget to remove the radio from the waistband.

It's dark outside when Anderson finally has permission to open the door. Holden bounds up the steps and into the drone control room, shaking hands with all the drone operators and thanking them for their hard work. He shakes our hands last, and thanks us as well.

Anderson joins us at the table.

"Thank you for your help today. You solved some sticky problems for us, and it looks as if everything worked fine.

"Are you hungry? We've got a meal arriving in ten minutes. Come and join us, and we'll drive you back afterwards."

"Thank you, Sir."

We follow the drone operators out of the trailer, and across the field to the equipment tent. We drop our suits, masks, and radios in crates outside, and when we walk in the space has been transformed into dining area for everyone on site. One of the drone operators we worked with waves us over to a table, and we sit with the drone team as another lorry and trailer pulls up outside, and we're sent out in groups to collect boxes of packaged hot meals and bottles of water.

"Takeaway service to a tent in a field? This might be the most impressive thing I've seen all day!"

The drone operators laugh, and agree with me. The food is good, and hot, and everyone seems happy with the day's work. We talk about life at Camp Bishop, and the training we're giving to the new recruits.

After dinner, as we're leaving the tent, Brigadier Lee walks over to us and shakes our hands, Commander Holden at his side.

"Thank you for your work today, recruits. It's good to have local knowledge for an operation like this."

Holden waves a hand at the two of us. "These are Bracken's candidates for Lead Recruit. The best of his senior team." Miller can't help smiling at that.

So we're both in the running, are we? I'll keep that in mind.

The brigadier nods. "I've been hoping to meet Commander Bracken's people. If your work today is anything to judge by, you both have bright futures ahead of you." He looks at me. "I hope we can work together again." He smiles, but it doesn't reach his eyes. It's not comfortable, being on the receiving end of that smile.

Holden thanks us again, and sends us back to camp with our driver. The roadblock is still in place on the bypass, but the driver shows the soldiers his badge, and they pull back and let him through.

We're back before the tiny fighters, but the lights are on in the medical building and the kitchen, although the kitchen staff don't seem to be having their usual evening party. Maybe they only do that when they've spent all day with the kids. I know how they feel.

Miller and I make our way to the senior dorm, and I head straight to grab a shower and a change of clothes. It is a relief to wash off the sweat from the suits and the masks.

I think about our conversation today. Miller might not be Lead Recruit material, but I can't afford to ignore what he told me. If Holden thinks Bracken is considering him for the job, I need to make a move. I need to convince the commander to promote me again. I just need an excuse to show him how much he needs my help.

*****

"So! How was Birmingham? Did you give them hell?"

The coaches pulled in a few minutes ago, and Jackson is back in the senior dorm, fresh from supervising the unloading of crates of armour and guns from the luggage holds.

He smirks. "I was very responsible."

I raise an eyebrow. "Anything I should know about?"

"I nearly made Ellman cry." There's a smug look on his face.

"Oh?"

"She doesn't like the cameras. And she *really* doesn't like being called a front-line doll. When they print her photo in the paper, I'm going to pin it up all over camp. She'll cry then, for sure."

"Good work, Recruit Jackson!"

"I taught Sleepy a new skill, too. Radio ninja!"

I shake my head. "He is not! I don't believe you."

"You're right. He's not. He's hopeless, actually – but it kept him out of trouble."

I reach over and pat him on the head. "You and your hopeless puppy!"

He scowls.

Power

"Ketty! You must have done something right yester-day. Holden wants you back this morning, on the clean-up crew. Miller, Jackson – you're with Ketty. Pickup at the gate in 15 minutes.

"And remember – everything about this exercise is classified. You weren't there, you know nothing about it. No one hears about it from you. Understood?"

"Yes, Sir!"

We're standing in the Commander's office, lining up for our instructions for the kids' day off. There are as-signments for all the Senior Recruits, but we're the only ones heading off site. The others were given their jobs for the day in the dining room, but we've been sum-moned to the private office. Our involvement in the weapons test is not to be shared.

"You'll need your armour and guns. Check your air canisters and contamination panels, and grab new ones from stores if you need them. Woods is authorised to let you have what you need.

"You're to do whatever Holden and his team ask you to do. Your conduct today reflects directly on me, and the rest of my staff. Do not let me down."

"No, Sir!"

"Dismissed."

We hurry back to our dorms to collect our armour and guns, and meet at the gate. Yesterday's driver pulls up, and helps us load our crates into the Land Rover. We climb in, and he drives us back through the roadblock to HQ's field base.

Commander Holden is waiting in the briefing room. We introduce Jackson, and the commander waves us to the empty seats at the end of the table.

"Thank you for coming back – Smith, Miller: your assistance yesterday was invaluable, thank you."

"Today I need you on the ground. You three have been recommended for your physical fitness, your discretion, and your ability to follow orders.

"Yesterday, we placed the weapons into the target zone. Today, we need to collect them again for analysis."

He switches on the screen behind him. The diagram of the City Killer appears.

"The units will be disarmed before you reach them. You will scan them here," he points to the barcode, high up on the weapon's cone, "and ensure that they are safe to move. You will load them into your truck, and you will return them to a collection point in town.

"You will follow any and all orders given to you during the day. You will follow a pre-defined route. You will change that route only under instruction from me or my staff. You will consult your contamination panels, and you will keep your helmets on at all times.

"Remember: whatever you see, or think you see, in town – we have permission from the government to do whatever we need to do to test our weapon.

"You will not share with anybody anything that you see or hear in town today. This is a classified weapons system deployment test. You are here as trusted recruits, and you will not discuss today's activities with anyone. Understood?"

"Yes, Sir."

"Moreover, if you see any unauthorised personnel during your mission, you will inform HQ immediately. You will detain anyone you see, if it is safe to do so. You will hold them securely until a member of my team arrives to pick them up.

"You will not speak to them. You will not engage with them. You will not permit them to speak.

"Understood?"

"Yes, Sir."

"Good. Smith – I understand you have been trained to drive one of our all-terrain cargo vehicles?"

"I have, Sir."

"You're our driver, today. Miller – you're our tech support. Scan the weapons, make a visual check, make sure they are safe for your team to pick up."

"Yes, Sir."

"Jackson – you're the muscle. The physical safety of the weapons is in your hands. Ensure that they are handled with care, and stowed safely in the vehicle."

"Yes, Sir."

Holden steps back to the screen, and brings up the aerial view showing the locations of the weapons. He waves his hand over the eastern side of the town.

"Your job for today is to pick up the weapons in this area. You will follow the trained bomb disposal teams, and you will pick up the weapons only after they have declared them to be safe. Your route is as shown." A red line appears on the screen, joining the dots across our zone. "Changes to your route will be communicated to you via radio, and via this."

He picks up a tablet, and slides it down the table towards us. "Miller: you're also the navigator. Keep an eye on the route, and inform your driver if it changes."

"Yes, Sir", Miller says, picking up the tablet. There's a map of the town on the screen, and the same route is picked out in red. They must have set up a local network to communicate with it on the move.

"Jackson: you're on communications. You will monitor radio traffic, and inform your driver of any important announcements or changes. You will also check in with my staff as requested, and keep them informed of your movements and any problems you encounter."

"Yes, Sir."

"Is your armour black, or do you still have the grey recruit armour?"

"Black, Sir."

"No names visible?"

"No, Sir."

"Good. Get changed. The bomb disposal teams are already at work. When you're dressed, one of the drivers will assign you an all-terrain vehicle, and run through everything you need to know. There are changing rooms in the next trailer.

"Any questions?"

"No, Sir."

"Dismissed."

*****

We drive into town, and it's a mess. It looks as if they've bulldozed all the buildings. The roads are blocked by empty cars, and the ground is split and broken. There are fallen trees everywhere.

All morning, we load empty weapons into the truck. We drive back to the drop-off along our pre-determined route three times to unload, and then we set out again. Everywhere is the same. The buildings are rubble, the ground is crumpled as if something has tried to crawl out from under it. There are trees and cars and belongings blocking the roads. I use the all-terrain vehicle to mount curbs, drive along verges, drive over obstacles, and push past abandoned cars.

We're trying to get to the next location, in front of what used to be a row of shops, but the road is completely blocked. Several vehicles have collided, and there's no way to get past. I pull the vehicle up onto the pavement and drive along the edge of the road, pushing the cars out of my way. The noise would be deafening if we weren't wearing helmets.

I pull into a small car park, next to the weapon. We climb down, and Miller scans the barcode and declares it safe to move. He pulls down the tailgate of the truck and climbs up to stand in the back. Jackson and I lift the weapon to Miller, and Jackson follows it up. Together, they secure it with ropes and wooden panels, then jump back down to the car park. I roll my shoulders and stretch.

"Anyone hungry?"

"Sure."

"We should get back in the vehicle before we take our helmets off …" I protest, but it's too late. Jackson makes a show of checking his contamination panel, and taking off his helmet. He takes a deep breath, grins, and pulls a ration bar from his belt. My contamination panel shows a pale enough pink in the chemical section to allow a short exposure to whatever is they used in the test yesterday, and we all take our helmets off and enjoy a few minutes in the open air, out of sight of Holden's troops.

"They've made a mess of this place", Jackson says, pointing at the building in front of us.

He's right. There's nothing left. A couple of corners of brickwork, and a pile of rubble.

"Do you think the weapons did this?"

"No, Jackson. I think the fairies did this." I roll my eyes. Miller laughs.

"So how do they work? They don't look big enough to knock down houses."

"It's a network. If you put enough of them down and coordinate their actions, you can create localised earthquakes", Miller explains, and Jackson nods.

"You can release chemical agents as well", I point out, holding up my right arm to show the contamination panel.

"So you get the buildings and the people in one go?"

"They're called City Killers, Jackson. What do you think they do?" Miller and I are both laughing now, at Jackson's expense.

Jackson looks around. From where we're standing, we can see warehouses and industrial units reduced to metal skeletons. Cars jammed together on the road. Trees and lampposts on the ground.

He starts to grin.

"We're unbeatable! Look at this! Look!" He spreads his arms wide and indicates the destruction around us. His enthusiasm is infectious.

And then he's pointing at something on the floor, next to the building in front of us.

"War paint! We need war paint. We're *warriors*!"

There's a lipstick on the floor, next to the corner of brickwork. The idea is crazy, and we're all laughing, but Jackson walks over, points at the lipstick, and picks it up.

He pulls the lid off as he heads back towards us, holding it out like a sword. I realise that he's serious, and dodge out of his reach, but Miller isn't so lucky. Jackson catches his armour and puts a thick red stripe across his chest.

Miller looks down, hands in the air. "Hey! Bracken's going to be mad at this!"

"Bracken would be mad at all of this. We're not supposed to take our helmets off, remember?"

Jackson laughs, and lunges for me. I'm too quick for him, and he tries again and again, until Miller steps behind him and grabs his elbows.

I step forward, and take the lipstick.

"You want war paint? Stand still."

Jackson shakes out of Miller's grasp, and stands to attention in front of me. I steady his head with one hand, and draw three bold stripes down the length of his face. He roars and thumps his chest when I'm done.

"Miller?"

He stands still, unwilling to let Jackson hold him for me. I give him two bold stripes along his cheekbones. He looks good.

I use my reflection in the wing mirror to give myself one stripe down the centre of my face, hairline to neck. Jackson's right – this feels powerful and exciting, like being back at the party in the kitchen, dancing on the tables.

I'm laughing as I throw the lipstick away, climb back into the truck, and start the engine. The others climb in, and we put our helmets on again.

"Where to?"

Miller consults the map.

"That way", he says, pointing straight ahead, across the road blocked by cars. Jackson thumps his glove against the dashboard.

"Go on, Ketty! Smash us through!"

So I do. Rev the engine, aim for the gaps between the cars, and push them, screaming, out of the way. It feels powerful. It feels amazing. I'm laughing as we break through the second row of traffic and onto the side road beyond.

Doubts

We're on our second-to-last pickup of the day. I pull the vehicle into an empty driveway, and we climb out to check the weapon. Miller scans the barcode while Jackson and I wait.

We're on a residential street, but most of the houses are piles of rubble. The weapon is on a traffic island, in the middle of a junction. There are fallen trees, half blocking the road, and more belongings – shoes, bags, coats – on the pavements and driveways.

I step away from Miller as he performs his checks. There's movement, behind one of the fallen trees. I unclip my gun, and step towards it.

Carefully, turning round as I walk and keeping everything around me in sight, I approach the tree. Through the branches I can see a patch of colour, moving slightly as I get closer. Gun trained on the tree, I step round the branches and take aim at the movement.

There's a cry, and a girl – she can't be more than seven or eight – pushes herself back against the trunk. She's looking at me, and she looks terrified. I'm armoured up, helmet on, and I have a gun pointed at her. Her bright yellow raincoat stands out against the dark branches.

Slowly, I let go of the gun with one hand, and hold it up so she can see it's not aimed at her any more. I step closer, put one knee on the ground, and clip the gun to my back. I show her my hands, and she relaxes slightly.

Unauthorised personnel, Holden?

She says something, but I don't hear it through the helmet. I check my contamination panel, and crack the seal on my visor, enough to catch what she is saying.

"Are you going to kill me as well?"

I look at her for a moment. Why would she think that? Why would she even consider that? And what is a young girl doing in the middle of a weapon test zone?

I wave my hand at the surroundings.

"Is this your street?"

She nods.

"Where did everyone go?"

She points away, down the road. I look in the direction she's pointing, but the road turns a corner, and I can't see where it leads.

"I came back, though", she says. "I needed to find Grandma, but the soldiers wouldn't wait for her."

"Wasn't she with you?"

The girl shakes her head.

"Did you find her?"

She shakes her head again.

"I got scared. I hid in the car." She points at a very expensive people carrier in the nearest driveway. "There was smoke. It smelled funny. It made me cough. I closed all the windows and sat in the car until it went away. I think I slept all night in the car."

Smoke. From the weapons. From the City Killers.

Did Holden use chemical weapons on a civilian population?

That can't be right. They must have evacuated the people. I saw the soldiers on the screens yesterday, leading people from their homes and cars.

So what's this girl doing here?

"What's your name?" I ask, as I reach to activate my radio.

"Natasha."

"Well, Natasha, I'm going to call someone to help you. OK?" She nods.

"Unit Five to HQ, over."

"Go ahead, unit Five."

"Unauthorised person detained in location 135, over."

"Understood, Unit Five. Support is mobilised. Hold the intruder in place until support arrives. Do not engage intruder, over."

"Understood. Unit Five out."

"Ketty?"

It's Jackson on the private team channel.

"Jackson. Stay where you are. Get the weapon onto the truck. I have this under control."

"OK."

I look back at Natasha. She's watching me closely.

"There are people on their way to get you somewhere safe."

She nods.

"People like you?"

"People like me. They'll take care of you."

She nods again.

"There were people like you here yesterday, when the shaking happened. They told us to go with them. Are you the good guys, or the bad guys?"

I can't help laughing.

"We're the good guys, Natasha. We're here to take care of you."

"Good", she says. "Daddy says that I can trust the good guys, but I have to run away from the bad guys – the ones who blow people up."

"That's good advice, Natasha."

And I really hope it is.

There are footsteps on the road behind me. Several people running. I turn to see four soldiers in armour coming along the road towards us, guns raised.

I stand up and face them, hands in the air. I pull up my visor and shout.

"It's a kid! It's just a kid!"

They stop running and walk towards us, cutting off any escape we might attempt.

"Unit Five?" My radio picks up the transmission. I activate my microphone.

"Yes."

"Stand aside."

I look back at Natasha.

"It's just a kid …"

"Stand aside."

I step away from the tree.

One of the soldiers lowers their gun, and walks forward, holding out a hand to the girl. She looks at me, hands clasped behind her back where the soldier can't reach them. I nod to her.

"Go on."

She thinks for a moment, then stands up, and offers her hand to the soldier. He leads her away down the street, the other three following behind.

I run back round the tree to the vehicle, where Jackson and Miller are securing the weapon in the truck.

"Are we done?"

"Yeah."

They jump down, and we climb into the cab.

And I'm almost sure I hear gunfire, three shots, a little way down the street, before I close the door.

*****

We're heading back to the drop-off point with our final load of weapons. Miller and Jackson are arguing over the map – Miller thinks we've taken a wrong turn, and they're trying to direct me back to the approved route. I stop the vehicle at a deserted junction, and wait for them to figure it out.

There's a gap between the demolished buildings in front of us, and I think I see movement on the far side. There's a wide stretch of grass behind the rubble, and through the gap I see people in black armour, walking up and down, guns in their hands.

And there's something else, behind them on the grass. I don't have a clear view, but I can see what look like piles of clothing, colourful, heaped up on the ground.

Miller reaches a decision. Eyes on the map, he waves his hand to the right.

"Turn here, then turn left at the next junction. Then you'll be back where you should be."

I nod, and start turning the truck. I keep watching the view ahead, and as I swing round and speed up along the road, I realise that they're not clothes. They're people. Bodies. Piles and piles of them.

Unauthorised personnel. An entire town of unauthorised personnel.

*****

I focus on driving the truck. Miller and Jackson are still looking at the map on the tablet and arguing, and we've moved on, out of sight of whatever it was that I saw.

A couple of turns later, and we make it back to the drop-off point. We unload the weapons, and the officer in charge signs us off for the day.

"Good work. Drop the vehicle back with HQ, and report in with Commander Holden. And stick to your route on the way out of town."

"Yes, Sir."

We climb back into the truck. Miller consults the map, and directs me to the north and out onto the bypass. This isn't the quickest route back to HQ. There must be more places in town they don't want us to see.

I don't know what Miller and Jackson saw while they were discussing our route, and I'm not sure I want to find out. We drive back to HQ in silence.

We return the vehicle and the tablet, keeping our visors over our faces, and hurry to the changing rooms. I take off my helmet, and wash my face. As much as I like the war paint, Holden won't approve, and the cold water feels good against my skin.

I change out of my armour, stack it in my crate, and double-check my face for any traces of the lipstick. I meet the others outside, and we walk back to the briefing room. Holden and Brigadier Lee are waiting.

"Good work, recruits," says Holden, looking pleased. "The eastern section is clear, on schedule, thanks to you.

"As I said this morning, this operation is classified. You will not discuss what you have seen here today with anyone. Commander Bracken may debrief you. He is part of this operation, and he has the relevant security clearances. You have permission to speak to him.

"Whatever you saw, or think you saw, was done with the full permission of your government. Disclosure of anything you saw or did today to anyone outside this room, or Commander Bracken's office, will be severely punished. And trust me, you do not want to find out what that means. Understood?"

"Yes, Sir."

Holden glances at Brigadier Lee, who nods, and takes over. "This operation is now over. I am pleased to announce that we have successfully tested the most useful weapon in our arsenal. Thank you, recruits, for your contribution. I will be reporting back to Commander Bracken on your performance today, and my report will be glowing."

He smiles at me, and I can't decide what he's thinking. His smile is warm, but his eyes are cold.

"Thank you, Sir."

"Dismissed."

*****

The driver takes us back to camp, and drops us at the gate with our crates of armour. I'm aware that no one speaks on the journey, and the three of us all stare out of the windows, alone with our thoughts.

I'm starting to doubt what I saw. Were there really piles of bodies on the grass? And what about the gunshots, when I handed over the little girl? There has to be an explanation, for all of it. We can't be killing civilians now. I can't believe that.

Can I?

Whatever you saw – or think you saw. That's what Commander Holden said. What was he expecting us to see?

What's the plan behind all of this? Is there something bigger going on? Something I can understand?

"We've missed dinner." Miller sounds stunned, standing on the gravel path into camp. I hadn't realised how late it was.

"They'll have saved something for us." Jackson claps Miller on the shoulder. "We'll go and raid the kitchen. Ketty?"

I'm looking at Commander Bracken's office. The lights are on, but the blinds are closed.

"I'll follow you. Give me a minute." I look at Jackson. "Actually – would you mind taking my crate to the dorm?"

He shrugs, and holds his crate out. I stack mine on top.

"Thanks", I say, distracted, as the two of them walk away.

And I march over to the commander's office.

I'm starting to get angry. I want to know what he knows.

Challenge

"What did we do?"

Commander Bracken sits up in his chair, surprised to see me. Surprised by my tone of voice.

"Close the door", he growls.

I've never seen him like this. I hesitate.

"Close the door!"

His shout shakes me out of my uncertainty, and I push the door closed behind me.

"Sit down." He waves at the chair in front of his desk. I do as I'm told.

He rubs his hands over his face, as if he's trying to wash something off. There's a glass of something – whisky? – in front of him on the desk. He sits, hunched over, unable to look at me.

"What. Did. We. Do?" I ask again, through clenched teeth.

He shakes his head.

"Ketty … Ketty. There are some things you need to understand."

I sit back in the chair.

"Try me."

He nods. Takes a drink. Sets the glass carefully down in the centre of his desk.

"Yesterday wasn't an exercise."

So it's true. We did attack a town full of people.

"OK." I keep my voice neutral.

"It's all part of a larger plan." His tone is pleading. He's begging me to understand.

"A plan to do what? Win the war for the terrorists?"

He shakes his head again. Makes calming motions with his hands. Takes a deep breath.

"There was terrorist activity in town. We tracked them going in, scouting for an attack."

"So the town was full of terrorists? We just did what we had to do?" I can't keep the sarcasm from my voice.

He looks at me, and I see that he's close to tears, or to losing his temper. I keep quiet and nod, encouraging him to continue.

"HQ has been looking for a target. They wanted to test their wide-area weapon." He takes another drink. I sit quietly. I don't want to provoke more shouting. He shouldn't be telling me this, and I don't want him to remember that. I want to understand what's happened.

"When we tracked the terrorists into town, we had orders to leave them alone. We were told to contact HQ, and to stand by for instructions."

"And they sent Holden."

He nods.

"They asked for local liaison officers to be sent over, and they told me to clear the camp for the day. They sent the recruits to Birmingham, they gave the camp staff and medics an NBC drill, and they put their own guards on the gate. I ... I left them to it."

He runs his fingers through his hair, leaves them there. Rests his forehead on the palms of his hands.

"You didn't know?"

He shakes his head. "I wasn't certain."

"Who else knows?"

He shrugs.

So we're in this together. HQ has put us in this position.

"And they sent me, and Jackson, and Miller to clean up after them?"

He nods, slowly. I think through what HQ is doing. What they might be planning.

What we can do.

"So how does this work? Do we claim it was an accident? A demonstration gone wrong? Or do we claim that we've wiped out a nest of terrorists?"

"I don't know, Ketty." His voice cracks, and he sits up, cups his hands around his glass. "HQ will update me."

He sits in silence for a while, staring at the drink in his hands.

"You shouldn't know this", he says, quietly.

I say nothing. I know he's right, but I know what I saw in town. Things I can't forget.

"Can I trust you?" He looks up, meets my eyes.

And I see my chance. I see that he needs me. I see what I can do.

I lean forward in my chair. "Sir. As I understand it, your Lead Recruit would need to know this." I'm offering him my loyalty, and I'm asking for my job back. I'm taking a risk. I'm gambling everything on his need for an assistant to share this with. For someone to go through this with him.

I'm gambling that he's telling me the truth. I'm gambling on HQ having a plan to manage the situation. I'm hoping he wants me back. And I'm using the worst atrocity of this fight – of my lifetime – as leverage.

I feel sick. I'm terrified that he's going to say no, to send me away in disgrace. I'm horrified that this could be my ticket back into his confidence.

And then I realise that I have another lever to use against him. Behind him, on a low shelf, I can see a row of bottles. Two empty vodka bottles, and a half-full bottle of whisky, which must be what he's drinking now. He looks up at me, and follows the line of my gaze.

This is easy. This is what I've been doing all my life. Negotiating my survival with the alcoholic who holds my future in his hands.

Thanks, Dad, for the training.

He looks back at me, his expression begging me not to notice. Not to say anything. I hold his gaze, keeping my expression neutral. I raise an eyebrow, fractionally.

And I have to stop myself from laughing when he responds.

"Absolutely." He clears his throat. Sits up straight in his chair. "Absolutely, Ketty. You're right."

He reaches into a drawer in his desk, pulls out my file; opens it, pushing his drink out of the way.

"This could have happened in any number of towns. Anywhere we had evidence of terrorist activity. The first town to track terrorists on their streets. It happened to be on our doorstep."

He pauses, and nods to himself, thinking this through.

"That puts us in a unique position. We're under HQ's microscope, while this situation is being handled. We have an opportunity to step up and show what we can do."

He looks at me briefly, then continues.

"This changes things. We're not just running a kindergarten here any more. We're on the front line. We're not babysitting these kids. We're fighting a war." He flips the pages of my file until he finds the record of my work at Camp Bishop. "I'm going to need someone I can rely on. Someone with a strong stomach, and the willingness to follow through on whatever HQ does to handle this situation. Someone willing to take risks. To get their hands dirty. To do uncomfortable things." He glances behind him, at the bottles on the shelf.

"Yes, Sir."

He looks at me again, speaks slowly and deliberately.

"*We* need to be the team that exceeds HQ's expectations. *We* need to become the people they call to sort out their toughest situations. This could be good for both of us." He's looking me in the eye. "This could bring us to the attention of HQ. This could be my ticket to a promotion.

"And if I go to London, I want you to come with me." There's a hint of panic in his eyes, now. The begging expression is back. "We're a team, Ketty. I know I can trust you to do what needs to be done. Let's show them what we can do together."

He picks up a pen, and adds a line to my work record. Signs his name.

"Recruit Smith."

"Sir!"

"You are once again promoted to the role of Lead Recruit for Camp Bishop."

"Sir! Thank you, Sir."

"Your security clearance is reinstated. Your silence on this conversation, and all conversations with me going forward, is assumed and expected."

I'll keep your secret, Sir.

"Yes, Sir."

"And Ketty?"

"Sir?"

"Don't screw up again."

"No, Sir."

"Debrief will be at breakfast tomorrow. I'll pass on whatever I hear from HQ, and you will help me to enforce their orders, and their version of the events of the last 36 hours." He leans forward again, elbows on the desk. "This all begins tomorrow, you and me. And there's a ... complication I'm going to need your help with."

"Yes, Sir."

He looks as if he's going to say something else, but then he shakes his head.

"Dismissed. Go and get some sleep."

I stand up and walk to the door, my head spinning. I know that was a horrible thing to do. I took advantage of the situation, and of the commander. But HQ did this, not us. We're not the bad guys here. We're the ones who have to clean up for them and cover their tracks if we're all going to get through this.

And I deserve that job. The commander needs me, and I need him. It's going to take hard work, but I need to become indispensable. When he gets out of here, I need him to take me with him.

I'm committed, now, and so is he. And I can handle whatever we need to do.

Time to get tough, Ketty.

I leave the room, and make it out of the building before I allow the smile to show on my face.

*****

Jackson is in the Senior Dorm, feet up on the table in the dining room, empty meal tray next to him. I walk past, push his feet off the table, and sit down opposite him. He holds his hands out, offended.

"Hey! You're not the commander's enforcer any more." He starts to lift his feet up again, but pauses when he sees my face. "Aren't you?"

"Got my job back."

He plants his feet on the floor, and leans his elbows on the table.

"You … what? … How? How did you convince Bracken?"

"Long story. Convinced him I'm worth it. And here I am."

"Congrats. That's … that's brilliant."

"Yeah."

There's an awkward pause.

"Any news on today? On a debrief?" He asks, quietly.

I shake my head.

"Tomorrow, breakfast."

He nods, suddenly serious, and I wonder whether he saw more in town than he's letting on.

Lies

So that's how they're spinning it. They're using it as a false flag attack. They're blaming it on the terrorists.

We're all in the recruits' dining room – Commander Bracken, Senior Recruits, newbies. Breakfast is over, and Bracken is addressing the group.

"This morning, we have bad news. Today will not be the training day you are expecting. There has been an attack."

Woods is setting up the TV at the front of the room.

"We will not be following our usual route on the training run. The town is sealed off. The terrorists have struck on our doorstep, and we are only just coming to understand the severity of the attack.

"In the coming days, it will be our duty to assist the army in whatever capacity they require. You are no longer recruits. You have graduated to armed auxiliaries. The army can now request your service at any time.

"This is an extremely serious attack. It demonstrates that the rebels are no longer a background threat to our way of life. They are well-armed and very dangerous. We don't know where they will attack next, but we will be on call to help prevent future incidents, and to assist if they attack again."

Woods turns on the TV, and switches to the Public Information Network. A newsreader, her face white with shock and her hands shaking in front of her, begins to read this morning's only headline.

"Good morning. It with great sadness that we bring you a live report from the site of another terrorist attack. Early this morning, the terrorists struck the town of Leominster, in Herefordshire. It is not yet clear how this attack was launched, but what is clear is the near destruction of the entire town.

"Ruth Davis is on the ground in Leominster. Ruth – what are you seeing?"

The view cuts from the studio to a hand-held camera on a street in town. A reporter in a bullet-proof vest and helmet is walking along the pavement, picking her way over scattered belongings, past lines of empty cars. The camera takes in the rubble of the buildings, the damage to the road surface, the fallen trees.

There are gasps from the recruits. The reporter describes the scene, but the images are far more shocking. I wait to see what else the news will be permitted to show.

They switch to drone footage of the town, while the reporter explains what she is seeing. The scale of the destruction is more obvious from the air. I watch, carefully. I want to confirm what I saw.

And there they are. Piles of bodies in parks and open spaces. People killed by gas from the weapons after running from the shaking and following the soldiers to safety. Commander Holden's 'Unauthorised Personnel' were the residents of Leominster. All of them. There were no survivors. There was no safety for anyone unlucky enough to live in his test town. He may have had official permission for everything he did, but he didn't have permission from the people whose lives he took yesterday. From the innocent people who just happened to live in his testing range. I take some deep breaths to fight back the nausea.

So they're blaming it on the terrorists. An interesting move. A good way to promote our role in the fighting. To shift public opinion in favour of government forces.

The newsreader returns.

"Breaking news: the Prime Minister has just announced a heightened state of National Emergency, and the introduction of Martial Law. In the light of such an audacious terrorist attack, she has placed the security of the country in the hands of the army. Parliament will be dissolved, until such time as these attacks can be stopped, and the democratic process can be safely reinstated …"

That's it. That's the excuse they needed to put the army in power. No wonder Holden wanted a whole town to play with. He's tested his weapons, the government blamed the terrorists, and the army get all the reasons they need to take over the country.

And the people will be begging them to do so.

And Bracken and I stand to benefit.

As he said, yesterday. We need to be the team that HQ comes to, to sort out their toughest situations. We need to prove that we can handle this. We have the opportunity to turn this to our advantage.

This was a horrible attack. Cowardly. Unethical. But it has happened. It can't be stopped. I can't turn the clock back.

But I can use it.

Intruder

The commander sends the recruits to pack their belongings. Under Martial Law, they're considered to be an asset of the army, and they can be sent to fight alongside the real soldiers. Time for the tiny fighters to grow up.

Jackson and I walk back to the senior dorm, past crowds of shouting recruits. We sit down with the other senior recruits in the dining room and wait for our briefing. We've been here a while when the commander bursts through the doors, Woods in his wake. He looks round the room, and points at Jackson and me.

"You, and you. With me. Now."

We look at each other, and my stomach drops. We stand and follow Bracken and Woods out of the dining room, the other Senior Recruits whispering behind us.

It's been two weeks since we took Ellman for a walk outside the fence. I can't believe we're in trouble for that now – not after this morning's news. And it worked – Ellman's been the model recruit. No heroics, no rescues. She still visits Sleepy every night, but that's on her own time.

Is it something we did yesterday? Talking to the little girl? Messing around with the lipstick? Taking our helmets off? Or has the commander decided that he doesn't like me knowing his little secret? I think about the bottles on the shelf, the begging look in his eyes.

Bracken hadn't spoken more than a passing word to me in two weeks, until last night. I know he was angry with me, but I thought that had more to do with losing his Lead Recruit than a lasting grudge for what we did to Ellman and Sleepy. Or anything we did for HQ.

Jackson and I exchange nervous glances as we follow the commander across the field towards the empty dorm. There are lights on in the unused building, and for a moment I wonder how much trouble we're in. One of the gate guards is standing outside, and I try to ignore a sudden vision of the dorm as a prison for Commander Bracken's more troublesome recruits.

Please don't let me lose this promotion again. I won't get any more chances.

We follow the commander into the building, and Woods walks in after us, closing the door on the guard outside. The commander leads us into the dining room, then calls us to attention.

"Recruit Smith! Recruit Jackson!"

"Sir!"

"At ease."

He pauses. I wait for Woods to pull out handcuffs or discharge papers, but he waits by the door for Bracken to speak.

"We have a prisoner." The commander pauses, then continues. "We strongly suspect that this is one of the terrorists HQ has been tracking."

So this is not about us. I nearly laugh with relief. This must be the complication Bracken mentioned yesterday. The problem he needs help solving.

The first task for our team.

"She was caught, dressed in recruit fatigues, trying to walk into the camp on Sunday evening. She must have been desperate – she tried to walk in next to a delivery truck, hoping we'd assume she was supposed to be here.

"She might have succeeded on any other night. But on Sunday she tried to walk in before the coaches came back from Birmingham.

"We got lucky. The gate guards picked her up."

I concentrate on stifling a smile. We're safe. We're not in trouble. This is what Bracken decided not to tell me yesterday.

So what are we here for?

"We have some questions for the prisoner. We need to find out who she works for, and what they were doing in town. So far, she's refused to speak to us. We've tried being reasonable, and we've tried asking nicely. We need to try something else.

"Ketty, Jackson – I understand that you both have some experience with the use of fists as a deterrent to unwanted behaviour."

I nearly choke. The commander is all but winking at me. Is he talking about what I did to Jackson, or what we both did to Ellman? Does he know about Ellman's trip outside the fence?

"My prisoner is exhibiting unwanted behaviour. Namely, she is refusing to talk. I'd like you to help persuade her to answer my questions."

"Yes, Sir!"

"Woods and I will give her one more chance to cooperate. If she refuses, I'll give you two five minutes with her. No broken bones, but I want her scared. I'm sure you can manage this between you." He looks from me to Jackson and back. "HQ doesn't know about the prisoner. I want to have something of value to offer them before I report her arrival. I'm counting on you two to persuade her to talk."

"Yes, Sir."

HQ doesn't know? After two days? This is a hell of a risk, and if she won't talk, we're in trouble.

"Wait here. I'll call you if you're needed."

He turns and leaves the room. Woods follows him into the corridor.

I lean over, hands on my knees, and catch my breath. Jackson stares after the commander, then pulls out a chair and drops himself onto it. I grab another chair and sit down next to him.

"I thought we were toast," he says, eventually.

I nod. "Me too."

We listen to muffled voices from the corridor.

"So we're the scariest people at Camp Bishop, then?"

I laugh. "I guess."

We wait, while Commander Bracken shouts at the prisoner. Jackson kicks out a rhythm on his chair with the heel of his boot.

Footsteps in the corridor. Woods appears at the door.

"Your turn," he says, and leads us to the prisoner's room. There's a chair outside for a welfare officer to sit on and monitor the prisoner, but there's no one sitting here, and there's no one else in the corridor. The door at the far end slams shut as we follow Woods into the room.

She's got a room that would usually sleep four. There's a bed, a mattress, a table, and a chair. Plenty of space to work with. She's sitting on the chair, with the table in front of her, wearing muddy camouflage trousers and a regulation khaki T-shirt. The commander is right – she does look like one of the recruits. 17 or 18, shoulder-length dark hair, tall and slim. Sitting up straight in the chair. Confident.

Posh.

"These are my best recruits," says the commander. "I'm going to leave you with them for …" he checks his watch "… five minutes." He nods to us, and to Woods, and the two of them leave the room and close the door.

Jackson and I look at each other. I hold up a hand to stop him jumping straight in.

I address the prisoner. "Will you answer the commander's questions?"

She doesn't move. She sits, straight in her chair, her eyes fixed on the opposite wall.

"You're sure?" I try again. No response.

I shrug, and turn to Jackson.

He walks round behind her, lifts his foot, and kicks the table way. It tumbles, and slides across the floor. I step back to avoid it.

She flinches, slightly, but she doesn't move.

Jackson smacks his fist into his palm, right next to her ear. She doesn't react.

I step towards her.

When she moves, she's fast. She kicks the chair backwards as she stands up, catching Jackson in the stomach. She twists out of his reach and puts her back against the wall, hands up in front of her in a martial arts pose.

Great. She has training.

But there are two of us.

I step towards her, my fists raised, and she takes the bait. She turns to face me, ready to defend herself.

But she lets Jackson out of her sight.

He reaches out, grabs her wrist, and twists her arm behind her back. She's bent over, punching behind her with her free arm, her attention fixed on Jackson, but she's punching the air. I step forward and land a kick on her shins that sweeps her legs out from under her. She pitches forward, and nearly breaks her nose as she hits the floor.

Jackson's on her back in a heartbeat, pinning both arms behind her, his knee in the small of her back. She's fighting to keep her head up, and fighting to breathe.

I pause, and watch for a moment as I realise what it means to have one of the terrorists in our hands. One of the people who've been planting the bombs and messing up the country. She represents everything we've been fighting against, everything we've been training for, *and she's entirely at our mercy.*

Without thinking, I aim another kick. This one connects with her forehead, just above her eye, and breaks the skin.

I kneel down, next to her on the floor. I want to tell her how pathetic she is. How evil the terrorists are. How they're not going to win.

But that's not my job. I take a deep breath, grab a handful of her hair, and pull her face up from the floor.

"Are you ready to talk yet?"

She rolls her eyes, and stares past me.

I let go of her hair. Her head drops and her chin hits the floor. When she lifts her head again, her bottom lip is split and bleeding.

"How about now?"

She laughs, blood spraying from her lip.

I look at Jackson. He looks down, grabs her by the shoulder, and flips her over onto her back. Her head cracks against the floor, and her legs are tangled behind him. He kneels over her, and suddenly this is like a dance. We've done this before. We know these moves.

I reach over, take her arms, and pull them up over her head. I kneel on her elbows, press down on her shoulders, and flash Jackson a grin. He grins back, and throws a punch at her ribs.

There's a rhythm to this. He punches, she gasps, I hold her still. The feeling of power is back, intoxicating. Like Ellman, she's quiet. Just a winded breath with every punch. Unlike Ellman, her eyes are open, staring past me at a point on the ceiling. Staring through me.

It's unnerving.

There's a knock on the door. I realise with surprise that I have no idea how long we've been in here.

The door opens, and the commander's voice is loud in the bare room.

"Get her up on the chair."

Woods walks into the room and picks up the chair and the table, setting them back on their feet.

Jackson and I stand up, and lift the prisoner between us, one arm each. We sit her back on the chair, and pull the table in front of her. She slumps forwards, curling protectively round her bruised ribs, forehead on the tabletop.

Bracken steps forward and kicks the table. She lifts her head, and looks at him through a curtain of tangled hair. The graze on her forehead is starting to bleed, and blood from her lip is smudged across her chin.

"Ready to talk?"

With obvious discomfort, she sits up straight again in the chair, and sets her gaze on the far wall, silent.

Jackson lifts his fists and steps towards the table, but Bracken holds up his hand.

"Enough. Thank you, recruits. You are dismissed."

"Yes, Sir."

We turn to leave the room. I take one last look at the prisoner, and there's a fraction of a second when I meet her gaze as I walk past. Her face is calm, and she doesn't flinch when I look directly at her. It's as if we haven't touched her at all.

Missing

Commander Bracken sends us to help the camp staff in the recruits' dining room. We're handling assignments and answering questions from the kids. We're waiting for the army to contact us with a list of the skills and training they need from the Armed Auxiliaries, and in the meantime we're drawing up lists of recruits and their abilities.

The tiny fighters are piling their armour crates and rucksacks in the corner of the dining room, ready to be sent out if the army needs them. The vehicles in the car park outside are being loaded with supplies. The kitchen staff are all busy carrying crates and loading trucks, and the other Senior Recruits are helping them.

All the doors in the dorm have been propped open, and the noise from the corridor and from outside is loud and distracting. The Commander joins us, with a list of requirements from the army. He's recovered his air of calm authority since our conversation last night, and since our encounter with the prisoner. He seems to know what needs to be done, but the camp looks like an ant nest that's been poked with a stick, and whatever is going on in the car park looks like chaos.

I'm trying to concentrate on the paperwork in front of me over the shouting from outside when the alarm whistle sounds. Three whistles, from the direction of the empty dorm. Everyone looks up, as the guard and the welfare officer from the prisoner's dorm come sprinting across the field towards us.

"The prisoner is missing!" The guard's shout cuts through the noise from the car park.

Three more blasts on the whistle, and more shouting.

"Ketty, Jackson – guns, outside, now."

Bracken runs to the door, shouting to us and pointing at the recruits' armour crates. We're lifting crates, spilling them all over the floor and pulling out guns for each other as he runs out to the car park. We keep going through the crates until we find two guns with bullets in the magazines. I take the safety off as we run out of the building.

There's the sound of a truck engine starting, and we're outside in time to see one of the vehicles driving straight across the grass between the car park and the gate. One of the back doors is hanging open, and someone in a kitchen uniform is reaching out to close it while the truck lurches away from us. The driver is revving the engine, and the wheels are ploughing up the grass, but the truck is moving.

The passenger gets a grip on the door handle and pulls it towards them, looking back at us for a second before they close it.

And I recognise Ellman. Ellman in a kitchen uniform, breaking out of camp in a stolen vehicle.

It's absurd. For a moment, I doubt what I've seen, but then I see two of her little friends at the gate. Amy Brown is chatting to the guards, while Jake Taylor is quietly opening the gate behind them. They're in their own uniforms, but they're both wearing rucksacks. Are they expecting to get away as well?

And who else is in the truck? Who is *driving* the truck?

"Stop them! Use force if you have to!" The Commander is shouting at us, and waving us towards the gate. I sprint along the gravel path as the gate guards realise what's happening. They restrain Brown, who screams at the truck as it drives past, but it doesn't stop.

There are too many people on the path, and Jackson and I have to push them out of the way, shouting as we run. We finally get a clear shot as the truck straightens up and aims for the gates. Taylor has opened one gate, and the other is unlocked.

"Take the shot!" Bracken is behind us, running down the path.

We raise our guns and aim for the back of the truck. Bullets holes erupt in the tailgate, and the back window smashes, but the driver doesn't slow down.

Bracken sprints up to me, grabbing my gun as he passes.

The truck smashes through the remaining gate, and the tyres squeal as it turns into the lane. Brown and Taylor are watching in disbelief as the truck speeds away from them. The commander reaches the gates, throws his arm round Taylor's neck in a restraining hold, and presses the gun to his head, turning to make sure the driver can see what he's doing.

But the truck doesn't stop. The driver speeds away along the lane, away from the bypass, and disappears into the trees.

Questions

"Why didn't we see this coming?"

The commander's face is red with fury. He leans his fists on his desk and shouts at me and Jackson, standing to attention in front of it.

"What did we miss? Three recruits, driven out from under our noses. But not just three recruits – oh, no. They managed to smuggle out our extremely valuable prisoner. Our only link with the terrorists in this area. A prisoner who *walked herself into camp*, got herself captured, sat in silence for two days, and got herself beaten up just *spirited herself away* with three of our recruits as accessories. Not to mention my kitchen supervisor, who was apparently *driving the truck*.

"So what did we miss? *What the hell just happened in my camp*? Ketty? Lead Recruit? Any ideas?"

I shake my head. I'm still trying to piece it all together.

The prisoner escaped. Ellman and her gang had something to do with it. I have no idea why the kitchen supervisor was involved, and I can't figure out how the prisoner roped the recruits into her plan.

The only leads we have are Brown and Taylor.

"Let me talk to the kids we've locked up. Let me see if they can tell us what happened." It's all I can think of to do.

The commander flings his hands into the air in frustration, and sits down in his chair. He rests his forehead on his knuckles and closes his eyes.

"We need to know", he says, quietly, "who cooked up this plan. Who decided to get the prisoner out. How our missing recruits had any contact with the prisoner. And why my very grown-up and responsible kitchen supervisor was at the wheel of that truck."

"Sir, I …"

He waves his hand at me.

"Yes, Ketty. Permission granted. Interrogate the recruits. Just … don't damage them. I have to report this to HQ. They're going to be all over it, and they're going to want to talk to the kids as well. Let's not hand them children with bruises all over them."

"Yes, Sir."

*****

Brown and Taylor are in the empty dorm, locked in separate rooms. The commander escorts me into the building, and leaves me with the off-duty gate guards. Everyone he can spare is guarding the prisoners, and the camp is on lockdown until we can work out what happened. The recruits have been sent back to their dorms, and Bracken is controlling the chaos and waiting for answers before he passes this up the chain of command.

Time to get tough, Ketty. Show them what you can do.

I start with Brown. She's more likely to talk.

We sit in her room, facing each other across the table. The guards have taken her rucksack and her boots, and she's still handcuffed, hands resting in her lap. She's crying. Her eyes are red and puffy, and the neck of her T-shirt is damp with tears at the collar.

I sit in silence, and let her worry about what I'm here to do. She sobs quietly, looking down at the table.

"So."

She looks up at me, startled.

"Recruit Brown."

"S… Sir!" She manages, between sobs.

"There seems to have been some excitement this morning. Care to tell me about it?"

She chokes back more tears, and closes her eyes. Shakes her head, slowly.

My fists are balled in my lap. If I could use them, this would be so much easier.

You don't know how lucky you are that Commander Bracken has a conscience when it comes to his precious recruits.

"We'll try some easy questions, then. Who was in charge of your little gang this morning?"

More sobbing.

"Whose idea was it to drive away with the prisoner?"

Tears. Head shaking. I punch a fist into the palm of my hand under the table. She looks up at the sound, the colour draining out of her cheeks.

"Whose idea?"

She stares blankly at me.

"Was it Ellman?"

There's a pause, and then she nods.

"Thank you, Amy. This will be so much easier if you just tell me what I need to know."

She nods again, fighting back more tears. *Getting somewhere.*

"Let's try another question. Who was the prisoner?"

She shrugs.

"Some friend of Bex and Dan," she whispers. I have to lean forward to hear her.

I shift forward in my seat. This is interesting.

"So Bex and Dan knew the prisoner from before?"

"Yes."

The posh kids know each other. Could they have come from the same place?

"From school?"

She nods. "Maybe."

"Amy, how did Bex and Dan know she was here?"

She shakes her head.

"Do you know how they made contact?"

She takes a few deep breaths, and calms herself.

"I think Bex snuck into her room."

Ellman did what? I can't help shaking my head in surprise.

"You're saying that Bex came in here, past the guards, and talked to the prisoner?"

"I think so."

"When was this, Amy?"

"I don't know", she says, and the sobbing starts again.

I'm trying to think this through. The prisoner arrived on Sunday night. When did Ellman have the chance to break into the dorm, past the guard and the Welfare Officer, and talk to her?

"Amy – did Bex have help from someone? Someone at camp?"

She takes a moment to answer.

"I think maybe her friend from the kitchen." She's whispering again.

"Ellman's friend?"

She nods, slowly, and dashes tears away from her face with the back of one handcuffed hand.

This makes no sense. How did Ellman make a friend in the kitchen? She's the last person I'd expect to go partying with the staff. Was she playing mother to someone on the camp staff as well?

Or has she found someone to mother her?

"Amy. This is very important. Is Ellman's friend the kitchen supervisor? The older woman?"

The one who was driving the truck.

She's nodding quickly.

"They meet up in the evenings. They sit outside. By the kitchen."

Ellman's evening walks. That's where she was going, after visiting Sleepy.

"So she helped Bex get in here, and she's the one who drove the truck this morning?"

"Yes." She's whispering again.

"So what was the plan? You were supposed to go with them?"

And the tears come flooding back.

Of course you were supposed to go with them. You weren't expecting to be sitting here, talking to me. You were expecting to be out there – what? Joining the rebels? Getting the prisoner home safely? Earning good behaviour points with Mummy Ellman?

"What was the plan, Amy?"

I don't have time for more tears. I smack my fist into the table to attract her attention. She looks up, a look of terror spreading across her tear-streaked face.

"What. Was. The. Plan?" I thump the table with every word.

She shakes her head, aggressively.

"I don't know!" She shouts at me, her voice raw. "I don't *know*! OK?"

"You were helping, and you were planning to leave with them, and *you don't know where you were going*?"

"No." Her voice is quiet again.

Mummy Ellman cast her spell over you, didn't she?

"So let me make sure I understand this. Ellman came to you, and said 'My friend is being held prisoner, and my other friend is going to help us escape. Can you distract the gate guards for us? Don't worry – we'll stop on our way out and take you with us.' And you said 'yes'. You didn't say 'Where are we going, Bex?' You didn't say 'Who is the prisoner?' You didn't even say 'Why are we doing this?' You said 'Yes, Bex – and can I lick your boots while I'm here?'"

The sarcasm might be obvious, but it feels good, and it's having an effect.

She puts her elbows on the table, and her head in her handcuffed hands.

I can't help myself.

"What is it? What is it about Ellman that makes you all follow her around like puppies?"

She shakes her head again.

"What is it?" I shout, banging the table with both fists.

Brown whispers something into her hands, too quietly for me to hear it.

"Speak up!"

She drops her hands to the table and lifts her head to look at me. She meets my gaze.

"She's kind, and she's good, and she cares about us. She's my friend."

I stare at her. I feel as if she's winded me. She watches me, waiting for a response.

All this power, all this authority, and all this respect, and I can't even begin to compete with 'kind' and 'good' and 'caring'.

This shouldn't be possible.

I realise I'm staring back at her, and I don't know what to say.

Yes I do.

"If she's so kind and good and caring, then *how come she left you at the gate*?"

Now it's her turn to look winded.

"Where is she now?" I shout, waving my hands at the room we're sitting in, enjoying the weapon that Ellman has handed me. Good, kind, Ellman, who left her friends to face the consequences of her plan in her place.

"She *left you here*! She used you, and she left you here. She doesn't care about you at all!"

"Saunders does", she says, still meeting my gaze.

"Saunders? What's Saunders got to do with this?" I'm trying to understand what she means. What the connection might be.

"Wait – was Saunders in the truck?"

She nods, still watching me.

"Amy, who was in the truck?"

"Bex, Dan, Saunders, the prisoner, and the lady from the kitchen."

Of course they were. Ellman and her gang, busting out through the gates in a truck full of supplies.

She's looking defiant, now. As if she's realised that I'm not allowed to touch her. As if she's happy that her friends got away.

And I can't help laughing. It all seems so funny, suddenly. Our Mother Complex, our Whipping Boy, Mr Posh, and the prisoner, all smuggled out by the woman who runs the kitchen. All our problem recruits, vanished at once, stolen by the person who does our washing up. And two of her devoted followers left behind to learn what it means to be abandoned by their mother.

I laugh so hard that I have tears running down my cheeks when I finally stand up and leave the room.

Brown is still sitting behind the table, hands handcuffed in front of her, staring at me. But she's not crying any more.

She's angry.

Good.

*****

Taylor is next.

I've calmed down, splashed cold water on my face, and been shown into his room. We're sitting across the table from each other, but it's clear that he's not going to cooperate.

"Recruit Taylor!"

He stares at his handcuffed wrists on the table in front of him.

"Recruit Taylor!"

This time I punch the tabletop, but he doesn't respond.

There's an unpleasant smell in the room, and I realise that he's been throwing up. Someone has brought him a bucket, and it sits next to his chair, within reach.

"Final chance, recruit", I say, quietly. "Are you going to talk to me?"

Slowly, he shakes his head. I lean forward, and rest my elbows on the table. He doesn't look up.

Let's see how upset you really are.

"In that case, you can listen.

"Earlier today, Bex Ellman told you that she was breaking out of camp with her friend, the prisoner. She asked for your help. She gave you the job of opening the gates, while Amy Brown distracted the guards.

"For reasons that I am struggling to understand, given how this little adventure ended for you, you said yes."

He sits, motionless.

"Based on what Recruit Brown has already told me, you didn't know anything else about this plan. And you didn't ask. Ellman said 'jump', and you said 'how high?'"

He lowers his head. His black hair falls forward over his face. He doesn't make a sound.

"You conspired with Ellman, Pearce, Saunders, and Brown to smuggle a member of a terrorist group out of this camp. You broke … I can't even count how many regulations. You broke the trust of the commander, and of your fellow recruits. You let a terrorist go free."

I keep my voice calm and even.

"And here's the part I don't understand. You opened the gate. You let them get away. You waited for them to stop, so you could climb into the truck and go with them. And what did they do, your so-called friends? Did they stop? Did they risk life and limb to take you with them? Did they come back for you?

"Or did they drive away as fast as they could, *even though they knew the commander had a gun to your head*?"

I thump the table again. Taylor makes a small groaning sound.

"Bex Ellman, *your friend*, left you to die today. You'd played your part. She had no further use for you. She and her loyal gang drove away and left you to the commander's mercy.

"Do you know how angry he is? Do you know how close you came to ending your life *today* with a bullet in your head?"

In one fluid movement, he pushes his chair back, leans over the bucket, and vomits again.

You do know. I can use that. Keep pushing, Ketty.

He sits still, doubled over; his head over the bucket, and one elbow still resting on the table.

"Jake," I start again, more gently. "I'm here because the commander needs to know what happened. Whose idea this break-out was. Who was in charge. What, *exactly*, happened this morning.

"I think you can tell me."

He coughs, and shakes his head, still leaning over.

"There's no point protecting Ellman. She's gone. She left you behind, and she's gone. Pearce and Saunders, too.

"Who is left to protect? Other than yourself?"

Maybe you'll learn that that's the person you should always be protecting. No more Mummy Ellman to make everything better. Learn to stand up for yourself.

"Things are never going to be the same here for you. You screwed up. Might as well give the commander a reason to keep you alive."

No response.

"I think you understand what I'm saying. I think you can see how much trouble you're in here. So, is there anything else you can tell me?"

He sits up a little straighter in his chair, head still bowed.

"You can tell the commander ..." he says, his voice rasping, "you can tell him that I don't care."

I sit back in my chair.

"Oh?"

He turns his head to look at me.

"You can tell him I want to see Bex and Dan burn in hell. Tell him that all of you can go to hell. The terrorists can take this place and shake it to the ground.

"I. Don't. Care."

He spits his words at me. His voice is quiet, but the hatred he projects is real.

I can't help smiling. Mummy Ellman has lost one of her faithful followers.

Lost

The commander looks relieved when I walk into his office. He waves me to the seat in front of his desk. I can't help noticing that the bottles have gone from the shelf behind him. Part of me wonders where he's hiding them now.

"HQ is waiting for a full report. What have you got for me?"

"I've got names. We've lost Ellman, Pearce, Saunders, and the prisoner. Plus the kitchen woman."

He shakes his head. "Anything else?"

"I've got two upset recruits who had no idea what Ellman was planning, but somehow they were expecting to be miles away in a promised land of rebellion by now."

I can't keep the smug tone out of my voice as I lean back in my chair.

"They were planning to jump into the truck at the gates?"

"That's what they were told. Beyond that, they seem to know nothing."

"And the prisoner?"

"Brown thinks the prisoner was a school friend of Ellman and Pearce. I'm guessing she left to join the terrorists before the recruiters turned up on their posh boarding-school doorstep."

"Do we have a name?"

I shake my head.

"Nothing so useful. These two really have no clue. They took the whole plan on trust from Ellman. They did what they were told, and now they're both struggling to get their heads round the fact that they're still here."

"Any idea how they made contact with the prisoner?"

"That's the interesting part. Ellman seems to have made friends with the kitchen supervisor. She used her contact in the kitchen to get into the dorm and talk to her friend. I haven't worked out the timeline yet, but the kitchen woman was definitely involved."

The commander swears.

"How did this happen? How did we let this happen? How did we not notice what they were doing?"

I shrug. "We were busy. We were looking at the stuff going on in town, at the patrol in Birmingham. We weren't looking at our own staff."

He nods.

I think about HQ's base in the field. About the drones and the cameras. Could they have tracked the truck, and used it to find the terrorists? I sit up in my seat.

"Does HQ know where they are?"

"Not that they've told me."

"But you reported it?"

He sees what I'm hoping for. "Too late for them to track the vehicle. We lost them."

"But the drones …"

He shakes his head. "We were too late. Too busy with the kids at the gate. We didn't get the report to them in time."

"There must be a way …"

"We screwed this one up, Ketty. They've gone. Our recruits and our prisoner."

"We must be able to find them." I can't let this go so easily.

He waves his hand, dismissively.

"It's all up to HQ, now. I'll report what we know, and I'll wait for their instructions. For now, we're on lockdown. We've got no one in charge in the kitchen. We've lost three recruits, and there are two more we can't trust. No one goes in or out of the gates until HQ gives permission. We can't send any recruits to the army, and we can't take in anyone new."

He's given up. He's letting HQ decide how to handle this, while we get to sit around looking weak.

"What happened to showing them we can handle the tough situations? What happened to exceeding their expectations? Making ourselves indispensable?"

He sighs. "Let me talk to HQ. Let's see what they decide to do with us first."

I clench my fists and force myself to say nothing, but I'm struggling to keep my frustration under control.

This could be our chance to show what we're capable of. This could be our way out.

*****

"What are we going to do without them?"

Jackson and I have our feet up, facing each other across a table in the senior dorm. We've just finished planning the lockdown training schedule, now that we can't leave camp.

"Mummy Ellman and the Whipping Boy?"

"And the kitchen supervisor! Who's going to cook for me now?" Jackson pats his stomach. "We could starve!"

I laugh. "We could. This could be it for all of us. HQ might just lock the gates and turn the lights off."

They could certainly keep us working here forever.

"So what's the story? What's HQ going to do?"

I shrug. "Don't know yet. We're waiting for them to get back to Bracken with a plan."

I'm hoping the plan involves letting us handle the chase. Lets me get my hands on Ellman again.

"I can't believe they just drove out of the gates! Did they plan that in advance, or did they just steal a truck and run?"

"I think they planned it, but they must have planned it in a hurry. Brown and Taylor weren't in on the details, and they can't have had more than an hour or so to pull an escape together. I think the news this morning is what pushed them to make a move."

"Blaming the terrorists for the weapons test?"

I nod, thinking this through. "I think so. I think they realised what might happen to the prisoner if she stayed. They'll be executing even more of them now that they've gone to Martial Law."

"Couldn't face seeing their friend on the evening news?"

"I guess."

Jackson frowns. "Why did the prisoner turn up just when the weapons test was scheduled? Do you think she knew something?"

"Bracken said there were terrorists in town. That's why we got chosen for the test. Maybe she was trying to find out what we knew."

"She might have found out if she hadn't chosen the wrong day to play recruit."

He's right. A spy in the camp during the weapons test – that has to be more than a coincidence.

This has all happened so fast. The test, emptying the camp, the prisoner, the reporting, Martial Law – and Ellman's escape committee. There has to be something more going on here. Doesn't there?

I kick my heels against the table in frustration. "There's something we're not seeing. Something about this that we haven't worked out yet. There's a link, somewhere, between the test and the prisoner. The test and the breakout. But I can't see it."

"Maybe it's random. Maybe the terrorists were in town, so they sent someone into camp while they were here. Coming to town made the town a target, so the weapons test happened." He shrugs. "Nothing more than that."

"Maybe. But the prisoner knew Ellman and Pearce. That can't be a coincidence. Can it?"

He shrugs again. "You're obsessing. There's no conspiracy. The kids just got lucky this morning."

I need to think about this. I need to figure out how everything fits together.

I grin at him across the table. "You know the most important part of this?"

"What's that?"

I drop my feet to the floor and lean over the table towards him.

"Jackson's lost his puppy!"

"Shut up!"

"Jackson's lost his favourite puppy." He scowls at me. "Your sleepy puppy ran away! Who will you find to look after now?"

He holds up the training schedule we've put together. "Don't you have work to do? I think you need to take this to your favourite commander."

I stand up, take the papers from his hand, and walk out, ruffling his hair as I go.

Answers

Bracken has heard from HQ. I can tell as soon as I walk into the building. Woods is busy in the outer office, talking to someone on the phone and looking through personnel files. He waves me through to the commander's office.

"Ketty. Take a seat."

I put the schedule plans on Bracken's desk and sit down.

"You've heard from HQ?"

"I have."

"So what's the plan? How much trouble are we in?"

Bracken puts his elbows on the desk and steeples his fingers.

"I'm not entirely sure", he says, looking me in the eye.

I wait for him to say more, but he doesn't.

"So … what does that mean?"

He looks down, and pulls a sheet of paper from a file in front of him.

"We've been told to continue with business as usual."

"What …?"

He waves a hand to stop me.

"We've been told to continue training the recruits, as if nothing has happened."

"But we're under Martial Law! They're taking the recruits!"

"Not our recruits. Our recruits are staying here. Any of our recruits could be part of a terrorist conspiracy, or a terrorist cell, or just part of Ellman's secret gang, so the army doesn't want them. We're stuck with them."

Of course we are. Here, Bracken – keep your broken camp. Just keep your head down and stay out of our way.

"And what about the breakout? Are we still locked down?"

He shakes his head.

"We can come and go as usual. The recruits can go out on their daily runs. We can take deliveries. The kids can leave their dorms."

There's a note of wonder in his voice, and I realise that he doesn't understand this, any more than I do.

"It would be useful if you could plan a new route for the morning run, though. One that doesn't go into town."

I nod. "Absolutely. I'll get that sorted."

He looks at his watch.

"I think we should get the recruits back into their routine, as quickly as possible." He looks at me. "Assemble them in the dining room. The kitchen staff will be bringing lunch over in a few minutes. I'll come and explain things to them."

"What about Brown and Taylor?"

He thinks for a moment. "Let them sit tight in the empty dorm for now. See if they decide to tell us anything else. Send them back to their dorms tomorrow."

I sit up straight in my chair, unable to hide my anger.

"No consequences? They nearly absconded from camp, and they helped the others get away!"

Bracken shrugs. "HQ says to leave them alone."

"So that's it? Nothing changes, even after what happened in town? We just sit here and pretend that everything is normal?"

"Woods is arranging a new kitchen supervisor. We're keeping the recruits. Life goes on – until HQ decides to tell me what they're planning to do with us, long term."

So there's more to this than they're letting on.

"You think there's a plan?"

He nods. "I think this is too good an opportunity to waste. I think they're going to use these kids. I think they're going to use us. And when they do, we need to be ready. We need to exceed their expectations, and we need to prove to them that we can handle what they've got planned." He looks at me, watching my face. "Do you think we can do that?"

It's the opportunity we've been waiting for.

I can't hide my smile.

"Yes, Sir. I think we can."

AUGUST

Problem

The commander and I meet every day to discuss the recruits and their training, and keep track of our instructions from HQ. For a week, nothing changes. We're expected to keep to our normal schedule. Keep the kids fit, keep building their skills, keep them busy. HQ wants reports on any suspicious behaviour, and any troublesome recruits.

So we carry on as if nothing has happened. Morning run, gun practice, assault course, briefing sessions. The kids seem relieved – this is the life they know, these are the people they know. They've been given the chance to stay and improve their skills, and the repetition keeps them focused on their training. Repetition is easy for us, too. We get on with running our usual training sessions, I get used to looking away when I see empty bottles in Bracken's office.

A week after the lockdown, I'm running a briefing session scripted by HQ. The recruits are in the dining room. Brown has found herself a new group to sit with – all girls, who seem to find her sudden celebrity interesting. Taylor sits at an empty table alone, arms crossed defensively in front of him, eyes to the floor, his hair covering his face. He sits like this at every briefing session, and he never speaks. I have no idea why we're pandering to these two, and not keeping them locked up, but that's what HQ wants.

"Tiny fighters. Today we are talking about the terrorists. In his book *The Art of War*, Sun Tzu says 'know your enemy'. We can't fight the terrorists if we don't know who they are, or what their aims are.

"So. What do we know about the terrorists?"

Woods has found a flip chart and a set of pens for me, and HQ wants me to make a list of things we know, and don't know, about the enemy.

I wait for the recruits to make suggestions, but they sit in silence.

"Anyone? Something we know about the terrorists."

One of the girls at Brown's table raises her hand.

"Yes."

"They murdered everyone in town."

"OK." I write her contribution on the flip chart.

Wrong already.

"Anyone else? Shout out what you know."

"They want to destroy the country."

"They want to kill everyone who doesn't agree with them."

"They hate us."

"They hate freedom."

"They want to take over the government."

"They don't care what we think."

Their answers are coming faster than I can write. HQ would be pleased.

"Anything else? Where are they?"

"We don't know. They could be anywhere."

'Hiding', I write.

Spot on, kid. Thanks to Brown and Taylor, we have no idea.

"What weapons do they use?"

"Bombs."

"Against who?"

"Ordinary people."

"Civilian targets. Correct. Is that a brave way to fight?"

"It makes them cowards!"

"We've been out there in our armour, in public, while they sneak around. That's not very honest." One of Brown's new friends, whining.

"It's not a fair fight!" Another girl from Brown's table.

You have no idea.

"We're out there protecting the public. They're out there killing them."

"Which makes you," I turn away from the flip chart and point around the room, "all of you, the good guys. You're fighting to protect ordinary people. When you manage to remember your gun skills, and you do up your shoelaces and put your armour on properly to go on patrol, you're keeping people safe."

There's a murmur in the room as they realise that I've just paid them a compliment.

Don't get used to it, tiny fighters. I'm only doing what HQ wants me to do.

"So. That's what we do know." I fold the list over the top of the flip chart and expose a blank sheet of paper. "What don't we know?"

"What they want."

"Really? We know they want to bring down the government, destroy the country, take away our freedom. What don't we know?"

"What their plans are. What they want to do instead."

"Good. Keep shouting out."

"Why they're fighting us."

"Where they're hiding."

"How many there are."

I turn round in surprise. That was Taylor.

"Recruit Taylor! Nice of you to join in today." He's looking at the floor again, pretending to ignore me. "You made a good point. We don't know how many terrorists there are, but the fact that they crawl around in the shadows and use bombs instead of guns suggests that there aren't very many of them, don't you think? It suggests that they're afraid of us, and our soldiers."

There's a pause, and everyone in the room is watching him. This is the first time he's spoken in a training session since the lockdown.

He looks up at me through his curtain of hair, and smirks.

"They got four new recruits last week, didn't they? Who knows how many people are joining them? They could be hiding an army, for all you know."

Any other recruit, and I'd be putting them on report. Sending them to Commander Bracken. Demanding press-ups or taking away meal privileges. But with Taylor and Brown, my hands are tied. HQ wants us to ignore subversive behaviour from the would-be terrorists. We're supposed to carry on as if nothing happened, and report back on anything they say or do.

But the temptation to drag him out of his chair and remind him how lucky he is to be alive is very hard to resist. I bite my tongue, and try to control the situation.

"I think that's unlikely. Don't you? Don't you think we would have seen more terrorist activity if they had some sort of secret army?"

He smirks again. "Like you said, they wiped out an entire town, didn't they?"

There's a gasp from the other recruits. They're watching Taylor talk back to a Senior Recruit, and they're seeing no punishment. It must be obvious to all of them that this isn't business as usual. Worse, they think I can't touch him.

I'm the Lead Recruit. I'm the name the other Senior Recruits use to keep these kids in line. Taylor is publicly showing them all that my power is a myth. That I can't do anything to stop him.

My fists are clenched and I've taken a step towards him before Commander Bracken's voice cuts through my anger, and I step back to the flip chart.

"Recruits!"

He's been standing at the door. I have no idea how long he's been watching, but I'm grateful that he chooses that moment to step in. The kids rush to stand up, screeching their chairs out from the tables. Taylor doesn't move.

"Sir!"

"Enough for today. Lead Recruit Smith, please stick the lists on the wall, so everyone here can read through them at their leisure."

"Yes, Sir." I'm surprised how calm I sound.

"Recruits – return to your dormitories. You may take the next hour to read quietly, or rest. I don't want to hear conversation. I don't want to hear any sound at all. You may return to the dining room in one hour for dinner. Dismissed."

"Yes, Sir!"

The recruits glance at each other, and slowly make their way out of the dining room. We've never cut short a training session before. Free time gives them a chance to think, and assess what they're doing here. Commander Bracken tries to avoid giving them time to themselves, and they don't know what to make of this change to their schedule.

Taylor stands up and slouches towards the door, last to leave the room. Brown looks back at him before she leaves, but she doesn't try to talk to him.

At least one of you understands how to blend in and stay out of trouble.

"Ketty. With me." Bracken nods towards the door. I gather up the flip chart pens and follow him from the building. Jackson and Miller are waiting in the corridor, standing guard and making sure the kids don't start a riot before dinner.

"Rough briefing?" whispers Jackson as I walk past. I shrug, not trusting myself to speak, and it takes all my self-control to keep my fists down and keep walking when I notice the smirk on Miller's face.

You think you could do better? Think again, techie boy.

Trap

"You know what else Sun Tzu said?"

I've followed the commander to his office, and we're sitting across his desk from each other. He's poured himself a whisky, which I'm pointedly ignoring. I'm still trying to control my breathing and force myself to stay calm.

I shake my head.

"I was just using the script. I don't know who Sun Tzu is."

"Was. Chinese military strategist, two and a half thousand years ago. Generals still study his writing today."

I shrug. "OK."

"It's true that he said you should know your enemy. He also said that 'all warfare is based on deception'."

I think about that for a moment. "That's obvious, isn't it?"

The commander smiles.

"On one level, it is. You don't want your enemy to know what you're planning. You don't want them to know your numbers or your strengths. That's why both sides use spies – to try to find out the truth.

"But there's more to it than that. You and I know things that other people here don't. We have privileged information. We need to make sure we keep that information a secret – and not just the information, but the very fact that there *is* any secret information."

I nod, cautiously, glancing at the drink in front of him. *What are you getting at, Bracken?*

"The deception isn't all directed towards the enemy. Sometimes we need to withhold information from our own side. Tell them what they need to hear – not necessarily what they want to know."

"Sure. I haven't discussed the weapons test, if that's what you mean."

"Partly. But we also need to be the messengers for HQ. We need to deliver the briefings they send us, and we need to give those briefings *as if we completely agree with them*, whatever they say, and whatever we know."

I think back over this afternoon's session.

"That would be much easier if our two terrorist sympathisers were still locked up," I protest, watching his reaction.

He nods once in agreement.

"Our hands are certainly tied where Taylor and Brown are concerned."

"And there's nothing we can do?"

"We can report their behaviour back to HQ. I'll be giving them a full report on Taylor's disruptive episode later – and on Brown's willingness to knuckle down and stay out of trouble."

He watches me for a moment, studying my face. I feel like a sample under a microscope. Is he testing me?

"You've heard something, haven't you?" I lean forward. "Something from HQ?"

He takes a drink from his whisky. He says nothing for a long moment, and then nods.

Finally.

"What did they say? What's the plan?"

"This is Top Secret, Ketty. You, me, and Woods. No one else on site can know."

"OK."

"Can I trust you with this? Do you have your frustration under control, or will I have to step in again and stop you from assaulting a recruit?"

I take a deep breath.

"Sorry, Sir. Yes. You can trust me."

He nods.

"HQ wants us to catch some terrorists."

"Us? The recruits?"

This is insane. The tiny fighters couldn't catch a terrorist if they handed themselves in at the gate. We couldn't even stop our homegrown terrorists from stealing our vehicle and our supplies.

He smiles. "We're going to use the recruits as bait."

"We're … what?"

"Well – their armour, anyway."

"I don't understand."

He puts his elbows on the desk and leans towards me.

"HQ is going to send us out on patrol. As many patrols as it takes. We'll take a coach full of kids, and a luggage compartment full of armour and guns."

So far, so normal. I wait for him to continue.

"We give the recruits plenty of notice. Who is going, where they're going, when they'll be travelling. And we wait to see whether the terrorists track us down."

"How is telling the kids going to get the information to the terrorists?"

"That's how we'll start. HQ wants to see whether there's anyone at camp who's still in touch with Ellman and her friends."

I think about Brown and Taylor. If he's in contact with them, he's a better actor than I thought. Brown, though – obeying the rules and keeping her head down would be the perfect cover for a spy.

"And if they don't attack the coach?"

"Then we go on another patrol. HQ will leak the information through other channels, and we'll see who bites."

"So what's the point? If we travel with extra guards, no one will attack the coach, but the kids won't be able to detain a bunch of armed terrorist fighters. Do they all sit there and wait to be captured? Are they cannon fodder now?"

Bracken smiles.

"The kids do nothing. All they have to do is sit still and keep quiet. We're not after the fighters who attack the coach. We're after their base."

"You're planning to follow them back to where they're hiding out?"

"Not exactly."

He opens a drawer in his desk and pulls out a contamination panel – one of the components that clips into the armour, on the right forearm. The three coloured sections detect chemical, biological, and radioactive contamination.

He hands me the panel.

"Notice anything?"

I turn it over in my hands. Three sections, three colours. Clips on both ends. Just like the one in my armour. And yet …

The wrist end of the panel is slightly wider than mine. The coloured sections are slightly shorter. And there's a tiny hole in the panel, just below the displays, that I don't have on mine.

"Switch it on", he says. I activate the panel. No contamination, but there's a small red light set into the hole. It's hard to see in the bright room, but I cover the panel with my hand, and it's definitely there. Tiny. Hard to spot if you're not expecting it.

I look up at him.

"Tracking device?"

"Tracking device."

I turn the panel over again in my hand. Deactivate it. "They're going to lead us straight to them."

"That's what we're hoping."

"So no resistance when they raid the bus, then?"

He shakes his head. "We want them to steal the armour. We want them to take it all, and to think they've got away with it. We don't want to encourage a fight. Let them take the armour from the luggage compartment. Stay on the coach, keep your heads down, stay safe. Let the terrorists do our work for us. We'll get to them soon enough."

I put the panel back on his desk, next to his glass, smiling. "I think we can do that, Sir."

"I think you can, too."

Assignment

"Tiny fighters! Try to contain your excitement. You are going on patrol again."

Another day, another briefing. HQ has arranged patrol duty for us, less than 24 hours since they ordered Commander Bracken to use his recruits as bait. We're being sent to patrol outside a conference centre in Oxford. Big event, plenty of international visitors, lots of nervous organisers. And of course, big enough that we're not the only guards. If the trap works, we won't be getting there at all.

Like yesterday's briefing, Taylor is sitting alone, and Brown is with her new friends. Taylor actually reacts to the announcement, looking up and looking around at his fellow recruits. Brown watches me quietly, and doesn't contribute to the whispering that breaks out around her.

I explain the plan. I give them the name of the conference, the start and end times, and more of the arrangements than they will need to know. I give them the date, and the times of travel. I brief them again on the procedures for the day – what they should pack, where the armour and guns will be stored, who will be with them on the coach.

Most of them are too excited to take any of this in, but Brown is watching me calmly, and Taylor is paying attention. Either of them could be our spy – or any of the other kids here. Let's hope they remember everything I'm telling them.

The conference is five days away, on Wednesday. Five days should give anyone here enough time to pass the plans to their contact, and allow the terrorists to plan their raid. And it gives me plenty of time to run extra training, with a focus on obeying orders if something unexpected happens.

"Any questions?"

Taylor looks at the floor again, and Brown stares at her hands on the table. A couple of the other kids ask basic questions about their roles on the day, but nothing that could help spring the trap.

Jackson and I split the kids into groups and spend the rest of the session working on their communication skills. Radio protocol, dealing with members of the public, calling in emergency assistance. No one else asks questions about the plan.

*****

Two days later, gun training is focusing on managing weapons in public. The recruits are in armour, complete with helmets and their shiny new contamination panels. We're trying to train them to keep their guns safe, but combat-ready. Jackson picks a couple of the well-behaved kids, and challenges them to steal his gun. He demonstrates what to do if someone approaches, and successfully guards the weapon against their attacks. He protects the gun with his body, alters his grip to make it more secure, and uses the gun as a truncheon at close range, taking care to avoid hurting the kids or their armour.

The recruits pair up and try to take each other's guns. Jackson and I move round the field, adjusting their grips and demonstrating the moves we're trying to teach them. As usual, they're hopeless and frustrated. As usual, we're showing them the same actions, over and over.

I'm showing someone how to grip their rifle and use it as a truncheon when there's a shout from behind me. Jackson stops walking and sprints towards the noise, and without thinking I grab the gun and turn to join him.

There's a recruit lying on the ground, face up, visor open, pushing himself up with his elbows. Standing over him is another recruit, brandishing a weapon, and lifting it as if to fire. As I step towards them, I realise the recruit with the gun is Taylor.

"Stand down, Recruit Taylor! Drop the weapon!"

Taylor laughs, and my stomach tightens as he turns the weapon on me. I'm almost certain the gun isn't loaded, but unlike the recruits, I'm not wearing armour.

Jackson uses the other recruits as cover, and moves in closer to Taylor, but he's not close enough to disarm him. Taylor activates the gun, and grins at me before tightening his finger on the trigger. The red targeting laser flashes past my eyes. I start to lift the gun I'm holding, and everything moves in slow motion as I wait for him to fire. I can see each action in gorgeous, vivid detail, as if there's a spotlight on Taylor, or flashbulbs firing. Sound and colour drain out of the rest of the world, and I feel impossibly calm and focused.

I pull my gun up and aim it at his head.

He pulls the trigger.

I take a slow breath.

Nothing happens.

He releases his grip and drops the gun into the truncheon hold.

I start to walk towards him, gun levelled at his head.

He laughs, and turns to the recruit he's knocked to the floor.

Jackson starts to run towards him, from behind.

Taylor lifts the gun, and brings it down, hard, against the other boy's helmet.

I start to run, gripping the gun with one hand but dropping my aim.

There's an explosion of blood as the rifle butt bounces from the side of the helmet across the boy's face, and smashes into his nose.

He cries out.

Jackson rushes Taylor, tackling him at the waist and bringing him down, both of them landing across the other boy's legs.

I reach them. I lean down, and take the gun from Taylor. He lets it go without a fight.

Jackson restrains him, pinning his arms in the small of his back.

I take another breath, and the world rushes back.

Recruits are shouting, the boy on the ground is crying out, Jackson is screaming at Taylor.

And Taylor is looking up at me, and smiling.

Persuasion

We're back in the empty dorm. Taylor is behind the table, me and Jackson in front. There are guards outside the room, and outside the building.

"Want to tell us what that was about, earlier?"

I look at Taylor. He's sitting up straight, this time, watching us. His armour's been taken away, but he's still wearing his black base layers. He's got a bruise on his cheekbone – he must have hit the other boy's armour when Jackson brought him down.

"Not particularly." He taps his fingers against the tabletop, as if he's bored.

"Did you have a disagreement with your training partner?"

"No." He sounds as if I've asked him if he wants sugar in his tea.

"Did you have a problem with the lesson?"

He shakes his head, slightly. "Not really."

"So this was personal, then?"

A smile tugs at the corners of his mouth, but he controls it.

"This was about me. This was about you holding a gun to my head, just like the commander did to you."

He looks me in the eyes, and a wide, humourless smile spreads across his face.

I feel like the mouse, trapped by a cat who wants to play before he eats.

He's figured out that we can't touch him.

I lean forward, elbows on the table.

"So how was it, Jake? Did you enjoy pointing an empty gun at my head? Did you enjoy smashing another recruit's nose? Did you enjoy being knocked over by a Senior Recruit?"

His smile doesn't waver. He leans forward and hisses his answer at me across the table.

"Yes."

And Jackson moves. He's on his feet, past the table and behind Taylor before the kid can react. Jackson hauls him up by his elbow, then twists his arm up behind his back and pushes him forward. His face lands on the table next to me, and Jackson pushes a hand into the back of his neck, pinning him down. His face is a grimace. At least he's lost the smile.

I glance at Jackson, and we exchange a grin. There's that rush of power again. *We're good at this.*

I lean in, close to Taylor's face.

"Don't assume you're protected here, Taylor. Commander Bracken likes you. That's why he couldn't pull the trigger when he had his gun to your head. But us two?" I point at myself, and at Jackson. "We don't."

I pause. Taylor starts to say something, but Jackson pushes his hand harder against his neck, and it comes out as a grunt.

"Think carefully, Taylor. We run your training. We give you orders and tasks every day. We are in control of your activities, and your safety.

"How hard do you think it would be for us to make sure you have an … unfortunate accident?"

Jackson laughs. I can't help grinning. I don't feel like the mouse any more. I feel like a lion, and it feels amazing. By the look on his face, Jackson's feeling it too.

Taylor squirms in Jackson's grip.

"I'll tell him! I'll tell Bracken!"

I give Jackson a nod, and lean in closer, whispering in Taylor's ear.

"I don't think you will."

Jackson kicks the recruit's legs out behind him, so his full weight is resting on the table. He grunts as the air is knocked out of his lungs.

Slowly, I stand up, and walk round the table. I take my time, dragging the chair out of the way, and stepping towards his feet. He starts to panic, pulling forward with his knees and trying to get a grip on the floor with his toes. He's not wearing his boots, and his socks are slipping on the lino tiles.

Jackson pushes his arm further up his back, and leans heavily on his neck. I kick his feet backwards again, so his toes are resting on the floor.

Carefully, I use the toe of my boot to pull his ankle sideways, towards me. His foot comes to rest awkwardly on the floor, his toes turned inwards and his heel in the air. He tenses the muscles in his leg.

I plant my boot on the floor, and use my toe to press down on his heel, pushing it towards the ground, and twisting his leg and foot. Slowly, I twist his ankle further and further. He lets out a low moan, that becomes a scream as I push harder.

Jackson plants his boot on the back of Taylor's knee and starts to push with me, twisting his leg further. The screaming turns to begging.

"Please please please! Stop! Please!"

He sniffs, and I realise he's crying. I hold my foot still, and look at Jackson. He nods.

Slowly, we both release our pressure on his leg.

"Thank you! Thank you!"

Jackson lets go of his arm and neck, and he crashes to his knees on the floor, almost bringing the table over with him.

I feel as if I'm floating. I'm calm and electrified at the same time. I move his chair back into place, and we walk back round the table and sit down, watching him.

He stays on the floor, curled up on his side, hugging his knees. There are tears flowing down his cheeks.

"Sit up." Jackson sounds disgusted. "On your chair. Now!"

Slowly, Taylor unfolds himself from the floor, and drags himself onto the chair, using the table for support.

"Did you enjoy *that*, Taylor?"

He folds his arms across his chest and looks at me from under his hair. He shakes his head.

"Message received, then?"

He nods.

"If we can make that happen to you in here, with guards outside the door and nothing more dangerous than a table, what do you think could happen on the morning run? Or on the assault course?"

He nods again.

"Breathe a word to Bracken, and start looking over your shoulder. We know where you eat, we know where you sleep. We know where you are every minute of the day."

He shivers, and looks down at the floor.

"No more messing around, Jake. Take a leaf out of Amy's book." At the mention of her name, he looks up at me again, his eyes hard and angry. I lean on the table. "Keep your head down. Keep yourself busy. Keep yourself invisible. Keep yourself safe."

We stare at each other, and I can't help getting one more punch in.

"Do yourself a favour, and forget about Ellman. She's not here to help you any more. You're on your own. Pick yourself up, find some new friends, and blend in. Don't make us do this again."

He closes his eyes, and we leave him there, curled over in the chair.

*****

"Ketty. Sit down."

Bracken is busy with paperwork when I come to give him the day's report.

"I'm told there's a recruit in the medical centre. Anything I need to know?"

I make sure my voice is calm and steady.

"No, Sir. An accident."

He looks up at me. Puts the papers down.

"And Taylor?"

"Taylor had a discipline issue. We've seen to it."

"He's in the prisoner's dorm?"

I nod. "He is. Permission to keep him there overnight?"

He frowns at me. "If you think that's necessary. I know he's been disruptive, but you know what HQ wants. No special treatment."

"I do. And I think he'll get the message this time, if we give him a few hours to think about it."

The commander thinks for a moment. "Is that your formal recommendation, Lead Recruit?"

"It is."

He nods. "Permission granted. I'm glad you've dealt with this so effectively."

Kept it off your desk, and off the record?

"Thank you, Sir."

He shuffles his papers again.

"How is the patrol training? Are the Recruits ready to face the public again?"

"I think they will be, Sir. We've got two more days to make sure they all know what they're doing."

"Good." He nods again. "I'm going to pull Taylor from gun training for now."

"What?" I start to protest. The whole point is to keep Taylor and Brown in the unit, training with the rest of them. "We've made him understand. There won't be any more trouble."

Bracken cuts me off. "I think he would make a good replacement for Saunders, helping Jackson with the communication in Oxford. Don't you?"

Part of the unit, but not a wild card with a gun.

It's a good idea. I nod. "I do, Sir."

147

"Send him to train with Miller while the others are using guns. Make the changes to the rota, and make sure Miller knows what he's dealing with."

"I will, Sir. Thank you."

"And I'd like you to brief Jackson on HQ's plan. He'll be the other Senior Recruit on the bus with you, so he needs to know what's expected of him. Top secret, though. Make sure he understands."

"Yes, Sir."

He turns back to his paperwork.

"Dismissed."

Oxford

"So you're running all the tiny fighters?"

I nod. "I am. Commander Bracken thinks I can handle it. Unlike you."

Jackson wears a look of mock offence. "He's trusting me with the toughest recruit of all! By myself!"

"That's true. You should be afraid. He might *sulk* at you."

"There's a recruit in a hospital bed with a shattered nose who says otherwise."

"I think we've convinced him not to try that again. Don't you?"

Jackson brings up his fists, and pretends to examine them. "I think so."

"Just wave those at him if the sulking gets too aggressive. He'll think twice before he bothers you too much."

The coach draws up at the gate, and we pick up the first crates from the pile the kids left outside before breakfast, and carry them down to the guard hut. Miller joins us, carrying the radio equipment in a pair of metal instrument cases. The guards check the driver's ID and references, and he unlocks the luggage compartment. Between us, we load the crates under the coach and watch as the driver locks the hatches.

Not all the recruits are coming to Oxford with us. HQ is only prepared to risk one coachload of kids and equipment, so most of the Senior Recruits are staying at camp to run training sessions. We've selected the recruits by offering one-to-one coaching for the first thirty or so who volunteer to stay behind, with exceptions for Taylor and Brown. They've lost the privilege of making choices, and they're with us, whether they like it or not. Jackson and I are in charge, and the commander is trusting us to take care of the recruits, but give up the armour and guns. I've briefed Jackson on the plan.

Bring it on. I want to get this over with.

We load up the recruits, filling the coach. Bracken comes to the gate to see us off.

"You're ready?"

"Yes, Sir!"

He turns away from the gate and pulls something from his pocket, shielding it from the kids on the coach. He steps towards Jackson, and hands him a bundle of camouflage cloth. Jackson flips the cloth back and looks inside.

It's a handgun, with extra bullets.

"Take this on the coach with you. Make sure you keep it out of sight."

"Yes, Sir."

He looks at both of us.

"If they come after the crates, let them take what they want. But if they come after the kids, I want you to use that. Defend the coach, Jackson. I want my recruits back."

Like a momma bear, Commander.

"Yes, Sir."

I wonder whether HQ knows about this.

*****

It's a two-and-a-half hour drive. No motorways – only smaller roads, where we'll be most vulnerable to attack. This early in the morning the roads are clear, and it's obvious how easily someone could stop the coach.

Jackson and I sit at the front, alert for any sign of a raid. The kids are noisy to start with, but they calm down as we drive. Jackson slid the handgun into a cargo pocket on the right leg of his fatigues when we climbed on board, and his hand keeps moving to touch the pocket, making sure the gun is within reach.

"Do you think we've got a spy at camp?" Jackson keeps his voice down, and speaks close to my ear.

I shrug. "Who knows? HQ thinks so, so that's why we're here. Testing their theory for them in the open, while they sit at their desks and wait for our report."

"Amy?" He asks, glancing back over his shoulder.

I shrug again. "Could be. More likely than Taylor, I reckon – but this is just speculation. We might not find out who the leak is. Or there might not be a spy at all. Brown and Taylor might just be casualties of a bad plan gone wrong. Ellman might have got lucky, or maybe the prisoner organised the breakout. Who knows?"

He nods, and checks his pocket again.

*****

We make it to the conference centre without an attack. We're here to work, so I leave Jackson to get all the kids off the coach while I find the security office and figure out where we need to be.

"RTS Unit 77B." The security coordinator runs her finger down a list of names. "Commander Bracken's group?"

"Yes, Sir."

"And you must be Lead Recruit Smith?"

"I am, Sir."

"Sign in here." She slides a clipboard across the desk, hands me a pen and watches as I sign my name.

"Lead Recruit. Your group will be providing visible patrols on the perimeter. You're based here," she puts a plan of the site down on her desk and circles a building in the car park in red ink. "There are changing rooms and storage areas. You'll have power for your radio base. Your patrols will run from the main entrance, here," she marks each location on the plan with a cross, "to the side access here, and from there back to the car park. How you split the route, and your recruits, is up to you. Just make sure that each patrol group is visible to the groups behind and in front of them at all times."

She hands me the site plan, a file of information for the radio team, and a bag of ID tags for the recruits.

"We're not expecting trouble, but I assume your recruits know what to do in the event of an attack?"

"Protect the public. Get them to safety. Call the attack in."

She nods. "Thank you, Lead Recruit." She looks up at me and smiles. "I hope you have an uneventful day."

*****

We escort the kids to our staging area with their crates. Jackson and Taylor set up the radio equipment, I assign the recruits to their patrol teams, and they get dressed in their armour. I pair Brown up with one of her new friends, and she seems surprised to be given the assignment she wanted.

You're in luck, tiny fighters – I can't be bothered to deal with teenage hissy fits today. I have bigger things to worry about.

I give out ID tags and explain the patrol route. No one has any questions, so I send them out with instructions to walk the route until we call them back.

Jackson and Taylor are working the radios. Jackson has his recruit keeping detailed records of all the orders given and received, and checking each patrol's frequency for activity. Taylor is quiet to begin with, only grudgingly giving Jackson feedback on what he's doing, but by mid-morning he's dropped the sulking and started engaging with his tasks.

I spend the morning liaising with the security coordinator, and putting together a rota for pulling the recruits back for breaks and food. By the time we call the first team in for lunch, everything is running smoothly, and Taylor is taking an interest in the tasks Jackson gives him.

We cycle all the teams through a lunch break, and by the time the last team heads out again, it's half past two.

"Four hours to go."

I'm checking in with Jackson, and keeping the clipboard up to date while Taylor takes a break.

"We've done OK, haven't we?" Jackson looks around at the empty building. "No one's freaked out, or had a tantrum, and there's no sign of the terrorists."

It's true. The recruits are reacting well to their duties, and we're making a good impression on the organisers of the conference. Even Taylor is on his best behaviour. We couldn't ask for a better patrol.

Except that we're here as bait, and no one's biting.

*****

It's two hours from the end of our shift, and I'm writing up the day's activities, when Brigadier Lee walks into our building. I jump to attention, and salute. I had no idea he would be here.

"At ease, Lead Recruit Smith. As you were."

I sit down, and he sits across the table from me.

"Anything I can help you with, Sir?"

"I'm just doing the rounds, Lead Recruit. How is it out there?" He waves his hand at the door.

"Fine so far, Sir. No problems."

He nods, and looks around the room.

"You run a tight operation, Smith. You're a credit to the RTS."

"Thank you, Sir."

What is this? A courtesy call to the people you're us-ing as terrorist bait?

He looks me in the eye.

"I'm here because HQ has given me the job of taking a good look at the Recruit Training Service. Assessing the good and the not-so-good. Reviewing our processes. Checking our personnel."

I nod, not sure how to respond.

"What's your opinion of your commander?"

I look at him, surprised by the directness of the question.

So this is about Bracken. A close look behind the scenes at Camp Bishop while we're distracted, doing our best to catch your terrorists for you?

I struggle to think of a suitable response. Bracken is my ticket out of camp. He's promoted me, and I know I can make sure he takes me with him when he moves on. He's the person who saw potential in me when no one else did. He's the person who saw my determination and rewarded it with responsibility. He's also trusting me with his secrets. We're a team, Bracken and me.

And Lee wants me to casually discuss his strengths and his failings.

I take a deep breath.

"I work closely with Commander Bracken, Sir. I find him to be a good commander, and a good man."

And someone I can usefully manipulate.

Lee smirks.

"You don't think he's made a few mistakes?"

I think about the last few weeks. Bracken's trust in HQ over the weapons test. His failure to report the pris-oner, and our failure to make her talk. The recruits breaking out of camp under our noses. The undeclared gun in Jackson's pocket.

I force myself to shrug. "I suppose so, Sir – but we've dealt with some difficult situations recently. I'm not sure it's a crime to be caught off-guard once in a while."

He tilts his head, and gives me another uncomfortable stare. He waits, as if he's expecting me to say something else. I meet his gaze, and it's like looking into the barrel of a gun. He doesn't move or blink, and I force myself to maintain eye contact, battling the urge to look down, to run away. When I don't say anything else, he continues.

"Thank you, Lead Recruit. Good to know where you stand. Is Camp Bishop well-run under Bracken?"

Keep throwing me the hard questions, won't you, Sir.

"I think so. The recruits are well-trained, the camp is a safe place to be. We have order, for the most part. Only the occasional teenage outburst."

I push thoughts of Taylor from my mind. Taylor smashing his partner's nose. Taylor begging me and Jackson to let him go. Taylor curled in pain on the floor. I bite down on a smile.

You don't need to know about that.

Lee watches me, waiting to see if I have anything else to say. I sit quietly.

"And what about you? You were Lead Recruit, but Bracken demoted you, and now you're back in the job. What's the story behind that?"

I keep my expression neutral, but I can feel the blood rushing to my cheeks.

None of your business, Sir.

It takes me a moment to make sure my voice is under control. I can't meet his eyes. "A misunderstanding, Sir," I say, eventually. "The commander and I had a disagreement about recruit discipline. I believe we understand each other better now."

"So you and Bracken work well together?"

I think about the bottles on the shelf. The commander drowning his fears when things get tough.

"I believe so, Sir. I believe that we've developed an understanding."

"You make a good team." It's not a question, but there's a mocking edge to his voice.

"Yes, Sir."

I look up, and find that his gaze hasn't flinched. He's looking right into my eyes. It's a moment before he looks away.

"Well. Thank you, Lead Recruit," he says, standing up. I stand, too. "Anything else you can tell me. Background on Camp Bishop, on Bracken. Anything at all – give me a call." He hands me a business card.

"Thank you, Sir. I'll remember that."

He gives me another long stare, then nods, and walks away. I watch him leave the building. When he's out of sight, I sit down and gather my thoughts. I take a look at his card – his name, rank, and photo, and a phone number. London dialing code. I slip it into my shirt pocket, and I notice that my hands are shaking.

What do you know? And what are you expecting me to tell you?

*****

"You've got the gun?"

We're on the coach, heading back to camp. The day has been uneventful, and the kids have done their jobs perfectly. We're all tired – several of the recruits are asleep in their seats – but we can't afford to let our guard slip. There's nothing to stop the terrorists targeting us on our way home.

Jackson reaches for his pocket, and nods. "Ready and loaded."

"Good."

I'd love to close my eyes and rest, but an ambush is still possible. I focus on the road ahead and watch as we pass through villages and towns, past farms and fields and woodland. It's getting dark, and I'm increasingly aware that every shadow could conceal an attacker, every ditch and gateway could hide a terrorist gang.

By the time we reach the Leominster bypass, I'm exhausted. I notice they've put a black cover over the sign at the edge of town, and there are permanent roadblocks in place on all the routes in and out. It's as if the whole place never existed.

Commander Bracken is waiting at the gate. He sends the recruits to stow their crates and assemble in the dining room for a briefing before dinner. Miller arrives to take away the radio equipment, and Jackson helps him carry the boxes to the store room.

"How was Oxford?" Bracken asks as the coach driver locks up his empty luggage compartment next to us.

"It was OK. No problems. Everyone behaved really well."

"Even Taylor?"

"Even Taylor. I think Jackson has the magic touch, getting problem recruits to play their part."

The driver checks the coach for lost property, then gives us a cheerful wave from the front steps, and drives away. The commander returns his wave and waits for the engine noise to fade, then turns to me.

"But no attack?"

I shake my head. "No attack."

"HQ will be interested to hear that."

I bet they will. No spy at camp? Or no one we can trace this time?

"Does this mean we'll be given more patrol jobs?"

"That's what I'm expecting. I'll report back, and see what they send us next." He looks at me for a moment. "Good work, Ketty. These recruits are growing up and learning what's expected of them. We have you to thank for that."

"Thank you, Sir." I can't hide my smile.

Castle

The schedule begins again the following morning. No day off for the tiny fighters this time – they're straight back into their training, making sure they're ready for their next patrol.

Miller teaches Taylor every day while the other recruits are with Jackson and me, training with their guns and armour. After a few days, this feels normal, and no one seems to notice when he doesn't show up for our sessions.

The commander seems happy with our progress, and with Taylor and Brown. They're both keeping their heads down and training hard. We've had no more discipline problems, and no more violence from Taylor. He's still sitting alone at the briefing sessions, but he's paying attention – and most importantly, he's stopped talking back.

So I'm surprised when Bracken brings up Brown at one of our daily meetings.

"HQ has looked at my reports, and it seems that they agree with you about Brown. She's the most likely person to be in contact with Ellman and the terrorists. They want you to talk to her."

"Talk to her? You mean interrogate her again?"

He shakes his head. "It seems they have something more gentle in mind."

I can't help smirking. "What – like a woman-to-woman chat?"

"Something like that."

You have got to be kidding. They want me to play big sister with Ellman's loyal buddy?

"You're not serious."

He looks at me. "HQ is serious, so I'm serious. There's more to command than shouting orders and handing out discipline. You need to be able to talk to your recruits when they need it."

Amy doesn't need this. HQ needs this. And I need to show them I can handle it.

"Fine. What do they want to know, and when am I supposed to corner her?"

"They're interested in what she thinks is going to happen next. Whether she sees herself sticking around and joining the army, or whether her long-term aims are less aligned with our own. You'll need to ask some careful questions. She's not going to tell you everything you need to know, but how she answers the questions will tell you a lot about her expectations.

"And as for when – they've organised another patrol, for Monday. Taylor is on radios, with Jackson, and Brown is being assigned as your assistant. If you get there without incident, you'll need to find a time, and somewhere private, to start a conversation."

"Won't the other recruits be upset that the safe jobs are going to the kids who broke the bad guys out of camp?"

"I'm sure you can handle some hurt feelings, Ketty." He can't stop himself from snapping at me. There's frustration in his voice as he dismisses my concerns. "Orders from HQ are more important than temporary jealousy. Get Brown alone, and ask her how she's doing. See what she tells you."

*****

It's Monday morning, and we're loading another coach with armour, guns, and recruits. Jackson shows the commander the handgun, and puts it carefully back in his pocket before we join the kids on board.

"Best of luck," the commander says, his voice serious. "You both know what you're doing. Bring the kids back safely."

"Yes, Sir."

He stands at the gate and watches the coach drive away. He's still standing there as we turn onto the bypass. This time, we've shared the patrol information with the recruits, but HQ has leaked it as well. If anyone has a connection with the terrorists, they'll know where we're going.

We're heading for a castle in Wales, to provide additional security for an open day for schoolchildren. Every school in the area is sending children to the event, and we're the visible deterrent against a terrorist attack. Again, we're sticking to smaller roads, and again, they're unnervingly quiet.

I find myself sitting forward in my seat, watching the road. Every time we drive through woodland, I'm on edge, looking for shapes in the trees. This is where they could stage an ambush. It all feels too easy.

About an hour into the journey, we're driving through fields, and there's a track that joins the road. I can't see any buildings, but the track runs across the fields and away, out of sight. There's a Land Rover, parked a few meters into the field, with a good view of the road in both directions. There's an older man standing next to it, and two younger men further down the track.

They're not doing anything, they're not on their way anywhere. They're just watching the road.

The hairs on the back of my neck stand up. I nudge Jackson.

"I think we're being watched."

He sits forward, watching the men.

"Certainly looks that way."

I keep my eye on the older man as we drive. He watches the coach as we pass. His eyes meet mine through the side window before he drops behind us, and I feel my spine turn to ice.

I don't like being this vulnerable.

I turn to the driver. "How much longer? When do we get there?"

"About half an hour," he says, cheerfully.

That's a long time to wait for an ambush.

I settle back in my seat. There's nothing else I can do.

*****

Half an hour later, we're pulling into the car park at the castle. It's still early, but there are marquees and colourful gazebos on the lawn in front of the castle gates, and people in historic costumes are preparing for the schoolchild invasion. I leave Jackson and the recruits on the coach, and walk through the tents to the ticket office.

"Oh, you're here!" The woman behind the desk looks thrilled to see me. "You've brought us some brave recruits to guard the gates?"

She seems much too relaxed to understand what we're here for. She doesn't seem to be taking this seriously, and the chaos outside on the lawn is going to be very difficult to patrol effectively.

I can't help sounding cold and humourless. "I've got fifty recruits on a coach outside. They need a place to change, and space to store their personal belongings. I've got radio equipment that needs power and a place to set it up. I'm hoping you know where I can find all this." I don't smile.

My demands don't put a dent in her cheerful attitude.

"No problem at all! We've set up a marquee for you. Round the corner, at the far end of the car park. You can park the coach down there as well, out of the way." She waves her hand to indicate the general direction of the marquee, and starts ticking off points on her fingers. "We've run a cable, so you've got power and lights, and we've set it up exactly as we were told to. Changing areas, seating, tables, portaloos. You should find everything you need!" If anything, her smile gets broader.

I have to stop myself from rolling my eyes. She might have set up the marquee as requested, but the castle itself is not a secure area. We'll be patrolling without a proper perimeter. There's no way we can keep everyone safe.

"Are we the only patrol you've got, today?"

She looks confused. "Oh, no. We've got some soldiers here as well. They've got a marquee next to yours. Smaller, but that's what they asked for."

I resist the urge to start shouting, and force myself to be polite.

"Perhaps I could talk to them about patrolling today's event?" I wave my hand vaguely at the door.

"Oh, they're expecting you. They'll be waiting in the marquee. In your marquee." She smiles again.

I take a deep breath, and then flash her an unfriendly smile. "Thank you," I manage, teeth clenched, before turning on my heel and leaving the office. I have to control the urge to punch something on my way out.

I walk quickly back to the bus, ignoring the people in costume who seem to have time to wander about and gossip. I head straight along the path, fast enough that I force people to step out of my way.

Get used to it. You'll be moving out of the way for my tiny fighters all day, or you'll be answering to me.

I climb back to my seat, and direct the driver to the far end of the car park. We park next to two marquees, and a row of army vehicles. The woman in the ticket office was right – we're a long way from the castle gate.

We're expected to keep everyone safe, but we have to keep our distance.

Jackson directs the unloading of the coach while I head into the larger marquee. It's a huge space, with partitions for changing areas and storage, and lines of power sockets on the ground along one canvas wall. There are tables and chairs for two or three coachloads of recruits, and at one of them Brigadier Lee is waiting.

Are you here to spy on us? Or is this a personal visit?

"Lead Recruit Smith! Good to see you again."

"Sir!" I walk to the table and salute.

"At ease." I relax, hands behind my back, and stand up straight. "Welcome to Wales. We're looking forward to working with you."

"Thank you, Sir."

"So, what have you brought us today?"

"Fifty trained recruits, all with armour and guns. One radio operator. One radio assistant. One assistant for me."

"Very good, Lead Recruit." He smiles.

I nod, and wait to see what he's here to tell me.

"Obviously you're here to be the visible deterrent." I nod. "We'll need your recruits to patrol along the edge of the car park – from the driveway, past the castle gates, up to here, and back. While you're out there, we'll be securing the grounds to the rear of the castle, and keeping an eye on your patch as well. We expect the recruits to call in anything that requires our attention, and we'll make sure we're there inside a minute or two. But we're not here to babysit them."

I nod again. "I understand, Sir. No problem."

"We'll talk to your radio operators, when they've set up their equipment. We'll make sure we can contact you, and you can contact us. If we run into anything out back, we're going to need you to run an evacuation out front.

Get everyone into the car park and away from the castle. Can you manage that?"

"Yes, Sir."

"Good. Thank you, Lead Recruit." He stands. "Perhaps you could notify us when the radios are ready?"

"I will, Sir."

I stay where I am while the brigadier leaves the marquee, then head back to the coach.

No awkward questions for me this time?

Jackson and the kids have unloaded the boxes, and they're waiting for me to tell them what to do next. I send them into the marquee to get changed, and help Jackson with the radio boxes. Taylor and Brown are sitting at a table together when we walk in. They haven't brought armour or guns. Like us, they'll spend the day in fatigues, supporting the recruits on patrol.

I send all three of them to set up the radios, and head to the back of the tent. The changing rooms and storage areas are separated by canvas dividing walls, and the noise of fifty recruits getting changed is loud in the enclosed space.

As the first recruits emerge with their uniforms in their crates I send them into the storage area and then direct them to find a table and sit down. The other recruits follow, and soon they are all sitting at tables, waiting for me.

I walk to the front of the marquee.

"Tiny fighters!"

"Sir!"

No one reacts. It's as if they don't even hear the insult any more.

"Today, you are offering your expert protection to a swarm of schoolchildren. Seeing as you all used to *be* schoolchildren, I don't think I need to tell you that these children will be loud, unpredictable, and undisciplined. They will likely be allowed to run round on their own, without supervision. They will go into places they are not supposed to go. They will jump out from places when you least expect them. They will find you, and your armour and guns, particularly fascinating.

"For this reason, your guns are to remain deactivated while you are on patrol. Your first response to a dangerous situation today will *not* be to fire your guns. Your first response will be to use your radio and report to Senior Recruit Jackson. He and I will assess the situation, and we will tell you what to do.

"Anyone firing an unauthorised shot will face serious consequences. Please remember that.

"We are sharing today's patrol duties with soldiers from the army." There's a murmuring from the recruits. "Yes, tiny fighters. The actual army. Real soldiers."

"It goes without saying that any orders given to you by a soldier must be obeyed instantly, even if they directly oppose the orders given by me or Jackson." I look around the room, making eye contact where I can. "Instantly. Without question. In a situation like this, obeying or not obeying could mean the difference between life and death for you, for the soldiers, or for the schoolchildren in your care. Is that clear?"

"Yes, Sir."

"Good. When the radio equipment is ready, I'll call you up in pairs. I'll explain the patrol route, and the places you are not permitted to go. Make sure you pay attention – in here and out there. I don't want to be making apologies for your behaviour to anyone later – not to the organisers, not to the army, not to someone's parents. Understood?"

"Yes, Sir."

"Questions?"

Even though this is only my second patrol with these kids, it's already starting to feel routine.

Amy

The process of sending the recruits out goes smoothly. The first team calls in when they reach the end of the driveway and turn back, then the second, and the third. They're walking at a suitable pace, keeping other patrols within sight, and staying out of the way of the soldiers. So far, so good.

Jackson and Lee are confirming the radio protocols for the day, and we have an emergency procedure set up and ready to use. Taylor is rising to the occasion, sitting up straight, clipboard in hand, waiting for the brigadier to finish speaking. Brown and I find ourselves with nothing urgent to do.

Time to start a conversation.

I pick the table furthest away from the radio equipment, in the far corner of the tent. I make sure my radio is clipped to my belt and switched on, and then walk over and sit down. Brown, clipboard of rotas and information in her hand, follows me. We sit down at the table, both on the same side – I'm not in a hurry to recreate the atmosphere of the interrogation room. She puts the clipboard on the table and waits for me to speak.

This is not my comfort zone, Bracken. I need shouting and fear, and Jackson for backup. Not this.

"So, Amy. How are you getting on?" Inside, I'm cringing. I sound like the worst school counsellor. I sound fake and brittle.

She shrugs. "OK."

I shake my head, hiding my frustration. "I don't mean today. I mean at camp. Generally."

"Oh." She looks down. I think she's blushing, but it's hard to tell in the low light of the marquee.

"You've found some new friends."

"Yeah."

"You seem to get on with them. Are they helping you to move on?"

She looks up at me, coldly. "Move on from what?"

I could do without this, Bracken.

I want to roll my eyes and say something sarcastic, but that's not what I've been asked to do. Instead, I look her in the eye. This feels aggressive. This is something I understand.

"It must be a shock, having to find your way at camp without Bex and Dan. And then there's Saunders. You must miss them." My words are gentle, but the sustained eye contact is not.

I cannot believe that I'm here, playing Good Cop to my own Bad Cop routine – and that her interrogation was only three weeks ago. She's definitely blushing now, but this is anger, not embarrassment.

So much for Good Cop, Ketty.

"So. Is there anything you want to talk about? How you're doing a great job of getting on with stuff? What you hope to achieve, long term? What we can do to help?"

She keeps staring at me. She's gritting her teeth, and I'm guessing she doesn't trust herself to speak. She's furious.

"Amy," I keep my voice gentle, "we're really impressed with how you've put your head down and carried on with your training. Commander Bracken and I – both of us. You've set an incredible example for Jake," I glance over my shoulder to the group at the radio table, "and you're proving that you're stronger than we thought you were.

"You've been amazing, these past few weeks. No issues, no disciplinary problems, no pushing the boundaries. You've accepted the situation as it is, and you've moved on.

"I'm here to help, Amy. What do you need from me – from us – to excel at Camp Bishop?"

She lets out a long sigh. I guess she's been holding her breath. Her shoulders slump, and she sits back in her chair, eyes closed.

Come on, Brown. Give me something to take back to Bracken.

I look back at the radio team and give her a few moments to calm down. The brigadier has left. Jackson is talking to Taylor, and they're both checking something on the clipboard. Taylor seems engrossed, and Jackson seems calm. He really is working wonders with Jake's training.

I look back at Amy. She hasn't moved. She's resting her head on the back of her chair, and I realise that she's crying. She's quiet, and her eyes are still closed, but there are tears on her cheeks. She's trying to control her breathing.

This time I do roll my eyes. There's no one to see me, and this is all I need. A recruit in tears, when I'm supposed to be having a friendly chat.

"Amy," I try again, "I'm just trying to help. We want you to do well at Camp Bishop. We want you to succeed." She sobs, once. "There are opportunities for you, as a recruit. What do you want to do? Where do you see yourself going, after your training is complete? Are there some skills you'd like to develop?"

Nothing. I'm not getting through. Her face crumples and more tears flow down her face. She takes a ragged breath, and makes a choked-off sobbing sound.

Round of applause, Ketty. You're rocking this. Just what HQ wanted.

Enough. This approach is going nowhere.

"Recruit Brown!" My near-shout makes Jackson look up in surprise.

She makes a half-hearted attempt to sit up straight. She opens her eyes, but they're red and puffy. She's still crying.

"Sir!" It's a quiet croak, but it will do.

"One question, recruit."

"Yes, Sir."

"Tell me – where do you see yourself in a year?"

She closes her eyes again, and takes another deep breath.

"It's a simple question."

She shakes her head.

"One year, recruit. Where will you be?"

She puts her hands over her face and smears away the worst of the tears. I lean towards her, and ask her again, hissing into her ear.

"Where will you be?"

Her voice is tiny, barely more than a whisper, but I hear her confession.

"Out of here," she says, distinctly.

Return

I send Amy outside with a couple of bottles of water to wash her face and get herself under control. There's nothing I can do today, apart from getting her home safely, and passing my report to the commander. I can't tell whether she's our spy or not, but keeping her head down and making new friends is clearly an act while she looks for a way out. I stay near the door, keeping her within sight. The last thing I need is for her to walk away before I can get her onto the coach.

Jackson and Taylor have everything under control. I make sure they have the lunch rota, and before long they're calling patrol teams back for sandwiches in the marquee. The cheerful woman from the ticket office brings crates of food across to us, and checks that we have everything we need.

Everything except my assistant, thank you.

The brigadier comes back as I'm finishing my sandwiches. He sits down opposite me and leans his elbows on the table.

"How is everything going? Any problems?"

"Everything seems fine, thank you, Sir. Any trouble on your side?"

He shakes his head. "No sign of anyone who shouldn't be here. But then, that's half the reason for us being here, isn't it? An effective defence is an effective deterrent." He smiles at me, but his gaze is calculating.

"I suppose so, Sir."

He looks at me silently for a moment, then speaks again.

"So – what's a capable officer like you doing working for someone like Bracken?"

I'm so surprised by his question that I'm not sure I've heard him correctly. Is this the follow-on from our last conversation? I blink, stupidly, and try to think of something to say.

"I'm not sure what you mean, Sir."

He relaxes a little, and shakes his head.

"I mean that you're wasted in the Recruit Training Service, Smith. Look at the ease with which you've got this whole patrol system set up and working like clockwork. The recruits respect you, your radio team doesn't question your judgement, and apparently you can handle crying teenagers and nauseatingly cheerful staff without breaking stride. You know there'd be a place for you in the army. Something more challenging than this." He waves his hand to indicate the marquee, then lowers his voice. "It's a shame, what happened at Camp Bishop."

I look up. Apparently he's not done surprising me.

"The escape. The prisoner. The recruits. Bad luck." He shakes his head again.

I have no idea what to say. When I say nothing, he carries on.

"But it shouldn't affect your career prospects, Smith. You're not Camp Bishop. From what I can see, you're the person holding it together," he looks around the marquee, "but you don't have to go down with the ship." He winks at me. "Word to the wise. There's a place for you, if you want it. But don't wait too long."

Are you trying to promote me? And if so, what are you trying to do to Bracken?

"You know how to reach me. You've got my number."

"I have, Sir. Thank you, Sir."

"Think about it," he says, as he stands up. I remember to stand, too, as he walks away.

*****

The rest of the day runs smoothly. No terrorists, no careless children, no surprises. When the last coachload of children has left the area, we're free to pull the patrols back and head home.

Again, this should be the end of a tiring day, but again I'm on edge as we begin the drive back to camp. The gathering darkness makes all the woodland seem haunted, all the fields full of shadows.

I can't relax until we're back on the bypass, the lights of Camp Bishop shining through the trees against the darkness that used to be Leominster. The commander is waiting at the gate to meet us.

"Good day?"

I nod. "Good day. No problems." The recruits are collecting their crates and walking round us back to their dorm. Jackson supervises the process, and carries the radio equipment himself.

"No sign of our friends?"

I think about the Land Rover in the field, the men watching the coach as we drove past.

"I'm not sure. Maybe."

"Something you'd like to discuss, Lead Recruit?"

"Yes, Sir."

We thank the driver, leave the coach at the gate, and walk to the commander's office. The sound of the recruits sitting down to dinner follows us across the field.

*****

"So you told him about the terrorists?"

"We don't know that they were terrorists, Jackson. We only know that they were watching us. Maybe they were watching everyone."

I push my empty plate away, and unwrap the chocolate bar the kitchen has given us for dessert. We're alone in the senior dorm – the other Senior Recruits had eaten before we came home.

"What – they just like watching traffic? Come on, Ketty. That was the bad guys. That was Ellman's friends, sizing us up for an ambush."

"And they decided not to attack."

"They decided not to attack *today*."

He's right.

"One day at a time, right? If that's who they were, then they're thinking about stealing the armour. They're giving it some serious thought. They're researching our movements."

"And if they knew where we'd be, who told them? Do we have a spy? Or did the HQ grapevine do the trick?"

I shake my head. "I don't know. I can't figure it out."

"But Brown …"

"Brown said she wanted out. That doesn't make her the spy. We didn't see any terrorist scouts when we only leaked the patrol information to the kids."

"Maybe they were hiding."

"And maybe they didn't get the message, because Brown isn't a spy. She's barely keeping herself sane, without Ellman and Sleepy – who, by the way, she seems rather keen on." Jackson raises an eyebrow. "I doubt that she's running a secret messaging service as well as making herself invisible and plotting to leave as soon as she can."

"And are we letting her walk back in here, with no consequences?"

"We have to. HQ says we have to. The commander wants to keep her away from the gun sessions now, too, but that's it. She's going to train with Woods while we're running the gun training. Paperwork. Preparation. Being a good assistant."

"Clipboard skills?"

I laugh. "Clipboard skills. Very important, Jackson. Especially when you need to wake up sleepy recruits."

We both laugh at the memory of Sleepy, jolted awake by the crash of Woods' expertly handled clipboard. It seems a lifetime ago.

"And what was going on between you and the brigadier? He seemed rather *keen* on you."

Jackson pretends to leer at me, then leans on the table in a passable impression of Brigadier Lee's actions this afternoon.

"It's so good to *see* you, Ketty. You've got my *number*, Ketty." He mocks our conversation in a sing-song voice.

"It's nothing like that. I think he wants to offer me a job."

"Have a *job*, Ketty. Come and work for *me*, Ketty."

I throw the chocolate wrapper at him. "Enough, Jackson. It's not like that. And anyway, why would I want to leave the glamorous Camp Bishop?"

He grins. "I knew it. It's me! You can't leave me." His chestnut brown eyes grow wide. "You can't live without me."

"Yes, Jackson. That's why I stay. Your dubious charm is all that keeps me here. Don't ever leave me." I keep the delivery deadpan and sarcastic, but he keeps grinning anyway.

Which makes me laugh, in the end, because he's right. What would I do without him, and Miller, and Bracken, and the recruits? I've built a reputation here. I'm the go-to recruit scarer. I know how to handle the kids, and how to work with Bracken. Jackson and I make a slick team. When it comes to getting results from the tiny fighters, we work together so smoothly. I can usually tell what he's thinking, and he can usually work out what I want him to do. It's easy.

But is easy what I want? And is Bracken, with his schemes and his weakness, my only way out?

Can Brigadier Lee get me the promotion I need? And what's the price I'd have to pay for leaving Camp Bishop? Can I build myself a reputation somewhere else – somewhere I don't have Jackson to back me up?

Get it together, Ketty. You sound like Amy Brown.

I'm not my team. I may be a valuable asset to this camp, but I could be just as valuable somewhere else. Somewhere better. I'll give the brigadier a call, when this is over.

I stand up, and flash Jackson a grin as I walk away. He grins back, still laughing.

Bait

Another day, another patrol. Nearly a week after the last excursion, and we're loading the coach again. This time we're heading for Cardiff, to help at a football match. We'll be inside the stadium, and some of the kids are very excited about being able to watch the game. I'm going to enjoy explaining to them that their job is to watch the crowd, not the pitch.

Bad luck, tiny fighters. You're here to work.

Jackson, gun safely in his pocket, sits next to me in the front seat. Taylor, Brown, and the other recruits are behind us, settling in for the drive. Brown is grudgingly coming as my assistant, but she's sitting as far away from me as she can, on the back seat of the coach with her friends. On the other hand, I think Taylor is looking forward to helping Jackson again. They seem to enjoy working together, and Jackson is certainly bringing out the best in him. No more sulking, and no more broken noses.

What happened to iron fists and steel toe caps, Jackson?

The coach pulls off, and Bracken waits at the gate again until we're out of sight on the road. The sky is cloudy, and before long it starts to rain. It's a cold, damp day, and there are shadows everywhere. I can't help thinking about the men in the field last week, watching us.

If they knew about that patrol, they must know about this one. HQ has leaked the information to the same people.

We know what to do. We're ready for an ambush. But I hate feeling this exposed. I check the road ahead. We're surrounded by fields and farms. Good visibility.

I lean across to the driver.

"Pull over. Pull the bus over."

Jackson looks at me, his hand moving to his pocket.

"Trust me," I whisper. He nods.

"There's a layby up ahead. Pull in there."

The driver slows down, indicates, pulls the bus off the road.

I stand up and hold my hand out. "Keys, please."

The driver looks at me for a moment, then pulls the luggage keys from his pocket.

"Back me up, Jackson."

The driver opens the door, and Jackson and I hurry down the steps.

"Keep an eye on the fields." He's pulled the gun from his pocket, and he's holding it against his leg, out of sight of anyone on the coach.

I reach down and unlock the first luggage compartment door. I open it, and pull out the first crate. The lid opens with a popping sound, and I grab the rifle from the top. I reach inside, find a box of bullets, and pull those out as well. Training issue, so they won't cut through armour, but they'll hurt.

"Anything happening, Jackson?"

"No sign," he confirms, staring out at the fields.

I push the lid on and load the crate back onto the coach. Carefully, I close the compartment door and kneel down to lock it. I make sure the rifle is loaded, then put the spare bullets in a pocket and pick up the gun, concealing it behind me as I climb back onto the coach. I hand the keys back to the driver and sit down again, the gun resting out of sight against my knee. Jackson's gun is back in his pocket as the driver pulls us away, and back onto the road.

I sit back in my seat. I feel much safer now that we're both armed. I feel ready.

Bring it on, Ellman.

*****

An hour into the journey, and our route takes us through a stretch of woodland. The rain has stopped, but the sky is still cloudy, and there are puddles of water on the empty road. I'm watching the trees through the side window, looking for any signs of people or vehicles, when the road swings round a gentle corner, and the driver throws on the brakes.

Jackson swears, and reaches for his gun. Ahead of us, standing in the road, are two soldiers in patrol-style armour. Helmets on, visors down, rifles active and pointed at us. The driver pushes harder on the brakes, but we're speeding towards the soldiers. As he straightens the wheels, the coach begins to slide.

I'm gripping the bar in front of my seat as hard as I can to avoid being thrown towards the windscreen. Jackson steadies himself with one hand, holding tightly to the gun with the other. The coach skids along the road towards the soldiers, and the back wheels start to slide sideways. The driver struggles for control, but we sway from side to side, sliding on the wet surface. Through the windscreen we're seeing trees ahead of us, but the coach is sliding sideways, turning us round until we're almost blocking the road. The noise of the tyres screaming against the asphalt is deafening, and it drowns out the sounds of panic from the kids behind us.

We come to rest, the coach sitting diagonally across both lanes of the narrow road. The two soldiers calmly take a step backwards as we stop, guns still raised.

The engine stops, and the silence is shocking. No one speaks. No one moves.

The two soldiers make their way to the driver's side of the coach, and the sudden sound of gunfire brings shouts from the recruits. I duck down and watch the soldiers through the wing mirrors. As we expected, they're targeting the luggage compartments. If we sit still and stay calm, we should get through this.

Slowly, I push myself up and turn round so that I'm kneeling on my seat. I keep my voice calm, and I'm trying not to shout.

"Recruits!"

A few of them manage to respond.

"Sir!"

"Eyes on me. Listen very carefully. The soldiers outside want one thing, and that's our armour and guns. They're not interested in you. Stay quiet, stay still, and do exactly what we tell you to do."

Fifty faces watch me. Fifty shocked, terrified faces.

"*Extremely* quietly, I want you all to crouch on the floor. Crouch down, keep your heads down, keep out of sight. Now!"

Fifty recruits duck down and jostle each other to find space on the floor. Some of them end up crouching in the aisle, and some between the seats. The metal sides of the coach won't protect them from bullets, but at least they're not visible targets. Jackson swings his legs out into the aisle next to me, both hands on his gun. He looks back down the coach, and forward, through the windscreen. His heel is drumming against the seat.

I turn back and sit down. The luggage doors are open, and in the driver's wing mirror I see four men in plain clothes emerge from the trees. Two of them start unloading the crates, and two more start moving them away along the road.

All we have to do is let them get on with it. Every instinct I have is pushing me to raise my gun, shout warnings, and take out the attackers. The men without armour are defenceless. We could drop them in seconds – but that's not what we're here to do.

The soldiers step back to the front of the coach. One takes up position directly in front, gun pointed at the windscreen. The other moves round to the door, just in front of where I'm sitting. Through the wing mirror on the left of the coach I can see two more plain-clothed men already in place, aiming old-fashioned rifles at the door.

I was right. The woods are full of terrorists.

If Bracken is right, we'll be safe if we sit still, keep out of the way, and let our attackers take what they came for. So far, they've shown no sign of aggression towards the recruits, but the feeling of exposure is back, and my training is screaming at me to do something. To defend the coach. To defend myself.

I watch the soldier in front of me, and I realise he's wearing black armour. This isn't recruit armour. This is isn't the stuff Ellman stole when she took her friends out of camp. This is professional armour, like mine and Jackson's.

I'm trying to figure out how the terrorists have stolen professional armour, when I'm distracted by two vehicles approaching, ahead of us on the road. For a moment I think we're going to be interrupted, that we might have to factor civilian defence into the situation, but the two pickup trucks swing round in the road and park with their empty flatbeds facing the coach.

The two men with rifles move away from the door of the coach, slinging their guns across their backs as they go. Someone has dropped the tailgates on the trucks, and all the plain-clothed guards are helping to carry and stack the crates in the vehicles. The soldiers in armour are still pointing guns at the coach. I drop my hand to my rifle, tucked against my seat.

The soldier in front of us shifts his aim, moving his gun from the centre of the windscreen to the driver. The driver makes a small, frightened sound and lifts his hands from the steering wheel. Jackson's heel drums faster against his seat, and I realise that he's not going to stay still. He's at breaking point, trapped here on the coach.

I reach out to take his arm and stop him from making a move, but I'm too late. He stands up, raises the handgun, and fires a shot through the windscreen, cracking the glass and hitting the soldier in the chest. The soldier staggers backwards, but his armour holds. He'll be winded, but unhurt.

I reach out to grab Jackson, but he shrugs me away, turns, and starts stepping over the crouching recruits, heading for the back of the bus.

The soldier at the door looks distracted. I have no idea what Jackson is planning to do. I keep my eyes on the soldier, and wait.

All we have to do is let them get on with it.

There's a shout from Jackson. "Everybody stay down!"

The back door of the coach hisses open, and I watch in the wing mirror as he glances out, aims the gun at the soldier outside the front door, and ducks back inside.

Jackson! There's no threat here. Just let them take what they need.

But I can't stop him. I can't control this situation. All I can do is stop them getting onto the coach.

I reach for my gun.

The soldier outside the door swings round and points his rifle at the back door. He steps out of sight, closer to the front of the coach, and all I can see in the wing mirror is Jackson's hand holding his gun.

Come on, Jackson. Drop the momma bear act. The kids are fine.

There's movement near the pickups in front of us, and for a moment I think that they're getting ready to drive away. Instead, six of the men are running towards the coach, rifles pointing at the windscreen.

That's too many guns. I'm standing, stepping into the aisle before I can stop myself. I raise my rifle, activating it, and pointing it at the soldier in front of the coach. Slowly, he lifts his hands into the air, holding his gun above his head, eyes fixed on the windscreen. He doesn't step back, or drop his weapon. Six men behind him train their guns on me.

I look out at the vehicles, and there's a man standing in the road watching the coach. He looks at me, calm in the middle of all the guns, and I realise he's the man from the field. The man who was watching the coach as we drove past. The man who looked right at me while he planned this.

There's a moment when everything is still. The driver's hands are shaking gently as he holds them above the steering wheel. I can see the six men, watching me through the sights on their rifles. I can see the trucks behind them, loaded with armour. I can see the trees, branches swaying in the breeze. Light reflecting from a puddle in the road. I can hear my breathing.

And then a burst of gunfire shatters the silence. I crouch down, searching for the source of the bullets, waiting for the windscreen to collapse, but nothing happens.

The noise is coming from behind me.

Jackson.

I crane my neck to see the rear door in the wing mirror. The soldier is walking towards Jackson, firing again and again. Jackson fires back – two shots that miss their target and land in the woods. The soldier keeps firing, round after round, walking towards the rear door. Jackson pulls his hand back, and I lose sight of him as the soldier begins firing into the door.

We're not wearing armour. All Jackson has is his gun.

"Get back! Get inside, Jackson!" I'm shouting, and he's shouting, and the recruits are cowering on the floor.

I grab the driver by the shoulder. "Close the back door! Close it!"

He reaches down and presses a button, then lifts his hands again, shaking even more. There's a hissing sound as the door closes and the shooting stops.

"Jackson!" I'm watching the soldier in the mirror, walking back to the front door. I'm trying to keep my gun pointed at the soldier in front of me. And I'm trying not to let Jackson's silence distract me. I shout again, louder this time, and he answers.

"We're good, Ketty. We're good."

I wish I could believe him.

I'm standing in the aisle, at the top of the steps, watching the gunmen in front of the coach. Watching the driver, eyes closed, muttering something under his breath. Weighing up the odds. Trying to decide what happens next.

The driver and I both jump at the sound of something hitting the door. He raises his arms above his head, ducking down, eyes still closed. I look down, and see the soldier at the door pounding his fist against the glass, gesturing to the driver. I keep my gun trained on the soldier in front of the coach, and watch as the frightened driver presses the button and opens the front door.

Keep them off the bus. That's all we had to do.

We've lost control of the situation. Whatever happens next will not be my decision. I stand up straight, brace my elbows against the seats, and wait.

The soldier steps up to the door, and turns to brace himself against the doorframe, gun pointed into the coach. I keep my gun trained on the soldier outside.

The soldier reaches up with one hand and opens his visor, wide enough to shout through, but not wide enough to show his face.

"Drop the gun!" The voice is muffled, but it's definitely female. And definitely angry. I keep my gun on her friend in the road. If I'm right, this is about keeping him safe, and right now I've got him in my sights. The vulnerable patch, just at the side of his chest where his arm is raised.

"Drop the gun!" She shouts, again, and shifts her gun until she's aiming at my chest. She's in armour, so even if I can aim and fire before she does, it might not stop her. I'm in fatigues, so one shot is all she would need.

I make a decision. I don't want to die today. I don't want to die for HQ and this dangerous plan, for Jackson and his stupid decisions. I don't want to die for Bracken and his recruits, who shouldn't be here in the first place. Let Jackson defend the kids. I'm not dying today.

I drop the gun, keeping it close to my feet.

"Kick it to me."

That would leave me defenceless. But truthfully, I'm defenceless already. I kick the gun towards her, and it tumbles down the steps, coming to rest near her feet. She ignores it, and steps up into the coach.

"Sit down." She waves her gun at me, and I step back into Jackson's seat, moving slowly, hands where she can see them.

She climbs up, next to the driver, and looks down the coach, taking in the kids crouched on the floor.

The radio in her helmet squawks, and she turns her head, distracted.

"Not now."

Someone shouts at her, the words garbled by her helmet.

"Not yet. There's something I need to do." She speaks quietly, but I'm close enough to hear her end of the exchange. "Dan – can you cover the back door?"

Dan? This is *Ellman*? Kind, good, caring Ellman? It's all I can do not to laugh. Everything she does, every move she makes, is a move I've taught her. Me and Jackson. And now she thinks she can use that training against us.

Good luck, tiny fighter. We're not finished here. You're not safe yet.

I wait for her to make her move.

"Heads up! Back in your seats!" She shouts at the recruits, but no one moves.

You're not the authority here, Ellman.

She waits, then lifts her gun and fires a shot at the ceiling. The noise is shocking, and I flinch away before I can stop myself.

Jackson calls out from the stairwell at the back door. "Do as they say!" There's a rustling sound as the recruits scramble back to their seats.

What do you want, Ellman? You've got your armour. Take it and leave.

She steps up again, so she's standing next to me, elbow touching the back of my seat.

Careful, Ellman. That's a little too close for comfort.

The recruits are still moving, shuffling in the aisle.

"You!" Shouts Ellman. "On the ground!"

I can't see what's happening behind me, but I have a pretty good idea. She's picking out recruits. For what? Bargaining chips? Threats?

She looks around the coach. The recruits are quiet now.

She waves her gun at the kids, her elbow brushing my ear. "Stand up!" More rustling.

"You! And you! On the floor." She levels the gun into the aisle.

What's she looking for?

"Back row! All of you, in the aisle, now!"

Amy. She's after Amy. She's not leaving without Amy and Jake.

Stupid move, kid. That's the one thing we can't let you do.

"You! On the floor. The rest of you – back to your seats. Here's what's going to happen. These four recruits are going to leave the bus with me. They're coming in the trucks, and we'll drop them off a mile down the road. You can come and fetch them. But you fire on us; you try to stop us; you do anything stupid; and we take them with us. Understood?"

You're making this up as you go.

I stifle a laugh.

"Am I understood?"

"Understood, terrorist," Jackson shouts, his voice hard.

He's going to let this happen.

This is on me. I have to stop them.

I'm swearing before I can stop myself, and I'm reaching up and pushing hard against her elbow. I've got one chance to knock her off her feet. I stand up as I shove her aside, pushing her off balance and into the seat across the aisle. She's caught off guard, struggling to stand up.

The back door of the coach opens again, and someone fires. Someone shoots back, twice.

Ellman is still trapped against the seat. She's all gangly limbs and flailing rifle. Without thinking, I throw a punch at the visor of her helmet, and her head snaps backwards. Someone – Dan? – is shouting, and I realise that I can't hear Jackson. I risk a glance back down the coach as I draw my fist back for another punch, and Dan is standing in the aisle, a clear shot between him and me.

He raises his gun, pulls the trigger, and my knee blossoms into pain.

I hear the gunshot. I feel the impact. My leg is nudged out from under me and I'm falling backwards, down the steps. I'm dimly aware of impacts on my back, my arms, the back of my head, and for a moment I think the guards outside have fired on me, that this is it.

And then I'm lying on the floor next to the driver, bruised but alive. My leg is braced against the steps, and there's a rush of adrenaline that's starting to mask the pain. I turn my head, and see the barrel of my gun, propped against the steps where it landed. I reach out and pull it towards me, shift it into a combat hold, and point it up at the figure standing over me in the aisle.

Dodge this, Ellman.

It might not kill her, but it's going to hurt, and that's all I care about right now.

She stops, mid-step, gun dangling from one hand. She was trying to escape through the front door, but now she has to get past me. I want to laugh, but the pain in my knee expands, and I'm biting my lip to stop myself from crying out. My hands won't stop shaking, but I'm aiming at her visor.

With any luck, the visor being open will weaken it. I could get lucky. I tighten my finger on the trigger.

And the windscreen above me explodes. There's a crashing noise, and glass is showering down. Without thinking, I drop the gun and throw my arms over my face, closing my eyes and shielding myself from the stinging glass fragments.

The noise fades. The glass stops falling. When I move my arms again, Ellman is gone. There are shouts from outside the coach and then the sound of engines starting up. I listen to the sound of the pickup trucks driving away with our armour and our guns.

And our recruits.

Pain

"Jackson! Jackson!"

I'm yelling. Screaming at the top of my lungs, but there's no answer. The kids are silent. The coach driver is staring at me, a look of horror on his face, a criss-cross pattern of cuts from the flying glass starting to bleed on his cheeks and arms.

My hands are bleeding, too. Covered in tiny lines of red where the windscreen rained down on me. My gun lies next to me on the steps. My leg starts to throb, pain flashing from the gunshot on my right knee. I bite down on my knuckles and close my eyes.

Get a grip, Ketty. Make a decision. Clean up this mess.

First things first. Stop the bleeding. Fix a tourniquet. Stand up, and secure the coach.

Stop the bleeding.

I push myself up on my elbows, blocking out the pain as well as I can. I can't stop myself from crying out as I sit up and move my leg. There's a ragged hole in my trouser leg, and a growing patch of blood seeping into the fabric.

I turn to the driver.

"Give me your shirt." My voice is a whisper, and he doesn't react.

"Your shirt! Now!" I shout, putting all my effort into making myself heard.

He nods, and pulls off his sweater and the shirt underneath. He untangles them, and hands the shirt to me.

Carefully, I push myself up and backwards until I'm sitting against the front of the coach, broken glass crunching under me as I move. Spikes of pain drive into my leg as I shift position, and I bite down on a scream as I bend my knee and plant my foot on the floor.

I hold up the driver's shirt, until I find the middle of the back panel. I use my teeth to start a tear, and then pull the shirt apart. One half, I tie above my knee, as tight as I can. I keep pulling on the tourniquet, tugging it tighter and tighter until I can't move it any more, and the edges of my vision are turning black. I wrap the pieces round my leg once, twice, and then tie the tightest knot I can manage.

The other half, I wrap around the injury, as a bandage to protect the wound. I tie it as tightly as I can without blacking out, and this time I can't help screaming as I work. When I'm done, the driver is still staring at me, and there's a line of kids' faces, watching me from the aisle.

Secure the coach.

I blink back tears, and take a deep breath.

"Recruits!"

"Sir!"

"Whoever is sitting next to the back door, go down the steps for me and find Jackson."

There's a rustling, and the faces turn away to watch. Someone walks down the steps and jumps down onto the road.

I turn to the driver. He's pulled his sweater back on. It's inside out, but he doesn't seem to have noticed.

"Open the door," I say, pointing at the front door of the coach. He presses the button and the door hisses open.

"Jackson! Jackson! Get in here!"

There's a scrabbling sound in the road outside, and one of the recruits appears at the front door.

"Sir …" he says, sounding uncertain. "I think there's something wrong with Jackson."

My mind races. When did I last hear Jackson's voice? Was it before or after Dan came through the back door?

Before. Before the shots were fired.

I fix the kid with a meaningful stare. "Is he bleeding?"

The kid nods.

"Can he speak?"

He shakes his head.

"Is he sitting up? Lying down?"

He glances back down the coach.

"Lying down, Sir. In the road."

His voice is starting to shake.

Hold it together, kid. I need you. Today's not over yet.

He's wearing fatigues, and I look for his name patch.

"Mitchell! Pay attention!"

He jumps, and stands up straight.

"Sir!"

"I need you to go back to Jackson, and tell me whether he's breathing. You know how to check that?"

The kid nods, and disappears, footsteps running along the road.

I lean my head back against the frame of the windscreen, and I realise I'm crying.

The driver seems to pull out of the shock of the attack.

"Shall I …?"

Without moving, I grit my teeth and reply. "Go and help? Yes. Please."

He takes off his seatbelt, and mutters an apology as he steps over me and heads down the steps.

I close my eyes, and the world starts to turn and tumble around me.

Focus. Focus on the kids.

I force my eyes to open, and shout as loudly as I can.

"Tiny fighters!"

"Sir," comes a ragged shout. Not good enough.

"Tiny *fighters*!" I force myself to shout louder.

"Sir!" Better.

"Is anyone hurt? Any recruits bleeding that I don't know about?"

There's a muttering, but no one shouts.

"Check your neighbour. Check your partner. Check the seats in front of you and the seats behind you."

More muttering.

"Is anyone hurt?"

"No, Sir." I listen for a 'yes' in the chorus of negative answers, but none comes.

Mitchell appears again at the door.

"Sir? He's breathing, and the driver says he's got a pulse, but he says it's bad."

There's a lump in my throat, suddenly, and my voice comes out as a whisper. "Thank you, Mitchell. Go back and help the driver. Tell me if anything changes."

He doesn't move.

"He wants the first aid kit."

The dizziness is getting worse. The coach seems to turn around me.

"OK. Where is that?"

He climbs up onto the first step, pulls the green plastic box from the stairwell wall, and runs back to Jackson.

Right in front of you, Ketty. You're losing it. Stay focused.

"Tiny fighters!"

My eyes are closing. Everything is turning round. I feel as if I'm sinking into the floor, and someone is pounding on my leg with a hammer.

"Sir!"

"I need you to stay in your seats. If the driver needs someone to help him, go and help. One recruit at a time. Everyone else, sit tight, and stay quiet." I can hear my words slurring, but I can't seem to stop them. It takes all my concentration to raise my voice. "Is that clear?"

"Yes, Sir!"

"Good." It comes out as a whisper.

I don't know how long I sit, eyes closed, my back propped up and my arms braced against the floor. The kids stay quiet, and the only sound is the voice of the driver, talking to Jackson and Mitchell outside.

Come on, Jackson. Hang in there.

And then there's a faint sound in the distance. The sound of a vehicle approaching.

I wonder if I'm imagining it, but it grows relentlessly louder, until I'm sure it must be right behind me.

The engine noise dies, and there's the sound of car doors, opening and closing. Someone is shouting, and I know I should respond, but it's so hard to speak. I want to shout out, I want to call for help, but nothing happens.

Footsteps outside, and I can hear the driver talking to someone.

"There's a house, about a mile back …."

"… use the phone …"

"… be back as soon as I can …"

The doors open, the doors close, and the vehicle drives away.

I sink down into darkness and pain.

When I come to, someone is kneeling over me, asking my name.

I try to speak, but no sound comes out.

I try again.

"Ketty. Smith."

"OK, Ketty," says a reassuring voice. "We're going to move you now. I'm sorry – this is going to hurt, but it's what we need to do. Do you understand?"

"I … yes. OK."

Strong hands slide around my back, and under my knees. I feel enclosed and protected.

And then they lift me, and my leg moves, and I remember screaming.

Cornered

I open my eyes.

I'm in a hospital bed, in a hospital gown. My leg is propped up, somehow, under a blanket, and there's a tube and a needle in my arm.

The lights are uncomfortably bright, and there's someone calling my name.

I cover my eyes with my hand, waiting to remember what I'm doing here.

And then I do.

"Jackson!"

I'm sitting up, shouting, before I realise that I can't move. I can't move my right leg, and I can't get out of bed. There's a doctor standing in the room, and someone else.

Bracken.

"Ketty …" he begins, but I don't want to listen to him.

"Where's Jackson?" I'm shouting so loudly I can feel my throat turning raw.

"Ketty …"

"Jackson. Where. Is. He?"

Bracken steps forward, lays a hand on my arm. His eyes are bloodshot, his uniform is crumpled, and there's a faint trace of alcohol on his breath. I wonder how long he's been here.

"He's alive, Ketty. He's alive, and so are the recruits, thanks to you."

The fight drops out of me and I slump back against the pillows.

The details of the attack on the bus are flowing back into my mind. I feel like crying again. I stare at the ceiling.

"I lost four recruits. I'm sorry."

Bracken laughs.

"Ketty! We lost two recruits. The other two walked back to the coach. The terrorists left them in the road and drove away."

I shake my head. I know who came back, and who didn't.

"We lost Brown and Taylor."

He nods. "Brown and Taylor."

He doesn't sound surprised.

"Sorry, Sir."

"Don't you dare apologise, Lead Recruit. You're the one who made sure everyone stayed on the coach. You got treatment to Jackson in time. You kept the situation under control. You even treated your own gunshot wound," he gestures to my leg, "an act which the doctors here are officially calling 'hardcore'. And that's not something they'd say lightly."

I find I'm smiling, and so is the doctor as she puts a hand on my shoulder.

"Seriously hardcore, Lead Recruit. But you had surgery this morning, and now we need you to rest. We've got you, and we've got your friend. We're going to take good care of both of you."

I look at Bracken again. "The kids? They're OK?"

He smiles. "The kids are fine. A little shaken up, a little confused, but they're fine." He looks at the doctor, and then back at me. "We're going to leave you to rest, now. I'll be back to check on you in the morning."

But there's something else. Something I need to tell him. "Mitchell. Mitchell was amazing, Sir. He helped Jackson, he helped the driver. Get him an award, or something. He made it OK. He was my eyes and ears, and he did everything I told him to do."

I can't believe I'm getting this emotional about a recruit. Must be the painkillers.

Bracken is nodding. "I know. I'm working on it."

"And Sir? It was Ellman. Ellman and Pearce. They stole the armour, and they attacked us. Our own recruits, firing weapons at their friends."

His face hardens. "The recruits told us – the ones who went with the attackers. Thank you, Lead recruit. I'll be back to take a statement when you're well enough to talk."

I start to protest that I'm well enough now, but the doctor places a firm hand on my shoulder. "We need you to rest. Commander Bracken will be back tomorrow. We'll see how you're doing then."

Reluctantly, I agree. As the commander leaves the room, I feel tears on my cheeks. I raise a hand and brush them away.

Get it together, Ketty.

*****

Jackson might be alive, but when they finally let me see him, he's a mess. He's lying, eyes closed, in a bed surrounded by machines. There's a tube punched through his chest, draining blood and air into a bag. There are wires running from his body to the monitors, and there's a breathing tube jutting from his mouth. Like me, he's got tubes and needles in his arms.

I talked one of the nurses into bringing me here as soon as I could sit up, and he's standing behind me, hands on my wheelchair as I watch Jackson from the corridor. Now that I'm here, I realise that I don't want to see this, but I can't look away.

Dan Pearce did this. Pearce and Ellman. And for what? Armour and guns they won't have a chance to use against us, and two children who couldn't learn to take care of themselves.

Come on, Jackson. You're worth more than that. I need your iron fists. I need you to back me up.

He looks small and broken. Taped together and co-cooned in machinery. I can't see his eyes. His power, his energy – they're gone. This stillness – this isn't Jackson. He should be standing over me, mocking me for the bandage on my knee, the wheelchair, the nurse pushing me around. He should be reading my mind. Asking me what to do next. We should be planning our retaliation, not lying in hospital beds.

I hate this feeling of helplessness. I want to do something. I want to hurt the terrorists, like they hurt Jackson. I want to take someone important away from them. Leave someone else bleeding and weak and helpless.

"I'm done. Take me back."

The nurse hesitates. "Are you sure? We're not in the way here …"

I grab the wheels of the chair and start pushing myself away, ignoring the stabbing feeling from the needle in my arm every time I tense my muscles. There are dark bruises on my arms and my back from my fall on the coach, and dressings all over my hands and wrists from the windscreen glass. Everything pulses with pain as I shove the wheelchair forwards, but I keep moving. At least I can feel something.

"OK! OK. We're going." The nurse takes over, pushing me away from Jackson. Away from his empty shape in the bed.

I find I'm dashing tears from my eyes as we leave the ward and head back to my room.

*****

When we get there, Brigadier Lee is waiting.

Are you stalking me, Sir?

"Lead Recruit Ketty Smith," he says, as I'm wheeled past him. "I hear you're the hero of the hour!"

"Couldn't say, Sir," I manage, as the nurse tries to help me up into bed. I wave him away. I want to stay in my chair if the brigadier is here to talk. I don't want to feel like a patient. I want to be able to look him in the eye.

"May I sit down?" Lee indicates the chair next to my bed.

"Of course. Please."

The nurse wheels me round to sit next to him, checks my drip and the blanket over my knees, and makes sure I'm happy with my visitor before leaving us to talk.

Lee reaches down next to the chair and pulls up a bouquet of brightly coloured flowers. "I brought you these. I hope you don't mind."

"Thank you, Sir!" I can't hide the surprise in my voice. I think this is the first time anyone has ever bought me flowers. I take them from him, carefully. I'm not sure what to do with them.

Pull yourself together, Ketty. This is a professional visit. Handle it.

I take a deep breath, will my head to clear, and put the flowers gently down on the end of the bed.

"What can I do for you, Sir?" I ask, folding my hands in my lap, and sitting up as straight as my bruises will allow.

He leans back in his chair, watching me.

"How are you feeling, Lead Recruit? I gather the terrorists made a mess of your knee." He indicates the bulge of the bandages under my blanket.

I shrug. "It could be worse, Sir. Bullet grazed the bone. I've got some torn ligaments, muscle damage – nothing I won't recover from."

He nods. "And your colleague?"

Use his name. He's not dead yet.

"*Jackson* has a punctured lung, some smashed ribs, some other broken bones. He's … not awake yet."

198

"I'm sorry. As I understand it, that shouldn't have happened."

"No, Sir."

He pauses for a moment, then continues.

"If you ask me, you shouldn't have been in that position at all. A coach full of children, sent out to be attacked. I can't even count the number of things that could go wrong."

"No, Sir."

"Was it Bracken's idea?"

"HQ's, I think. But Bracken approved it."

"Did he protest the plan with HQ?"

"I don't know, Sir."

"And did he come with you? Share the risk?"

"No, Sir." I shake my head.

He leans forward, towards me.

"You and Jackson should be very proud of yourselves. You protected a coach full of recruits this morning, and made sure the terrorists left with the tracked armour. *You* should be proud of yourself, for directing the rescue and recovery effort while dealing with your own bullet wound. The kids I've spoken to were clear that none of that would have happened without you."

"Thank you, Sir, but I just did what needed to be done."

He smiles. "And that's why you'd be an asset to my team. Not many people could do what you did."

"Thank you, Sir."

Are you promoting me, Sir?

"Any idea why the terrorists came onto the coach? I thought the plan was to give them the armour, and sit tight until they drove away."

"It was, Sir." I think about Jackson, his heel drumming on the coach seat. His instinct to shoot the person with the gun to our heads. My failure to stop him. "It was a tense situation. Who's to say what set them off?"

He raises an eyebrow. "And the hostages? Do you think that was their plan all along, to take their friends off the bus?"

"I don't. I think they were making it up as they went. I think they saw an opportunity, and they took it. I don't think we could have stopped them. Not without more casualties on the coach."

"I agree." He leans back, watching me again.

"Ketty. I'd like to ask for your help."

Not a job offer, then?

"Yes, Sir."

He leans his elbows on the arms of the chair, and steeples his fingers in front of him.

"Confidentially. Understood?"

"Yes, Sir."

"Commander Bracken is putting together a proposal for HQ. He wants to be the one to track the armour, find the terrorists, and take some prisoners. He wants to make sure that, after everything that's happened, he's the one to deliver the bad guys to us. I think he knows he's made too many mistakes, and I think he wants to make one, final pitch for a promotion. We know he wants out of the RTS. We also know that he plans to take you with him."

I try not to react.

"Bracken's proved that he can't be trusted with an RTS camp. He's made too many mistakes, and he hasn't learned from any of them. But I don't need to rock the boat to get rid of him – I think that if I give him enough rope, he'll hang himself. So I'd like to give Bracken this one last chance, because I think he can't handle it. I think he'll screw up, publicly, and prove to all of us that he's not up to the job."

My stomach sinks. All this time, he's been after Bracken. And now he sees a chance to take him down.

"But I need the operation to work. I need Bracken to fail, but I can't let the terrorists get away. We need our armour back, we need our guns back, and we need to destroy their base of operations. We're only dealing with one, local terrorist cell, but we need to make sure we crush it while we have the chance."

I nod, trying to understand what he wants from me.

"I need someone on the inside of Bracken's organisation. I need someone to plan with him, to encourage him, and go with him to the terrorist hideout. I need someone who can do all this to support him, but keep me in the loop on everything that happens.

"Bracken needs to screw up, but I need to be waiting, ready to march in and complete the mission. And to do that, I need you."

He smiles, and watches my response.

You're good, Ketty. You're brave, Ketty. I'd like to employ you, but first I need you to betray your commander.

I think about Bracken. I think about the chances he's given me. The responsibility. The trust he's put in me. And I think about how easily he was manipulated when HQ attacked Leominster. He didn't even know what was about to happen on his own doorstep. He didn't ask. He was so hungry for attention that he jumped through all their hoops, and he didn't ask why.

Like Brown and Taylor at the gate, manipulated by the person they cared about.

Like me and Jackson, on the coach, trying to show HQ that we could handle the terrorists.

And here's Brigadier Lee, manipulating me to get to Bracken. I shake my head.

"Forgive me, Sir. I'm just trying to sort this out in my head."

He nods, and waits for me to continue.

"You want me to give you Bracken. You want me to help him to screw up. But you said yourself that Bracken is my ticket out of the RTS. He'll take me with him if he

201

gets his promotion. Surely I should be protecting him – making sure he doesn't go through with this plan."

Lee watches me, saying nothing. And I realise he's enjoying this. He's enjoying watching me reason this out.

He's pitched this to me while my head is foggy with painkillers, and he knows I'm worrying about Jackson. He wants to see how good I really am. He wants to watch my performance. He's using the disaster on the coach to push me into a corner and see how I respond.

This is it. This is the test. This is where I prove to HQ that I can solve their difficult problems. That I can handle tough decisions. That I can do what needs to be done.

He's right. I'm better than Bracken. I deserve more than Camp Bishop. I could leave the tiny fighters behind, and finally make a difference with the real fighters. I can make this work for me.

I could sit here and refuse. I could worry about Bracken. But if Bracken is already in Lee's crosshairs, where does that leave me? If Bracken goes down, then surely I go with him. All Lee's flattery means nothing if I'm still working for Bracken when the hammer falls. When he makes his final mistake.

As much as I owe Bracken, as much as he's given me, I could lose it all by sticking with him. I need to start looking out for myself. I need to find a new way out of Camp Bishop. Brigadier Lee might be my only option, but so far he's done everything he can to flatter and manipulate me into helping him.

Let's see if this manipulation works both ways.

I nod. "I could do this for you. I could handle Bracken. And I could make sure the operation to catch the terrorists has a satisfactory conclusion.

"But in doing so, I'd lose the person who's coached me this far. I'd lose the person who promoted me and gave me a chance. I'd lose the one person who saw something in me, and gave me the opportunity to build on that.

"Respectfully, Sir, if I do this, if I give up Commander Bracken – what do I get out of it?"

Lee's smile becomes a smirk, and he looks at me for a moment. His eyes are cold, and his gaze makes my skin crawl.

"*Respectfully*, Lead Recruit, you get to keep your job. You get to walk back into this war, and you get to play a part. Working for me, if you'd like to. I'll make sure that you get that chance, rather than – say – a medical discharge, and a one-way ticket back home to Daddy."

And there it is. The punch in the gut. He's seen my file, he knows my weak point, and he knows just where to hit me. I know he has the power to make it happen. He could end my career today.

Help me, or go back where you came from.

Flattery and arm-twisting. Flowers and steel toe-caps. Carrot and stick. He's using my own techniques against me. For a moment I feel dizzy, as the reality of what he's saying sinks in.

He's got me. I'm trapped, and I hate it, but what choice do I have?

I'm in a corner. I'm bandaged and medicated and stuck in hospital room.

Come on, Ketty. There's a way out of this. He doesn't own you.

I try to think this through, to get ahead of Lee and his plans. Bad situations don't have to end badly. Like the weapons test, I can use this. I can use *him*. I can still get out of Camp Bishop. It's this, or the end of my career.

I make my decision. I smile back, as brightly and confidently as I can.

"If that was a job offer, Sir, then I accept. I would be delighted to work for you. And I'll bring you Bracken.

I'll bring you the terrorists, too. I have some scores I'd like to settle with their newest recruits."

His smirk becomes a broad smile. He's got what he came for.

"I'm glad we can work together on this, Ketty. I'll be in touch." His voice is mild, as if he's talking about some paperwork, or a new training session. As if he hasn't just threatened to destroy my future.

He stands, shakes my bandaged hand, and steps round my wheelchair to the door.

He turns back, his hand on the door handle. "I know I don't need to remind you of the consequences of sharing this with anyone else, Lead Recruit. Consider this conversation confidential and classified. You work for me, now, and the sooner I have Bracken, the sooner we can fit you into my team in London.

"Welcome aboard."

"Yes, Sir."

As the door closes behind him, I fight the urge to scream.

Determination

I'm lucky. The injury to my knee is messy and painful, but the bullet did relatively little damage. The doctors are pleased with the results of the surgery, and by the time Bracken comes back for my report, the morning after the attack, they've got me bandaged, but walking. It hurts, and I have to use crutches, but it beats the wheelchair. They've taken the needle out of my arm, and only the worst cuts on my hands are still covered.

Bracken arrives before lunch, a bag of clothes and toiletries in his hand. I make him wait in the corridor while one of the nurses helps me to get dressed. It's a relief to be wearing my uniform again. I brush my hair and tie it back neatly. I'm amazed by how much better I feel – I feel human, even in the hospital bed.

After walking this morning, the doctors want me to rest my knee. The nurse helps me to sit up straight on the bed, and props my leg up with a stack of pillows. She sends Bracken in, and he stops at the door.

"That's the quickest recovery I've ever seen! Casualty to soldier in …" he checks his watch, "five and a half minutes."

"Thank you, Sir!" I can't help smiling.

"How's the lead poisoning?" He nods at my knee as he sits down, moving the chair so it faces the bed. His eyes are bloodshot again, and puffy, as if he hasn't slept.

"Could be worse. Could be better."

His face is serious. "I gather that bullet was a present from one of our recruits."

"Yes, Sir. Dan Pearce."

"You're sure about that?"

"I am. I was restraining Ellman, and this was his way of getting her off the coach."

"Is he responsible for what happened to Jackson, too?"

"Yes, Sir."

He nods. "Thank you, Ketty. I'll make sure I mention that in my report." He pulls a notepad from his pocket. "Can you run me through what happened?"

So I do. I lose a few of the details of Jackson's response, and play up the idea of a chaotic situation. Jackson doesn't deserve the blame for this – it wasn't his idea to put us all on a coach and leave us to be ambushed. I make sure Bracken knows that he was doing his job, and protecting the kids.

"How's Jackson doing?" Bracken closes his notepad and slips it back into his shirt pocket.

"He's a mess, Sir. He's … messed up." I shake my head and wait for tears, but this time it's anger that flares at the mention of his name.

"They told me Dan shot him at close range, with one of our rifles. He's lucky to be alive."

"Have you seen him, Sir?"

He shakes his head.

"With respect, 'lucky' is the last thing he looks."

Bracken looks at me. "I'm sorry, Ketty. I'm sorry. I know you two …"

You know nothing. You know about black eyes and teaching sessions.

I wave his comment away, and try to stop myself from shouting. "He's my friend, he's my colleague, and he's the person I trust most at Camp Bishop. He has my back. And right now he's breathing through a tube because a spoilt schoolboy decided to play soldier for the bad guys, and Jackson was brave enough to stand in his way. So no. I don't think he's lucky. I think he's brave, I think he's loyal, and I want him back."

And I want Dan to pay.

Bracken nods. "We're doing what we can."

I take a calming breath. "Have they tracked the armour? Do we know where Ellman and Pearce are hiding?"

"I'm told they're getting close. We should know in a day or so."

"What's the delay? Surely they just have to follow the tracking signals?"

"They're not sure. They've got a general location, but the signals keep dropping out, for hours at a time. HQ is trying to make sense of it. It shouldn't be long now."

"Will you tell me when they figure it out?"

"Of course."

"I'd like to be there when they find our recruits."

"Ketty, you're injured. We'll keep you up to date, but …"

I lean towards him, my voice firm and quiet. "I was on the coach. I took a bullet. I want to be there."

I want my chance to hurt them.

He watches me for a moment, then nods. "I'll see what I can do."

*****

"We've had a request to discharge you."

The doctor is back, checking up on me and making sure I haven't moved. She checks the bandage, and gently moves my knee to check the range of movement.

"Any pain?"

"Sure." I'm gritting my teeth, but she doesn't need to know that.

"OK." She sets my leg back on its tower of pillows. "We're not going to let you go until we're happy that there's no infection, and we know you can walk unaided."

"Who made the request?"

She checks her clipboard. "Commander Bracken. He says there's a medic at Camp Bishop, and he's happy for you to be treated there."

Thank you, Bracken. One step closer to having my boots on the ground.

"When can I go?"

She nods towards the door. "When I'm happy that you can walk the length of the corridor on a single crutch." I start to get up, reaching for the crutches next to my bed, but she puts a hand on my shoulder. "No more walking today, Ketty. I'm sending the physiotherapist to see you in the morning. You can start then. For now, I want you to stay here and give the swelling a chance to go down. Your leg was a mess, and it will take time to heal. Don't push it."

"I can start tomorrow morning?"

"Tomorrow morning. I'll put it on your notes."

*****

"Miss Smith! Miss Smith, please. I need you to come back to your room."

"Ketty? Ketty, please. Come back and lie down."

"Someone call Dr Grace!"

I block out the voices around me, and ignore the nurses who are standing in my way. They'll move, if I keep walking.

It's half past five in the morning, and I'm starting my own training. Let the physio turn up when they want to. I'm starting now.

I'm on two crutches, and so far I've made it to the end of the corridor. I turn round, and start walking back, past my room, past the nurses' station, and into the tiny common room. I turn around again, and start to retrace my steps.

Every step sends a bright shaft of pain up and down my leg. I'm putting as much weight on my knee as I can, but the muscles that hold it steady as I walk are damaged, and it's only the bandage that stops my leg from folding up under me.

I refuse to be helpless. I refuse to wait.

I carry on walking.

I got myself dressed this morning. It took twenty minutes to get my trouser leg over the bandage, and another ten to keep my balance while making myself decent and fastening my belt. I refuse to be a casualty. I'm a fighter, and I'm going to fight my way back to camp.

"Ketty …"

The nurses are standing along the corridor, now. I ignore them as I walk to the end of the ward. And again, I turn round, I keep walking.

It's just me and the pain. And I can walk through the pain, if it means I get to face Ellman and Pearce and their friends. If I can be there to help Bracken and Lee. If I can bring a message from Jackson.

One step, then another. One step, then the next. Keep walking.

I don't know how long I walk up and down. The pain comes and goes, and the nurses decide to let me walk. They're keeping an eye on me, but they're not chasing me any more.

My balance gets better. I use the left crutch less and less, and put more and more weight through my right arm, balancing carefully and making sure my leg can take the weight. I turn round in the common room, and as I walk past my room, I throw the left crutch in through the open door and keep moving.

The nurse who pushed my wheelchair drops the file he's carrying on a chair and runs up to me as I start to wobble. I shift my weight back to my good leg, and lean on the crutch while I sort out my balance.

"Ketty, please. Wait for the physio." He reaches out to help me, but I take another step, and another, and it hurts. But I don't stop. I keep taking steps. I put my hand out to the wall when my balance shifts, but I keep moving.

The nurse walks with me. He keeps his distance, but he's there. At the end of the corridor he gives me a round of applause, and it's enough to make me smile. I meet his eyes, and he smiles back.

We walk together. End to end to end of the corridor. The pain doesn't go away, but my balance improves, and every time I turn round, he's there, cheering me on.

At breakfast time, he finally convinces me to sit down, but I sit in the common room, and I refuse to go back to bed. I'm leaving today, and I'm not wasting any more time. After breakfast, I walk again.

Dr Grace arrives at eight fifteen, just as I'm passing the nurses' station. She stops in the corridor, and watches me walk up to her, turn around, and walk back. She follows me to the common room where I turn again, and it takes her hand on my shoulder to make me stop.

"OK, Ketty. Point made. The nurses told me you've been doing this for hours."

I nod. I'm exhausted, I'm sweating, and I need a shower, but none of those things matter. I look her in the eye.

"I'm going home today."

She laughs. "I think you're right. I need to check the knee for infection, but you've proved that you're ready to walk out of the building. Come back to your room. We'll make sure you're ready to leave."

When she unwraps the bandage, I think I'm going to scream, and it takes all my willpower to close my eyes and keep quiet. She checks the scar, pokes and prods me while I grit my teeth, and finally stands back, snapping off her disposable gloves.

"There's plenty of swelling, but I think we've got the infection under control. We'll keep you on antibiotics." She looks at me, shaking her head. "You're lucky that you haven't pulled any stitches with that stunt. I'm going to discharge you into the care of the medic at Camp Bishop." I let out the breath I've been holding. I'm going home.

"But Ketty?" I nod. "Listen to your physiotherapist. I understand what you did here today, but you need to take care of yourself. We'll assign someone to work with you at the camp. Look after yourself, and give yourself a chance to heal. Agreed?"

When I've kept my promise to Brigadier Lee. When we've made our move on the terrorists.

"Agreed."

*****

Commander Bracken comes to pick me up at lunchtime. I walk out on my own, on a single crutch, my knee bandaged again.

Bracken carries my belongings, and the nurse hands him my flowers in a plastic bag.

"Secret admirer?" He says, raising his eyebrows at me.

"Something like that."

You have no idea.

On our way out, we pay Jackson a visit. There's no change. He still has the breathing tube and the chest tube, and all the needles and wires and machines. He's still not really Jackson. I turn and walk away, and the commander has to catch up with me in the corridor.

I'll get them, Jackson. I'll make them pay.

Rest

"I can't work out why you're my problem now, Lead Recruit. Why aren't you still in hospital?"

"I can walk, and I can work. No point staying there when I could be doing my job."

I adjust the pillows under my knee, and behind my back, until I'm sitting up straight. Lead Medic Webb checks my notes from Doctor Grace.

"But you shouldn't be walking. Not with this kind of injury. You've got damage to muscles … ligaments …" he turns a page, "tendons … cartilage … bone. This is a mess, Ketty."

I shrug. "Dr Grace let me go. I need to get moving, and I need to fix this. I want to be walking properly by the weekend."

He laughs. "And I want a pony and a chocolate factory, but that doesn't make it so. You need to give this time. You'll get there, but you need to be patient."

We'll see how that goes, Doctor.

*****

"I heard you were back. How are you?"

Miller stands at the door to my room in the medical centre. I wave him in, and he sits down on the other bed.

"I've been worse."

He nods, and looks round the room.

"You've done OK here. How come you get the presidential suite and the soft pillows, and the rest of us are still in dorms?"

I spread my arms, showing off the space. "Welcome to my new office! Doctor Webb gave me a room to myself, so I can hold meetings and parties without getting out of bed." I flash him a grin and drop my voice to a whisper. "Haven't you heard? Camp Bishop revolves around me, now. You lot just have to get used to it."

He laughs. "Camp Bishop always revolves around you, doesn't it?" He's joking, but there's a hard edge to his voice.

This isn't a courtesy call. This is you finding out how soon you can take my job.

"What can I do for you, Miller? Don't you have recruits to babysit?"

He looks at his watch. "I've got a few minutes." He looks down at the floor. "How's Jackson?"

I give him a cold stare. "Jackson's bad, Miller. Dan Pearce shot him twice in the chest with a camp-issue rifle. Pearce was wearing armour. Jackson wasn't."

"Mitchell said he'd been shot. He said the coach driver saved his life, but I wondered …"

"It's bad."

He nods, still looking at the floor.

"And Taylor?"

"Taylor's gone. And Brown. They finally found their way back to Ellman and her friends."

He looks at me again, an unfriendly, smug smile on his face. "You let them go?"

Really, Miller? Looking for another excuse to replace me?

I turn up the sarcasm. "Yeah. I let them go. I packed their little lunches, I gave them their warm coats, and I pushed them out of the door. I kissed them goodbye and waved them on their way. Oh – and as a thank-you, their friend put a thoughtful bullet in my knee."

He smirks, and I can't hide my anger.

"No, Miller – we did not *let them go*. Jackson and I defended the coach. We both took bullets for those kids, and the terrorists kidnapped them anyway. You want to shoot the breeze in the senior dorm about who should have done what, that's fine, but you weren't there. You weren't on the coach, you didn't have guns pointed at you, you weren't trying to keep the kids safe. You don't get to tell me what I should have done."

The pain in my knee flares, and I realise I've been tensing my leg muscles, leaning forward to make my point to Miller. I sit back against the pillows.

He stands up, the smirk gone from his face. "Good to see you, Ketty," he says, and walks out of the room. I stare at the ceiling, waiting for the pain to fade.

Like you could have done better.

*****

I'm still calming down when Webb puts his head round the door.

"Does my stubborn patient feel like eating? The kitchen's sending dinner."

I force myself to smile. "Sure."

"You're due some painkillers, too. How do you feel? Do you want those now?"

Thanks to Miller, I do.

I nod. He brings me a cup of water and a couple of tablets. When I've swallowed them, he puts his hand on my shoulder.

"How are you feeling? I know the last few days have been … eventful. Don't forget to let yourself stop. If you need to take some time off, I'm here to be your body-guard. I can send people away before they bother you. I can even send Bracken away, if you want me to. If I say you're resting, even the commander can't overrule me." He smiles.

We're trying Good Cop now, are we? Flattering me into staying in bed?

"I'm fine, thank you. I'd rather stay busy."

He nods. "I thought so – but the offer's there. Let me know if you change your mind."

One of the women from the kitchen arrives in the doorway with a tray.

"I'll let you eat," he says, taking the tray and handing it to me.

I eat alone, and it's hard. Jackson should be here, laughing and joking with me. Poking fun at the kids. Keeping me on my toes. Challenging me to do better. Iron fists and steel toe caps, each of us pushing the other to be the best, to keep the recruits in line. To do what needs to be done, and demanding nothing in return.

I push the tray away. I used to have the backbone to do this by myself. Keep myself going. Push myself to do better. And now – what? I need Jackson to do it for me?

Come on, Ketty. Push yourself. You're stronger than this.

But when Webb signs off for the night, and a duty medic takes over at the desk, I can't sleep. Every time I close my eyes I see Jackson, motionless, surrounded by machines.

And I miss him.

Progress

Bracken arrives after breakfast, a file of papers in his hands. The nurse brought me a waterproof sleeve for my bandage, so I've finally had a shower, I'm dressed in a clean uniform, and I'm ready to get to work.

"I gather I have to come to you now, when I want to hold a meeting?"

"You do, Sir. Doctor Webb has set me up in his finest conference room. Pull up a chair and tell me what I can do for you."

He raises an eyebrow at my playful insubordination, but he sits down.

"We've found them." He can't hide his smile.

"Ellman?"

"And all her friends."

For a moment, I can't think of anything to say. I close my eyes, take a deep breath, and breathe out slowly.

"That's good news, Sir."

"It is. It means the plan worked. What you did on the coach – that was worth it."

I shake my head, thinking about Jackson.

Let's hope so.

"So where are they?"

"On a farm, we think. Somewhere in Wales. We're sending surveillance teams over today."

I take another deep breath. There are tears pricking at my eyes.

Almost there. Almost ready to round up our missing recruits. Go on, Mummy Ellman. Get out of this.

"So what's the plan, Sir?"

"HQ is checking it as we speak. I want to hit them in the middle of the night – cut the power, cause maximum confusion, and flush them out of their hiding place. We'll try to take prisoners, but we'll have a backup plan in case we meet more resistance than we're expecting."

"And what are we expecting?"

"That's what we're hoping the surveillance will show. We'll keep an eye on people coming and going, get a feel for how many people we think there are on the farm. Then we'll send in troops, and take as many of the terrorists as we can for questioning."

"Questioning? Surely the point is to make an example of them? Show them off on the news. Broadcast the firing squads."

We waves his hand. "Sure. We'll get to that. But first we'll see what they can tell us about their organisation. Who else is out there. What they're planning. See if we can find out who's in charge."

Sounds good to me.

"So do we have plans of the site? Do we know what we're walking into?"

"We're working on that as well. When we've confirmed the location, HQ will trace the owner. We're going to see what information we can dig up on the property. Buildings, power, water. Whatever we can disrupt and use against them."

"How long before we make our move?"

"As soon as HQ approves. When we know what's out there, and we've confirmed our plans, we go. No point giving them enough time to get spooked and move on."

"No, Sir."

He stands up. "I need to get back. HQ will have questions, and I need to be on hand to answer them."

"Yes, Sir. Will you let me know what they say?"

"I will." He stops at the door. "And Ketty? I'm going to need you. I'm going to need your input on this. I'm glad you're here."

"Thank you, Sir."

I'm glad I'm here, too.

*****

"Go back to bed, Ketty!"

"Not yet. I told you – I need to be walking by the weekend."

Doctor Webb shakes his head. "And I told you – ponies and chocolate factories. You're doing yourself more damage. At least wait for the physiotherapist."

"When they get here, they can help."

I'm walking up and down the medical centre corridor, a single crutch in my right hand. It still hurts to walk, but I'm pushing myself through the pain. Doctor Webb sits down in the waiting area, watching me and shaking his head. The nurse sits at the reception desk, trying to look busy.

"Do I have to order you back to bed?"

"I wouldn't advise it, Sir." I'm concentrating on keeping my balance, and taking the next step, and the next.

"You are one bloody-minded woman. You know that?"

"I do, Sir."

"Normally, I'd respect that. But now?"

The door to the medical centre swings open, and one of the gate guards pushes his way inside. He lifts a green plastic medical supplies crate onto the desk. The nurse looks up in surprise.

"What's this? New kit?" Webb jumps up and goes to inspect the crate.

The guard looks at Webb in surprise, as he fishes in his pocket for the delivery note. He puts it down on the desk. "It's for her, Sir," he says, nodding at me as he leaves.

Webb looks at me.

"First flowers, now medical crates? Something you want to tell me, Lead Recruit?"

Nothing I can think of.

I keep walking.

"Expecting a delivery, Ketty?" I shake my head. "Can I see what's inside?"

"Sure. Suit yourself."

Webb snaps the lid off the crate, pulls back a layer of packaging, and lets out a cry of excitement.

"Katrina Smith! Someone likes you."

I make my way back along the corridor to the front desk, crutch tapping on the floor as I walk, and look over Webb's shoulder. He reaches in and lifts out a brown cardboard box. It's mostly plain, with a serial number and an illustration of a running stick figure, and it's sealed with tamper-proof tape.

He looks at me again, eyes wide. "Someone else wants you to be walking by the weekend."

Brigadier Lee?

He puts the box on the desk and opens the lid. A grin creeps over his face. "I don't think you're going to need the physiotherapist."

The nurse stands up. "Is that what I think it is?"

Webb sounds excited. "I think so!"

I'm tired, my leg is hurting, and I want to get back to walking. "What are you talking about? What is it?"

Stop messing with me. I have work to do.

He touches the plastic-wrapped items in the box reverently, one by one.

"This is battlefield tech. This is top of the line." His eyes widen again. "This is *expensive*."

I reach out and rest my hand on the desk.

Enough already.

"Do you want to tell me what's going on?"

He snaps the box shut. "Better than that. I can show you."

*****

I'm sitting up in bed, dressed in a T-shirt and a blanket. Doctor Webb carefully peels back my bandage while I grit my teeth and clench my fists. The release of pressure makes my leg pulse with pain. The stitches burn as the bandage pulls away, and the patchwork scar feels like a red-hot bar against my skin.

"Hurts, doesn't it?" He says, glancing at me. "Sorry about that. But you'll thank me."

He reaches for the box, and pulls out a plastic package. "This? This will seem like magic. I promise."

He opens the package, and pulls out a white gel pack, a little thicker and longer than a sheet of paper. He gently lifts my leg, and wraps the gel around my knee, as if he's applying a new bandage. The wound is covered completely, and the gel sticks to itself. After a few seconds, the join is invisible. He smooths the edges of the gel onto my skin, making sure that all the damage is covered. The wrapping feels cool against the scar, but the pain is still there.

He reaches back into the box and brings out a tube of stretchy black fabric. He tears open a Velcro-style fastening, and wraps it around my leg, on top of the gel. He adjusts it until it sits tightly above and below the knee, and snugly around the wound. It hides the gel completely.

He pulls a third package from the box – a small black box with a short cable running from it. He holds it up, grins at me, and slips it into a clip on the outside of the fabric tube. He leans over, picks up the cable, and plugs it into a port just below the clip. He watches my face as he locates the power switch, and turns it on.

The gel turns instantly cold, and stiffens slightly. I'm watching the bandage, and I can feel the cold spreading through my knee. It's fast, and it's pushing deep into the joint. It feels strange – almost ticklish – and before long everything under the bandage, through to the bone, is cold.

And the pain is gone.

He grins at me, and I can't help grinning back.

The pain is gone.

*****

Commander Bracken rushes out to meet us as Doctor Webb and I walk across the field towards his office. Webb is at my elbow, carrying my crutch, but he hasn't had to steady me at all. I'm walking on my own.

The gel is washing the pain away, and the fabric support is keeping my knee steady. It's awkward. I'm limping, and I'm moving slowly, but I'm walking without a crutch.

"Ketty! What …?"

Bracken waves his hands at me, at my knee, hidden under my trousers. Doctor Webb is grinning again. I stop in front of Bracken and stand at ease, my weight slightly shifted to my left side.

"Someone at HQ likes your Lead Recruit, Commander. She's the proud new owner of a PowerGel Battlefield Recovery System."

Bracken's eyes nearly pop out of his head. It's all I can do to keep a straight face.

"HQ sent you a PowerGel?"

"Yes, Sir."

"That's … that's amazing."

"I need some more practice, Sir, but I'd like to request again that you take me with you when you go after the terrorists."

Bracken nods. "Get practising, then! If you're ready, you're coming. HQ wants you there. I want you there. Go on! What are you waiting for?"

I'm walking up and down the corridor again, and this time Webb is encouraging me.

"Try to walk naturally. The gel will support you. I know it takes some getting used to, but don't be afraid to put more weight on your leg."

I walk again, and again, front door to back door and back. And every time, it gets easier. I'm still limping, but I'm slowly getting better at balancing my steps.

I've been walking for a while, and I'm half way along the corridor, when the woman from the kitchen arrives with a tray of food. Webb checks his watch. "Dinner, Lead Recruit?"

My steps are more confident now. The PowerGel is hidden under my clothes. I don't need to eat on my own in the medical centre – I need to show my face in the Senior Dorm. Let Miller and the others see that I'm fit for duty. That my job's not up for discussion.

I walk to the door, thank the woman, and take the tray. She turns to go, and I catch the closing door with my elbow and follow her out, moving slowly down the steps. Webb runs to the door behind me.

"Lead Recruit! Where are you going?"

I start walking across the field, concentrating on keeping my balance and carrying the tray. Making it look easy.

"I'm going to eat in the Senior Dorm." I carry on walking.

Webb gives a grunt of frustration. I hear the door close, and his footsteps on the grass as he jogs to catch up with me.

"You need much more practice before you go swanning off across uneven ground without help. At least let me carry your tray."

"No need. I've got this." I keep walking. Miller and the others need to see this.

Webb laughs, and shakes his head, walking next to me. "So much for taking it slowly. Any idea who your friend at HQ might be?"

I shrug, carefully, as I walk.

No one you need to worry about.

We reach the Senior Dorm. Webb insists on helping me up the steps and opening the door for me, and leaves me to walk in and stand opposite Miller. I place my tray carefully on the table, and look around, meeting the eyes of everyone in the room.

They're all watching me. All the Senior Recruits, staring as I sit down and pick up my knife and fork as if nothing has happened. I look up at Miller, and smile.

His face is grey. The colour is draining from his cheeks. From the expression on everyone else's faces, I'm guessing he's been bragging about his chances of being promoted to Lead Recruit.

Good luck with that, techie guy.

I start eating. I'm amazed at how comfortable my knee feels, even when I'm sitting down and bending it. The gel seems to flow around the joint to where it's needed, and the cold sensation never fades away. I'm also amazed at how hungry I am, now that I'm not forcing myself to ignore the pain.

"So, Ketty. You're walking." Miller tries to sound friendly, but he can't keep the chill from his voice.

"Looks that way," I say, around a mouthful of potato.

"Does it hurt?"

I pretend to consider his question. "Not really."

"Commander Bracken said you had some sort of battlefield medical tech."

I nod, still chewing. "Something like that."

He shakes his head, and lets out an unkind laugh. "How did *you* get that? How does a glorified babysitter get her hands on battle-grade kit?"

Babysitter? Really?

I take my time. I finish my meal, take a drink of water, and lean my elbows on the table. I fix him with a cold stare. He watches every move I make. Everyone in the room is watching, and no one makes a sound.

"I guess HQ thinks I'm worth it, Miller."

I grin. He stares back at me, his cheeks burning.

I pick up the chocolate bar and the bottle of water from my tray, and look around the room again. I stand up, carefully, the gel tingling on my skin as it flows around my knee.

"Well, it's been fun. Good to see you all. I'd stick around, but I have a job to do."

I put the chocolate and the water into my pockets, and walk out, leaving a silent room behind me.

And as I walk back across the field, I'm laughing.

*****

I have to take the gel off to sleep. The doctor needs to clean the wound, and I only have a limited number of gel packs. Battery power is limited, too. This isn't a miracle, but it will get me where I need to be.

And there's a price.

Webb switches off the battery pack and starts to remove the fabric from my knee. The gel softens, and the cold feeling begins to fade. As he releases the pressure, the gel peels away, and I can't help crying out as the pain slams back.

It's like being shot all over again.

"Sorry, Ketty. I know. This part's rough."

My knee looks white and puffy, and the stitches dig in like staples, pulling tight against my skin. Everything hurts. The muscles are on fire. The pain stabs into me, and it's a moment before I can speak.

"Can I get you some painkillers?" Webb looks concerned.

"Yes. Painkillers would be great." My voice comes out as a whisper.

He fetches two tablets and a cup of water, and I swallow them as fast as I can.

I nearly scream again when he straightens my leg, cleans the wound, and wraps my knee in a bandage.

"This feels worse, now. Why does it feel worse?"

"You've been pushing yourself, Ketty. You need to practice, but you're running before you can walk. Marching across the grass? Using the steps without a crutch? You're not ready for that yet. Concentrate on walking – on getting up and down the corridor. You can move onto uneven ground when you're ready. You could do permanent damage if you push too hard. Just give it time."

I shake my head.

I don't have time. I have a few days, and this is not going to stop me. Just keep the painkillers coming.

Planning

Webb hands me my crutch as I leave the medical centre after breakfast. I use it to walk down the steps, then carefully lean it against the outside wall and walk away across the field. He shouts after me, but I keep walking. I'm not meeting Bracken looking like an invalid. He needs to know I'm ready to confront the terrorists. He needs to see me, not my crutches.

When I reach the commander's office, the door is closed. Woods sends me in, and I'm surprised to find Brigadier Lee sitting in one of the guest chairs. Both men stand, and I carefully bring myself to attention, and salute.

"At ease, Lead Recruit. Take a seat." Bracken waves at the other chair, and I sit down as smoothly as I can, paying attention to the gel around my knee.

"Good to see you, Lead Recruit," says Lee, settling into his chair, no hint of threat in his voice. "How's the PowerGel working for you? The Commander tells me you've been training hard."

"I'm getting used to it, thank you, Sir."

"I thought it would put you back in the game. Give you the chance to help us out with the terrorist problem."

So it was you.

"Thank you, Sir. I appreciate that."

"It's not perfect. You need to get used to it, and I know that taking it off at the end of the day can be a shock, but I'm sure it's nothing you can't handle." He smiles, and it's not entirely friendly.

So you know what you're asking me to live with. I'll keep that in mind.

"No, Sir. Thank you, Sir."

Bracken clears his throat. "Brigadier Lee is here to run through the current intelligence on the terrorist base. I wanted you to hear it first-hand."

I nod. Lee sits back in his chair.

"We've traced the armour trackers to Makepeace Farm in mid-Wales. We haven't been able to get close – they've got tight security in place – but we've used historical records and photos to piece together what we're expecting to find.

"The place was an arable farm until the 1970s, when the current owner bought it, and planted it up for forestry. Sitka Spruce, mostly, right up to the back door of the house. From what we can see, the trees are pretty dense, and it's hard to get a clear view of anything on the ground.

"There's a farmhouse, a yard with a barn and some outbuildings, and lots of woodland. Because of the trees, the only way in with vehicles is along the main driveway, and that's under constant surveillance – we assume from inside the house.

"The owner is a William Richards. Stereotypical grumpy farmer, according to the neighbours. Keeps himself to himself, and waves a shotgun at you if he finds you on his land. We don't know whether he's involved with the terrorist activities, but he lives on site, so it's a reasonable assumption.

"As for numbers – we're not sure. We've only seen a few people coming and going, but I have a hunch that we're dealing with a sizable group. They've got plenty of space to be hiding in, and as they bothered to steal fifty sets of armour, I think we can assume that they intend to use them.

"So. More than we knew three days ago, but less than we'd like to know. We'll be going in partially blind, and we'll need to think and act on our feet."

"Has HQ approved the plan?" Bracken sounds anxious.

Lee nods. "With a few alterations. We'll hit them at night. We'll take down the power, and we'll raid the house. See what we find. Beyond that, we're in the dark. We've got acres of woodland to search, and we want prisoners if we can find them and disarm them.

"They want you to go in first with a couple of troop carriers. Raid the house, search the outbuildings, see what's there. Round up the terrorists, hopefully get your recruits back, and secure the site.

"I'll be off site with the backup team. If the terrorists are armed, or we encounter anything unexpected, I'll have a range of options to send your way. Nerve gas, flamethrowers, squads of soldiers on foot. We'll be ready for whatever they've got waiting for us."

Lee leans forward and gestures at Bracken.

"You're up, Commander! HQ wants you front and centre on this one. You helped us with the armour, and it's your recruits who got us into this, so they want you there to tie everything up. You, Ketty, whoever else you need.

"Congratulations. Your plan is going to catch us our terrorists."

"Thank you, Sir." Bracken is smiling. He thinks this is his chance. He thinks he's going to get back into HQ's good books by walking in blind and leading the cannon fodder on this mission. "Ketty. What do you think? Are you ready to take a command role in this operation?"

"Absolutely, Sir."

Couldn't turn you down if I wanted to, Sir.

I keep my eyes on Bracken, but I can feel Lee's gaze on me, challenging me to stick to the script. His threat of a one-way ticket home hangs over me like a shadow. He can take away the PowerGel, and he can take away my career. I don't have a choice.

"Can you be fit to leave at short notice?"

"Yes, Sir. When are we planning to make our move?"

Lee answers me. "We're waiting for confirmation, but the plan is to raid the farm on Saturday night, and be done bar the sweeping up by Sunday morning. Think you can manage that?"

Two days. Two days to be ready.

"Yes, Sir."

I don't have a choice, do I?

*****

Brigadier Lee pays me a visit in the medical centre before he leaves. He checks the corridor and closes the door as he comes into my room. I'm sitting up in bed, still dressed in my uniform. He walks in and takes a seat facing me. I swing my legs over the side and stand up, but he waves me back to bed, so I sit on the edge, facing the chair.

"So this is it. You're going to be ready?"

"Yes, Sir."

"And you haven't changed your mind?"

"No, Sir."

I have no sudden desire to move back to my child-hood home, if that's what you mean.

He hands me a small package.

"Take this with you. Wear it when you suit up, and keep it on you during the raid."

I look at the plastic-wrapped piece of tech in my hand. It's black, small enough to fit into my closed fist. I flip it over. It's an earpiece.

"It's a private radio. You can trigger it with your glove – I'll give you the channel setting on the night. Use it to keep in touch with me. I'll use it to give you orders. Remember – my orders trump Bracken's. He can't know what you're doing for me. I'll try to arrange it so that he won't miss you and your team.

"I'm going to give you five soldiers. You'll be ex-pected to pass on my orders to them, preferably by voice, not over the radio. Five plus yourself should be sufficient for what we need to achieve. Steadman's my tech guy – he'll be with you. If I need him, I'll let you know where to go. The others are reliable people. They know to do as you say.

"While you're following my orders, you're going to need to keep Bracken happy, too. I'll try to keep him off your back, but if you need to bluff it, can you do that?"

"I think so, Sir."

He looks back at the door, and drops his voice.

"Here's what Bracken doesn't know."

I sit forward on the bed.

"We know more about the farm – and the owner – than we've put in the briefings, and we have reason to believe that there's a cold-war era nuclear bunker at Makepeace Farm. Private, not military. We have reason to believe that it's the bunker, not the farmhouse, that's the terrorist base.

"Bracken's plan is a raid on the farmhouse. What I need you to do is run the raid on the bunker."

So nothing that Bracken will blame me for, then?

"We think there's a gatehouse, somewhere in the trees at the back of the house. That's the primary target. Secondary target is the ventilation system, but we haven't located that yet. You'll have Steadman for the ventilation – he knows what to do. But you'll have the first chance at the bunker.

"Get me inside, get me to whatever they're keeping down there, and you'll have done your job."

"Yes, Sir."

"I'm not going to tell you how to do it. I need you to be flexible. I need force and persuasion. I need whatever works. I've seen you run your recruits. I know you can handle whatever these people throw at you. Get out there and get us inside. Can you do that?"

Iron fists and steel toe caps. Not forgetting the velvet gloves.

"Yes, Sir."

"I don't want casualties – I want prisoners, but I'm not stupid enough to think we can do this without breaking some eggs. Persuasion first, shoot later. Understood?"

"Understood, Sir."

"Good. And Ketty? Not a word. Not to anyone. You understand."

I nod. "Yes, Sir. Absolutely."

Still not planning on going home, Sir. You've got my attention.

"Good. I'll see you on Saturday. Fighting fit and ready to run that PowerGel into the ground."

"Yes, Sir."

You have no idea.

Webb

"No way, Ketty. No way."

"I'm doing this, whether you help me or not. I can do it with you, and maybe get away with some pain and discomfort, or I can do it without you. You said yourself, this could do permanent damage to my knee. So help me, and keep me safe, or I'll help myself. Help me, or move out of my way."

Webb stands up straight and shouts into my face.

"Katrina Smith! Stand down! I'm ordering you …"

I wave him away. "Call Brigadier Lee if you want. He'll authorise this."

Webb takes a deep breath, and forces himself to speak calmly. "Brigadier Lee is not the medic here. I am. And I say that you do not have medical clearance to push yourself this hard."

"Noted," I say, "and ignored."

I look out at the assault course. I'm standing at the start line. The recruits are inside for their daily briefing session, and I've got the field to myself. Webb and I have been training on uneven ground for a day and a half. He's been happy to help me so far. I know I can walk if I need to. I can even jog for short stretches of time.

But now I want to test myself. Check that I'm ready for tonight. I want to run the assault course.

I'm not planning on trying for a personal best. I'm not trying to break any records. I know it's going to hurt. I just want to know that I can do it.

Webb runs his hands through his hair, and looks at the assault course with me.

"Ketty …"

"I've done this a million times. I know what I'm doing. I just want your supervision."

He sighs. "Fine. Fine. But you walk, and you take it slowly, and if I say you need help, you wait for help. Agreed?"

"Agreed." And I start walking.

I reach the cargo net, and pull myself up. It takes me a second to adjust to the tightness of the PowerGel round my knee, but I work out how much I can bend it as I climb. At the top, I drop down into the trench, left foot first, and start to run through the freezing water.

"Walk, Lead Recruit! Slow down!" Webb sounds angry. I drop my pace, dragging my feet through the mud towards the wall.

He reaches the wall before me, and makes a stirrup with his hands. I'm offended – I can do this by myself. I roll my eyes, but I give him my left foot, and reach up to haul myself over. I drag my right leg up, and roll onto the ledge at the top. Webb walks round the wall to watch my progress.

I hold onto the rope line at the top of the wall and hook my left foot over the rope to hold myself in place. I swing my right leg up, and rest it on top, ankle over ankle. Hand over hand, I drag myself over the water drop to the wall on the other side.

So far, I'm not straining my knee at all. I'm moving it carefully, but I haven't put much weight on it. So far, I'm hardly breaking a sweat.

Onto the wall, gently placing my feet, and turning carefully to the zip line. I grip the runner, the bruises in my shoulders complaining loudly as I lift myself up by my arms.

The zip line sings as I rush towards the ground. Webb is shouting – something about lifting my knee – but I'm already moving to touch the floor with my left leg.

Left foot out, right leg bent, I make contact with the ground, but I can feel myself messing up the landing. Without my right foot out to take a step, I fall forward. I let go of the zip line, and the ground swings up towards me. I catch myself on my elbows, and my forehead hits the mud.

Webb is at my side in seconds. He flips me over and takes a look at my face.

"You OK?"

I shake my arms out and bend my legs. I'll have some extra bruises, but nothing I can't deal with. I'm on my feet again before I can think too much, Webb hauling on my elbow.

"Careful, Ketty. I want you to go slowly through the tunnels."

I nod, and start walking towards the barbed wire. I drop carefully to my knees, lie down, and start crawling, keeping my back low. There's a lot of twisting in this motion, and before long I'm feeling spikes of pain from both knees. I slow down, and keep moving.

"Lead Recruit! Stop pushing your injury! I can see you slowing down. Use the left knee, rest the right knee."

There's no easy way out of these tunnels. I have to push through, or go back, and going forward is much easier. I look ahead, and all I can see is the vicious spikes of the barbed wire above me, mud below me, and the narrow exit from the tunnel. It seems impossibly far away.

The PowerGel has its limits, I'm learning. As a pain-killer, it seems less effective when I'm twisting my knee like this. I don't want to admit it, but Webb is right.

Gently, I straighten my right leg, allowing the cold sensation to dull the pain again. I dig my fingers into the mud and drag myself forwards, pushing with my left leg. The bruises on my shoulders flash with pain. My right leg is a dead weight behind me. My world narrows to one motion. I keep crawling forwards.

Push with my foot. Pull with my arms. Keep myself flat against the ground. Reach out, push with my foot, pull with my arms. Reach, push, pull. Over and over.

I crawl out from the end of the tunnel and pull myself clear of the barbed wire. I roll over, lying on my back and sinking my shoulders into the cold mud. All the bruises on my back are pulsing with pain, and even my fingers ache from the effort of pulling myself along.

Webb is standing over me.

"Still going, Lead Recruit? Or are you ready to stop?"

One more obstacle to go. I'm finishing this. I sit up, and Webb takes my hand to help pull me to my feet. I turn, and walk to the over-under bars.

"Take the easy option, Ketty," calls Webb.

No chance.

I duck down, under the low bar. The recruits go under the high bars and over the low bars, but I'm not settling for that. Left knee down. Lie flat on the ground, pull myself under the bar. Stand up. Over the high bar. Back on the ground again.

"Slowly, Lead Recruit!" Webb is yelling, but I can see the finish line. I can do this.

Under. Over. Under. Over.

I stand up. There's nothing between me and the end. I walk to the finish, and Webb meets me there.

"You're going to push me to early retirement, Ketty Smith," he says, shaking his head. "You OK?"

I take a deep breath, stretch my arms and roll my aching shoulders.

"Never better, Doctor."

My knee, cocooned in its ring of gel, feels fine. Everything else hurts, but I don't care. I'm floating above the pain. If I can complete the assault course, I can walk into the terrorist base tonight. I've proved I can do this, and I know I can trust myself later.

"Am I released to go with Commander Bracken tonight?"

This is the final formality. I need medical clearance to join the attack on the farm.

Webb shakes his head again. "Ketty, I ..."

"Am I fit to go? Can I do what Bracken needs me to do?"

He shrugs. "I don't have much choice, do I? What with Bracken and Lee breathing down my neck."

"Not really. But I hope I've proved to you that I'm not going to let this hold me back."

He thinks for a moment. "Sure, Ketty. Sure. You're released. I'll let Bracken know. But don't push yourself tonight. Keep in mind the things you can't do – not just the things you can."

I nod, and I can't hide a smile. "Yes Sir. Thank you, Sir. I appreciate it."

I'm ready.

Action

The troop carriers roll into Makepeace Farm just after one in the morning. Bracken sends three teams to search the house, breaking down the door and storming inside by torchlight.

We cut the power to the site on our way up the driveway, and the farmyard is in darkness when we arrive. Bracken sends another team to set up floodlights and a generator in the yard, but that takes time. We're all using torches, and the radio is busy with commands.

My team gets assigned to the house, but as soon as we're through the door, Brigadier Lee calls me on the private channel.

"Get your team through the house and out to the back."

"Yes, Sir."

"Keep walking along the path. We think you'll find an outbuilding, probably concrete. Probably small. That's your target. You know what to do."

"Yes, Sir. Leave it with me, Sir."

*****

The outbuilding is right where Lee expected it to be. We find it to the side of the path – a small concrete box with a metal door, chinks of light showing round the edges of the doorframe.

One of the soldiers pulls the door open, and we're met by bright lights and a shower of bullets. Someone inside is firing at us. Rounds rattle off the chest plate of my armour, winding me but not hard enough to knock me down. The soldier next to me fires a shot at the man inside, and the firing stops.

Lee is right. This is the gatehouse. They have backup power – enough to run the lights – and in the far corner I can see a security shutter, large enough to hide a wide doorway.

I wave the soldiers to stay behind me, and step up into the bunker, gun raised. The guard is slumped on the ground, propped against the wall, no armour to protect him. His rifle is on the ground, and he's clutching his stomach. Blood is seeping between his fingers.

I kick the rifle backwards, and someone behind me picks it up. I swing round, my gun sweeping the small room. There's a bank of surveillance screens in the corner next to the door, and sitting in front of them is a young recruit in camouflage trousers and an RTS T-shirt.

I blink. It's Sleepy. And he's unarmed.

Sleepy is in charge of security for the bunker. I can't help laughing. I lower my gun and raise my visor. Sleepy stares at me, fear and bafflement crossing his face.

"Mister Saunders."

He says nothing. I nod towards the shutter.

"Care to tell me what's back there?"

He swallows hard, sits up straight in his chair, and shakes his head emphatically.

"Really, Sleepy? Nothing you want to share?"

He shakes his head again.

I glance behind me, raise my gun, and shoot from the hip, planting another bullet in the guard. It hits him in the leg, and he grunts. I swing the gun back to cover Saunders.

"Last chance, Saunders. What's behind the shutter?"

He pulls himself up to his full height in the chair, his face a mask of terror and growing determination.

"Nothing, Sir." His voice shakes, but he puts force behind the words.

I take a step towards the shutter, keeping the gun on him.

"You won't mind opening it for me, then?"

Two more soldiers step into the gatehouse, and I wave them back. Saunders' eyes flick between them and me, and he starts to panic.

"Saunders! Over here!" I shout, and he looks back at me. "Open the shutter for me. I want to take a look inside."

He's distracted by the soldiers. He's gripping the arms of his chair. His breathing is shallow and rapid.

Come on, Sleepy. Do the right thing.

"Recruit Saunders!" He jumps, and focuses on me. "I can put another bullet in your friend here. I can put a bullet in you. Or you can open this shutter."

He glances at the guard on the floor, at the barrel of my gun, and back at me. He closes his eyes. His hands grip the arms of the chair and his knuckles turn white.

"You and your friends have caused me a *lot* of trouble, Saunders. Do *not* test me on this.

"Now. Open. The. Shutter."

"No."

I breathe out, carefully.

"What are you protecting? Stores? Weapons?" I pause. There's a pencil sketch resting on the desk under the screens. Even from a distance I recognise Ellman, Pearce, Brown, Taylor, and Saunders, posing in their armour.

A smile spreads across my face. I've got them.

"Or maybe your friends are sleeping down there."

His eyes flick open.

"Bex? Dan? Jake? *Amy*? They're down there, aren't they?"

He freezes, rigid in the chair.

I laugh. "They are. All your friends, tucked up in bed. Are you willing to die to protect them?"

Because I'm happy to take you away from them.

My mind jumps to Jackson in his hospital bed.

"Mummy Ellman owes me a friend or two." I take a step towards Saunders. He grips the chair, his breath ragged. His eyes meet mine.

"You can't have them." His voice is clear. Determined. "You can't have *her*. I'm their guard, and I'll *die* before I let you through."

I shrug. "OK."

And I pull my trigger.

His body jerks backwards, his eyes wide. His mouth gapes in frozen surprise. He looks down at his chest, at the small, neat hole in his T-shirt. At the spreading patch of red. His breath catches in his throat, and there's a rough rasping sound, then his head slumps forward and his hands fall away from the chair.

I don't move. I don't expect to be stunned, but I can't move. The stain spreads slowly across the front of his shirt.

I want to laugh. I want to shout. I want to run.

I've killed someone, Jackson. I've killed Sleepy.
This is for you, Jackson. This is for you.

Slowly, I force myself to lower my gun. I step forward, and nudge Sleepy's shoulder. He slips down in the chair and slides sideways onto the floor. I kick him onto his back. He doesn't react.

One for one, Ellman. Man down.

I push his chair away and step over to the surveillance screens. They're dark, and at first I think they're switched off. But then I notice torch beams flickering on two of the screens, faint, but obvious when you know what you're looking for.

The shooting when we opened the door tells me that Sleepy and the guard suspected an attack, but it's clear that they haven't been able to track our movements. They've been in the dark in here, trapped in their bubble of battery power.

With any luck, they haven't had the chance to sound an alarm.

I cross over to the shutter, searching for a control panel, but there's nothing. I cross back to the desk and check for buttons or switches, but the only switches I can find control the monitors. My search knocks the pencil sketch to the floor, and I leave it lying next to Saunders.

I'm stepping away, when all the screens jump from black to blinding white. It takes them a moment to adjust to the new light source, but when the images settle, I can see what's going on outside.

The cameras overlook the farmyard, and lit by Commander Bracken's floodlights I can see two women in pyjama trousers and sweaters waiting in the yard as the soldiers search the house. There's a guard with a gun next to them, and they're watching Bracken as he stands at the door, shouting orders to the people inside. Like the other people in the yard, they're shielding their eyes from the bright lights. I lean closer to the screens. Who have they found in the house? Ellman?

The images are in black and white, and they're grainy. I look carefully at the two women as they drop their hands from their eyes.

Not Ellman, but one of them looks like the prisoner we lost from Camp Bishop. She's young, with the same shoulder-length hair and slim figure under her sweater. The other woman I don't recognise. She's older, and she stands up straight in the courtyard, ignoring the soldier behind her.

I look back at the guard, still slumped against the wall but still breathing. I walk over and kneel down next to him. He's watching the screens, but he turns his head slightly and looks at me. His eyes are hard with anger in his pale face.

"What about you? Are you going to open the shutter for me?"

He stares. He opens his mouth to speak, and whatever insult he's about to throw at me is interrupted by Brigadier Lee, shouting in my ear.

"Are you inside, Lead Recruit? Do you have access to the bunker?"

I touch the transmitter.

"No Sir. I'm trying …"

"Never mind. We're out of time. Get your team to the service location. Report back when you find the inlet pipes."

"Sir, the terrorists are inside. I've confirmed their location. They're sleeping in the bunker. If I could just …"

"Lead Recruit. This operation has moved on. Take your team, and get to the ventilation pipes. We'll solve our terrorist problem that way."

My shoulders slump. "Yes, Sir."

I'm so close. I can deliver Ellman and her friends alive. The kitchen woman, too – and whoever else is down in the bunker – but Lee's attention has moved on. Now the mission is about gassing them as they sleep. Easy. Painless. They'll never know who found them.

"Any complications, Lead Recruit?"

I look at the guard. I don't think he's capable of moving, but he's alive, and he might have information that Lee could use.

"One, Sir. There's a guard in the gatehouse. He's wounded, and he's not going anywhere, but he might be useful."

"Acknowledged, Lead Recruit. I'll send a couple of soldiers to bring him in. Take your team and get to the air intakes. Call when you locate them."

"Yes, Sir."

I cut the transmission and turn back to the guard.

"It's your lucky day. Opening that shutter just became a low priority. Our commander is sending someone to talk to you, so I suggest you sit here and think about what your next move might be." I drop my voice to a whisper. "I'd recommend cooperating. It beats taking bullets."

He coughs, blood trickling from the corner of his mouth.

"Taking bullets ..." he coughs again, and shifts his position against the wall. "Taking bullets beats shooting at children." His cold eyes follow mine as I stand up.

It takes all my self-control to keep my gun lowered as I turn and walk out of the gatehouse.

Breathing

We walk back into the woods, visors up to give us as much light as possible. We leave the gatehouse for the brigadier's guards, when they arrive. Not our problem any more. The farmyard is behind us, and so are the floodlights, so we're picking our way along the path with torches.

We're looking for a small building – a hut, or a shed – where the air supply for the bunker comes up from the ground. With the trees growing so close together, finding it feels impossible, but the brigadier is convinced it will be near the path, somewhere to our left.

Our six torches don't throw much light, but between us we're lighting up as much of the space between the trees as we can. On our first pass, we walk right past it. The path widens and the trees disappear, and we're standing on the shore of a lake.

I activate the private channel to Brigadier Lee.

"Sir? Sir – we're at the edge of the woods. No ventilation pipes."

"Lead Recruit. Nice of you to check in. Describe your surroundings."

I look around, swinging my torch over the path and the water in front of us.

"It's a lake, Sir. The path splits and heads round both sides, but we can't go any further without getting wet."

There's a pause while he checks his records.

"That's too far. You need to come back and look again. It should be less than half way between you and the gatehouse. Closer to the lake, but not by much."

"Understood, Sir. We're on our way."

"Ketty? Hurry. Bracken's not getting anywhere with the prisoners, and we need to make a move before anyone else wakes up. We don't know what kind of warning system they have in the bunker."

"Yes, Sir."

We walk back along the path, stepping into the woods to shine the torches into hollows in the ground and check out fallen trees. I'm making the most of my PowerGel, walking between the trees, climbing over roots and rotting logs, when someone shouts ahead of me.

"Lead Recruit! Take a look!"

I follow the waving torch beam through the trees, and join the rest of the team. We're looking at a heap of evergreen branches, piled waist-high next to a fallen tree. Close to the path, but hard to spot in the darkness. Two of the soldiers step forward, and start to pull the branches away from the top of the pile while the rest of us hold the torches.

They've pulled a layer of branches off the top when the front of the pile topples, and falls towards us. Underneath is a small wooden box, about the size of a supply crate, with panelled sides and a waterproofed roof. I can't help smiling.

Got you.

We all step in and pull the rest of the branches away.

"Steadman. All yours. Tell me what we've got."

Steadman drops to his knees in front of the box, and we all aim our torches at the wooden panels in front of him. He pokes the edges and the joints in the wood, but nothing moves. He reaches up and pushes against the lid instead, and I let out a breath as it lifts away, pivoted on hinges at the back. He pushes it all the way back, and it falls and rests against the fallen tree. He reaches inside and slides back the bolts on the front panel, which drops outwards onto his knees, exposing a bundle of metal pipework.

"Is that it, Steadman? Is that what we're looking for?"

He bends down, shining his torch between the pipes. I'm holding my breath.

"I think so, Lead Recruit." He straightens up. "I think we've got them."

I'm smiling as I give Lee the good news.

"Thank you, Lead Recruit. Ask Steadman to verify the fittings and the connections. I'll send the equipment to your location. Wait for my instructions."

"Yes, Sir … Steadman! The brigadier wants to know what connectors we need. Can you work it out?"

Steadman pulls a roll of tools and tape measures from his belt and lays them out on the ground, then leans his head into the mess of pipes and starts to assess the sizes of the inlet filters.

I'm in control. I'm in command, and I'm going to give Lee what he's waiting for. The feeling is electric.

"Give me a few minutes."

"I'll give you two." I walk over to the box and shine my torch onto the pipework. "Everyone else? Torches on the path. We'll have company in a moment. The help is heading our way – make sure they can find us."

I watch Steadman work. He's kneeling over the pipes, torch in his mouth, feeling out the connections with his fingertips in the dark.

"Can we do it? Are the filters here?"

He takes the torch from between his teeth and grins at me.

"I think so. And I think it's going to be easy."

This is it, Ketty. This is where you show Lee what you can do.

"Sir!" I can't hide my smile as I call the brigadier again. "Steadman says we're go." I glance at Steadman and he gives me a nod. "Officially requesting the nerve agent, Sir."

Lee takes a moment to respond, and it's all I can do not to repeat myself.

"Understood, Lead Recruit. We're moving into position. Stand by."

We're going to get them. We're going to take down a terrorist cell, and we're going to take Ellman and her friends with them.

Sleep tight, Recruits. Sweet dreams.

I stand with Steadman, watching as he unscrews the end of a thick pipe with his fingertips and pulls out a cylinder of grey plastic with layers of metal mesh at each end. There's a serial number on the side.

"Got it. That's the intake filter." He puts his head down, level with the pipe. "Standard equipment should do it."

This is going to be easy. This is going to work.

"Thank you, Steadman."

"Lead Recruit! Status!" It's Bracken, calling on a private channel.

Bracken, who doesn't know I'm back here.

Breathe, Ketty. Stay calm.

"Sir!"

"Status, Ketty. Where are you, and why aren't you in the farmyard with the rest of the team?"

They must have finished searching the house.

Be confident. This is Lee's problem, not yours.

"Sir. Sorry, Sir. Just checking out something in the woods."

There's a pause. "In the woods?"

"Yes, Sir. Something caught my eye. We're checking it out."

I'm wincing as I speak. I can't believe how casually I'm admitting to disobeying orders.

"Lead Recruit! Get your team back here. Now!"

"Yes, Sir."

Come on, Lee. Help me out.

Steadman looks up at me.

"Problem?"

"I'm not sure. Keep working. I'll sort this out."

Keep it together. Stay in control.

I hesitate, wondering what to do. I can't leave the ventilation pipes, but I can't let Bracken figure out what I'm doing. I'm about to call the brigadier when my radio activates again.

"New orders, Lead Recruit. Lee wants your assessment of whatever it is you're looking at. Keep going. We'll call if we need you."

Bracken sounds hesitant, unsure of himself. But now I know that Lee is monitoring communications. And I know he's got my back.

You can do this, Ketty.

There are voices on the path, and more torch beams sweep over the ventilation box. The equipment is arriving.

*****

We're surrounded by crates and tools and pieces of metal. It's getting crowded on the path – the soldiers who brought us the crates are waiting for the order to connect the gas tanker to the ventilation system, but they're waiting here in case the order is to abort. Seven crates need fourteen people to carry them.

Steadman is working quickly and calmly, and the rest of my team is helping out – handing him tools, holding torches, searching through crates and boxes for the things he needs.

This is what I'm good at. Keeping everyone focused. Getting things done.

And it feels good.

I've updated the brigadier twice, but he's gone quiet. It's frustrating to be stuck out here, away from the action, away from Bracken, and away from the prisoners.

Come on, Lee. Talk to me.

I watch my team working together. "Steadman. Where are we?"

"We're good," he calls back to me, a screwdriver held in his teeth. There are three of them, kneeling in front of the pipes, hands inside the tangle of pipework, working together to fit a collar to the inlet filter as quietly as they can.

This is *my* team. No fuss. No drama. Getting the job done.

Steadman drops the screwdriver, pulls his hands away and gives me a thumbs up. "We're ready. The collar is attached. I just need the first length of hose." The others pull their hands out and stand up, rolling their shoulders and shaking life back into their arms. They've been kneeling there for ages.

I step between the crates, searching for a short length of hose with a metal collar on each end. I find it on the path, where several of the crates have been unpacked.

"This?" I shine my torch at the component in my hand.

"That's it. Thanks!"

I walk it over to him, and watch while he connects it to the intake filter. It's a quick, neat job, and when he tugs on the hose to test the connection, nothing moves. He grins at me, and I grin back.

"Nice work, Steadman. Thank you."

Lee's voice shouts into my earpiece.

"Report, Lead Recruit."

Come on, Ketty. This is where you show him what you can do.

"Sir, we're ready. The connector is in place. All we need now is the hose."

"Send the teams back, Lead Recruit. You and Steadman, stay where you are, but send the others back to me."

"Yes, Sir." I cut the connection.

"Listen up!" I shout into the woods. "You're needed back at the farmyard. Head back, and wait for instructions. Steadman – you're with me."

The other members of my team jog away with the soldiers, back towards the house. Steadman and I make a start at putting equipment back into the crates.

I realise I'm laughing to myself. In a few minutes, we'll have them. We'll be sending our poison into the bunker, and there will be nothing they can do to protect themselves. The feeling of power hits me again. There's nothing they can do to stop us. Lee's mission will be a success, and the terrorist cell will be gone.

There's a noise from the path. I look up, to see torch beams returning. I'm about to step out and help with the hose, when I realise that the soldiers are back too soon. I haven't had an update from Lee, and there shouldn't be anyone else on the path. I wave a torch at Steadman and gesture him to move back into the woods.

I switch off my torch, hook it back on my belt, and unclip my gun. Keeping the barrel pointing downwards to hide the targeting light, I activate the power, and move towards the path as quietly as I can, challenging the PowerGel as my foot slips on the uneven ground.

The pain stays away. I take another step, testing the way ahead with my foot.

Concentrate, Ketty.

The torches are approaching. I can see figures, lit by the torch beams.

Figures in armour. Guns in combat-ready holds, rucksacks were their guns should be.

This isn't Lee's soldiers.

This is the terrorists, making their escape in the armour they stole from the coach.

Walking right past me.

Not today, kids. Not on my watch.

I step out onto the path, ahead of the quiet figures, my gun raised.

Someone at the head of the group cries out as their torch picks out my armour against the darkness of the trees, and they notice the light from my gun. Everyone stumbles to a halt.

I look at the figures in front of me. It's hard to tell in the dark, but I think some of these are kids. I think these are my recruits, and their new friends. Not many of them, but that works for me.

Maybe Lee will get his prisoners after all.

And maybe I can be the one to bring them in.

I take a deep breath, and give my best parade-ground yell.

"Tiny fighters!"

There's a gasp from the figure in the lead, and I'm dazzled for a second by a torch beam playing over my face.

Take a good look, recruit. Understand who is standing between you and escape.

A torch beam flashes across the lead figure's face. His visor's up, like mine, to make it easier to see in the dark. I watch as he blinks, staring at me.

It's Taylor.

Perfect.

I feel as if I'm back at Camp Bishop. I know who's in charge here, and so does he.

I give him a recruit-scaring grin.

"Always a pleasure, Recruit Taylor. What have you got for me today? Insults and insubordination? Crying with a side of begging?" I crane my neck to look at the armoured figures huddled on the path behind him. "Have you brought me some friends to play with?"

He raises his gun and points it at my chest.

I run a quick head count. Twelve of them. One of me. But Taylor is the only one with his gun raised. If these are the guns from the coach, then they're only using training bullets. I'll be safe in my armour.

Your move, Recruit.

There's the sound of a twig snapping in the woods next to me, and from the corner of my eye I see the light on Steadman's gun barrel come on. He steps away from me, back along the path, and fires a warning shot over the heads of the group behind Taylor.

There are shouts and screams, and the group starts to move, running past me and Taylor towards the lake. I aim into the air and pull my trigger, and the confusion spreads.

Stay in control. Stay calm.

Steadman starts to call for help on the radio. The others run past us, but Taylor stands, gun aimed at my chest, unaffected by the panic. When torch beams touch his face, his expression is cold, determined. Chilling.

Big, brave Taylor. Go on then.

Steadman steps out onto the path behind him. Taylor takes a step towards me, and Steadman fires. His shot grazes Taylor's shoulder, and splinters of shattered armour spring up from the impact.

Afraid yet, Recruit?

Taylor stumbles forward. I step back, and he pulls the trigger as he stands up.

Three shots.

Three times, he sends bullets towards me.

Crack. A bullet thuds into the ground next to my foot.

Step back.

Crack. A bullet grazes the armour on my right calf.

Another step.

Crack. A bullet whistles past my knee.

There's a tiny sound, where the bullet touches something as it passes.

I look down, distracted, while Steadman fires again, and Taylor turns his fall into a run, pushing past me and following his friends along the path.

There's shouting from behind me, but something is wrong with my knee, and I can't turn round.

Move, Ketty.

I'm frozen, and I don't understand what Taylor has done. Everything is happening in slow motion.

Taylor is shouting, and other voices are joining in. I stare at Steadman, in front of me on the path, and I watch as the chest panel of his armour dents twice, and then explodes. He staggers backwards, tripping as he goes down, and falls away between the trees. The sound of gunfire is loud in my ears, but I'm not processing things properly. I'm not paying attention.

The pain is back.

And it's the pain that saves me.

My knee lights up with all the damage I've done this week. All the pushing and testing and training I've made myself do, so I could be here tonight. So I could stop the kids from getting away. A ball of white light pushes its way outwards from the centre of the dead PowerGel, and I stagger forwards. My right leg can't support me, and I pitch over onto the path, my gun still held in a combat grip.

My chin hits the ground, and my neck twists. There's blood in my mouth, and my hands are still on my gun as my nose bounces off the floor.

I'm trying not to scream.

Bullets are snapping past me, Taylor and his friends aiming much too high to hit me, now that I'm on the ground.

Move. Get off the path.

I let go of my gun with one hand, and focus on getting myself into the trees. At first I can't move, then I think about the barbed wire tunnels on the assault course, and I know I can do this. I start to drag myself forward with my fingers while pushing with my left foot. My right leg drags behind me, carrying a white-hot flame in my knee.

Keep moving.

I can't drag myself and carry the gun. I pause, lift the rifle, and throw it into the trees. Then I'm back into the rhythm again, pushing and pulling myself over the rough ground.

The bullets have stopped. Torch beams play over the tree trunks above my head, but I'm on the ground in black armour. Once I'm off the path, I freeze, clenching my fists against the pain.

You're safe, Ketty. Keep your head down.

There's angry shouting from the path behind me.

Taylor.

"Let me go! Let me find her. I'm going to kill her. I'm going to put a bullet in her."

Another voice.

"Jake, come on. We're done here. We need to keep going."

"Let me *go!*"

"We're making too much noise, Jake. We need to stay quiet. We need to move on."

Move on, Taylor. Walk away.

Someone is crying, and shouting at the same time.

"Jake! No more! No more shooting. We can still get away."

Brown.

And I realise that if they've made it out of the bunker, they came out through the gatehouse. They've seen what happened. They know about Sleepy.

And Amy's the one holding Jake back.

I'm lying, flat on my face in the woods. I've lost my gun. My knee feels as if it's tearing itself apart from the inside, and when the adrenaline wears off I'm going to start screaming.

And Taylor wants to kill me.

He's a few meters away, armed and angry, and he's not using training ammunition. I replay what happened to Steadman. Taylor has armour-piercing rounds in his rifle – his bullets will slice right through my suit. All he has to do is find me.

And I'm alone.

Steadman's gone. Jackson's gone. Bracken and Lee might as well be on the other side of the world. All I can do is stay down, and stay quiet.

Every instinct I have tells me to turn and fight, but without my PowerGel, I'm useless. I can't even stand up. I can't get to safety, and I can't eliminate the threat. He's behind me, and I can't see him. I'm cowering like a child, waiting for his bullets to rip me apart. I'm vulnerable again. I'm an easy target, and this time I don't have a gun.

My heart is exploding in my chest. Cold sweat beads on my face, and I'm breathing too fast. My fists are clenched tight, waiting for the bullet.

This is fear. This is the worst feeling in the world.

I've seen defeat in other people's eyes, but never in my own. I think about Dad at the kitchen table, kitchen knife within reach, begging me to stay. I think about Ellman, surrendering to her beating. I think about Saunders. The look of surprise on his face as one of my bullets stopped his heart.

Easy. Quick. Devastating.

I think about the gun in Taylor's hands. The power he has in this moment. The power I've lost.

Make your choice, Jake. Get out, or take your shot at me. Every minute you wait, every minute you argue, is a minute you could spend walking away.

You could get out of here tonight, or you could throw away your advantage and come after me.

Live or die. Your decision. There is nothing I can do.

I close my eyes, and dig my fingers into the carpet of pine needles. I wait, my pulse pounding in my ears.

I feel as if I'm waiting forever.

Then the voices fade. The torch beams disappear. I'm on my own in the dark.

For a moment, all I can do is breathe. I let myself relax, push the tension out of my muscles. Take deep breaths and wait for my heartbeat to slow.

I'm alive.

But I can't stay here, face down in the dirt. I'm too close to the path, and I need to watch for movement. I need to face whoever comes this way. Twelve people can't be the whole terrorist cell. There will be more of them coming. I'm an easy target, here – I need to get further into the woods. I need to give myself a chance.

Move, Ketty.

I pull myself deeper into the trees, the pain in my knee growing with every movement. Away from the path, I pause for breath and force myself to roll over and sit up, my back against a tree trunk. My knee is screaming for attention, but I make myself reach for the torch at my belt.

And it's gone. Dropped somewhere between here and the path. I've lost my torch, I've lost my gun. And I've lost my PowerGel.

No time for self-pity. Concentrate. Figure out what's wrong.

I reach down and gently touch the edge of my knee. There's a tear in the stretch panel of the armour, and through into the base layer. I can feel the PowerGel fabric under my fingers. I poke gently at the exposed layer, but it's whole. No damage. I run my fingers up and down the fabric, trying to understand what's broken.

And then I find the clip. Where the battery pack should be, I find broken shards of plastic. The batteries are gone. There's no power to the gel.

There's nothing between me and the pain.

I can't help screaming. I bite down on my knuckles to stifle the noise, but the frustration and the overwhelming, nauseating pain is too much for me.

I can't believe this is happening.

I need to call for help.

I don't want to tell Lee I've screwed up, but I can't walk back on my own.

Call it in Ketty. Call for backup.

And then there's a voice on the radio.

"Ketty, where are you?" Bracken. He sounds panicked. "We've got a situation here ..."

I'm trying to think through the pain. I'm trying to understand.

Lee's voice cuts across Bracken's, louder, into my earpiece.

"Abort, Lead Recruit! Abort! Contamination protocol – we have nerve agent in the air. Repeat, we have nerve agent in the air."

Concentrate, Ketty.

I'm too busy pulling down my visor and starting my air supply to respond to Lee's command.

"Lead Recruit! Get yourselves back here. Visors down, oxygen on. We have a contamination event in progress."

I switch on the private channel transmitter, but Lee is still shouting.

"Lead Recruit! Respond! Get yourselves back here!"

"Can't Sir." It's all I can manage as I try to focus.

"Report, Lead Recruit."

Tell him, Ketty. Tell him you've failed.

"Shot, Sir. PowerGel damaged."

There's a pause, and Lee swears.

"Steadman. Send Steadman back."

"Steadman's gone, Sir. Steadman's dead."

Another, longer pause.

Breathe, Ketty.

"Lead Recruit, are you reporting enemy contact?"

Breathe. Tell him what happened.

"Yes, Sir. Twelve people, including recruits. They're gone, Sir. We lost them."

"Lead Recruit, stay where you are."

I can't help laughing. The motion pulls my knee, and it turns into a gasp of pain.

"I can do that, Sir."

And he's gone.

There's a moment of silence before my radio starts up again. Bracken's voice. Shouting.

"Katrina Smith – are you *working* with this man?"

There is fury in his voice, and disbelief.

Just what I need right now.

I take a calming breath.

Careful, Ketty.

"What man, Sir?"

"Are you working with Lee?" He bellows into the radio.

I let out a long sigh. I can't deal with this.

"Sir …"

"Straight question, Ketty. Yes or no."

"Yes, Sir."

"And are you working *for* me or *against* me?"

My mind is foggy. I'm trying to find the right words, but all I can think about is the pain.

"I'm working for both of you, Sir."

"What does that mean?"

Say something. Convince him.

"I'm trying to make this operation a success."

He makes a disgusted noise, and cuts the connection. I reach for my glove, and activate it again.

"Sir ..."

"After everything I've done to get you here!"

I shake my head. I can't do this now. I can't do this here.

Tell him, Ketty.

"Sir, I need help."

His tone changes. There's a note of concern in his voice.

"Where are you? What's going on?"

"In the woods, Sir. I've been shot. The PowerGel's not working, and I can't move. I need help."

He sounds angry again.

"You'll have to wait, Ketty. We've got enough going on here. We can't run an ambulance service."

It feels as if he's thrown a punch.

"Commander ..." I can feel the tears starting. The exhaustion kicking in, as the adrenaline fades and the pain keeps growing. It feels as if my knee is exploding, blood and bone crashing out from the inside. I've pushed myself to be here. I've worked and trained for both these men. I'm here because Lee will send me home if I refuse, and because Bracken needs me.

Bracken needs me. And he's leaving me here in the dark.

"You will wait!"

And he cuts the connection again.

Home

When they come for me, the sky is already light. I've been in and out of consciousness, blacking out, then coming to. I don't know how much time has passed.

A medic arrives, and two soldiers to carry the stretcher. He gives me a shot of something that makes the pain float away, and I watch the tops of the trees pass overhead as they carry me back to the farmyard.

The terrorists have gone.

When they broke in, the bunker was empty. Stores, food, personal belongings, but no people. They think the rest of the terrorists walked out, ten meters from where I was sitting, and vanished into the dark.

The body count is three to one. We lost Steadman, and our guards at the gatehouse – that's where Taylor picked up his armour-piercing bullets. They lost Saunders, and we don't know what happened to their gatehouse guard. We've gained two prisoners – the women from the farmhouse – and some of our guns and armour. They'd sprayed it black, to look like professional armour, and leaving it out to dry let the trackers broadcast overnight.

I'm back at Camp Bishop. Webb changes my bandage twice a day, and keeps me on a morphine drip, but he doesn't speak to me. No one is letting me out of bed, and I couldn't walk if I tried. My knee is twisted and broken, and I'm going to need months of rest and therapy before I use it again.

I'm angry. I'm frustrated. And I'm in constant pain.

My PowerGel is beyond repair, and there's been no word from Brigadier Lee on getting me a new unit. No mysterious deliveries. No more flowers. He knows what this means for me, and how much pain I'm in, and he's leaving me here without comment. I guess he doesn't need to explain.

No one else wants to let me loose with a PowerGel again until I allow my knee to heal on its own.

I did what I had to do. I'll get fit again. This will not finish me.

It's a warm day, and the windows in my room are open. I can hear the kids training outside on the field, Miller shouting instructions at them.

Miller, Camp Bishop's new Lead Recruit. I still roll my eyes every time someone calls him that.

Learning to be tough, yet, techie boy?

"Recruit Smith!" Bracken puts his head round the door. "How are we today?"

"Sir. Good, Sir."

Same as any other day. Stuck in a hospital bed.

He's come to update me on Brigadier Lee. Lee, who hasn't spoken to me since the night at the Farm. Who blames me for the escape of the terrorists, and the failure to break into the bunker. Who hasn't forgiven Bracken for salvaging the mission and bringing home two prisoners, including the one we lost. For not hanging himself. For getting another chance from HQ.

He sits down next to my bed.

"I've persuaded him," he says, and watches my face for a reaction.

I can't hide my relief.

"So he's not sending me home?"

He smiles. "I convinced him that would be a waste of a good officer. He's not happy, but he's letting you stay."

"Thank you, Sir. You won't regret it."

"I'd better not." He puts a hand on my arm. "I think you're better than that, Ketty. I don't think you'll pull anything stupid like that again. I know what he threatened you with, and I know what the stakes were for you. Next time, come to me first?"

I nod. "Yes, Sir."

"You have my word. When my promotion comes through, you're coming too. If I'm going to London, I want you with me."

Because you need my help, or because I know too much?

I smile. "Are you sure you wouldn't rather take Miller? Surely your Lead Recruit has first refusal on a promotion?"

Bracken smiles back. "I think Miller has some learning to do first. You know he still uses your name to get the recruits to behave? One day you're going to have to go out there and shout at them, just so he doesn't lose all his credibility." He pauses, and shakes his head. "He doesn't know me as well as you do, Ketty. I can't … trust him, the way I trust you." He sounds grateful. He sounds frightened. He gives me a half-smile, and briefly tightens his grip on my arm.

And I realise the truth. Bracken needs me, and I need Bracken.

This is my team. This is where I choose to stay.

I nod. "I'll bear that in mind, Sir."

"And Ketty? We have some news on the terrorists."

Tracking

They've been walking for days. We've caught sight of them on CCTV cameras here and there, but we've always been too late to pick them up. They're heading north, and HQ wants to know where they're going.

So we let them walk.

We can't catch them, but we've got the prisoners from the farmhouse to work with instead. It's not what Lee wanted. It's not what any of us wanted.

And while they walk, I'm confined to a hospital room. I put everything I had into getting myself fit for that night, and I nearly lost everything when I confronted my recruits on the path – recruits who are supposed to be afraid of me.

I'm useless, I'm broken, my career's on hold, but I'm alive. I'm still here, I'm still in uniform, I'm still fighting, and Bracken is fighting with me.

It's not what I wanted.

But maybe it's enough for today.

Note

Alcoholism is not a weakness – these are Ketty's words, not mine, and they come from her unique understanding of her childhood experiences. Addiction in any form is acknowledged to be an illness, not a choice. I do not advocate treating alcoholism as a weakness, any more than I intend to present Ketty as a perfect role model.

**Darkest Hour
(Battle Ground #3)
is available now from Amazon.**

Keep reading for a preview!

Chapter 1: Dreams

Bex

We're shifting boxes again. The morning delivery is in, and Dan and I are stacking the goods in the store room. Neesh is taking the delivery – we're staying out of sight. Our pictures are all over the news again, and we can't risk anyone seeing us. We've been doing this for weeks, and we've turned it into a slick operation. No more asking where each item goes. No more stacking stuff in the wrong place. We know what to do and we put our heads down and get on with it. The sooner we're done here, the sooner we can have breakfast and figure out what else needs doing today.

Someone slams the delivery truck doors, and there's the sound of the engine starting up. The truck drives away, and Neesh walks back inside.

"All clear, you two. Thanks for making a start on this. There's a couple of pallets outside the door – can you handle the rest?"

Dan assures her that we've got it in hand, and she heads back to the shop.

I stand up and lean backwards, stretching and straightening my spine. Dan rolls his shoulders and leans against a stack of boxes.

"You OK, Bex?"

"Yeah. Just aching from the heavy lifting."

He shakes his head. "That's not what I meant."

I turn to look at him, at the look of concern on his face.

"I didn't, did I?"

"Twice. Woke us all up with the screaming, but when Charlie checked on you, you were still asleep."

I can feel the blush rising on my face. "I'm so sorry …"

"Don't be. It's not your fault. We just … we worry about you."

I nod. "Yeah. Thanks." I lean against the boxes, next to him.

"Was it Saunders?" He asks, gently.

I have to think for a moment. What was I dreaming about last night? Which nightmare woke everyone up this time?

"I think so. Saunders and Margie. Leaving people behind."

It's always about leaving people behind. Jake, Amy, Saunders, Margie, Dr Richards. There's always someone I can't take with me. There's always someone I can't save, and it is deeply, horribly upsetting. Sometimes it's people I know are OK, and I think I'm losing them, too. I've dreamt about Dan before, and Mum and Dad. People I could still lose. People who could still suffer from my mistakes.

Dan puts a hand on my arm.

"Come on. The truck's gone. Let's get some fresh air."

My hands are shaking as we walk back to the loading bay. Dan grabs two hoodies from the hook next to the door, and we put them on, pulling the hoods up to hide our faces. Bright lime green, with 'Morgana Wholefoods' printed across the back, the hoodies aren't subtle, but most people will be paying attention to the colour rather than the people wearing them.

We step outside. The service road is empty, so no one will notice if we're not working. The sun is just rising, and the clouds are streaked in orange and pink, with deep, purple shadows. It's beautiful, and it's wonderful to be able to stand in the open air, just for a moment.

*****

I start climbing the stairs back to the flat. Dan cracks open the back door of the shop and gives Neesh a wave, keeping his face hidden, and she waves back. The delivery is stacked. The pallets are leaning against the wall, the hoodies are back on the hook, and we've closed the shutters on the loading bay. Time for breakfast.

Charlie lets us in, toothbrush held between her teeth as she negotiates the locks on the door.

"How'd it go?"

"Good."

"You thirsty? Kettle's on." She grins, and waves a hand at the kitchen as she walks back to the bathroom. "Mine's a tea, thanks!"

I close the door and reset the locks, then follow Dan into the kitchen. He's pulling mugs and teabags from the cupboard, so I lean into the fridge and pull out the milk. The fridge shakes as I push the door closed with my knee, and the biscuit tin on top rattles.

The biscuit tin that holds two handguns and a pile of bullets. Our desperate attempt at buying ourselves a last stand, if the government tracks us down.

I take the milk to Dan.

Amy walks in, still in pyjamas, still yawning. She walks over to me and gives me a warm hug. When she pulls back, I see that her eyes are puffy and red.

"Was it Joss? The dreams?"

"Yeah." I nod, closing my eyes. Amy's the only one who knew Saunders' first name. In all the time I knew him, I never thought to ask.

She hugs me again, and this time I hug her back.

"We'll get through this, Bex," she whispers. "It's not your fault."

*****

We didn't talk about the night at the bunker. Not until we got here. Not until we felt safe again.

On our long walk north, each of us lived with what had happened alone. We walked. We split up to walk through towns, we joined up again on quiet country roads. We slept under bridges and in disused buildings. We kept ourselves out of sight, and we kept walking, putting more miles between us and the farm. Between us and Saunders, who died protecting his friends. Protecting us.

We didn't have a destination in mind. We just wanted to get away. I thought we might cross the border into Scotland, but we realised it would be too dangerous to try. The guards on our side of the border would catch us, and we'd be handcuffed and sent to London for questioning. Used to get to the people who took us in.

But someone was watching. Another resistance cell tracked our progress, and when they had the chance, they picked us up and brought us here. At first, we thought we'd been found, that the government had tracked us down. Two cars pulled up, blocking the country lane, and when we turned back, two more drove up and stopped behind us. We all reached for the guns, buried in our backpacks, but before we could get to them we were surrounded. The rebels searched our bags, and questioned us at gunpoint until they were happy with our story, then they bundled us into their cars and drove us to Newcastle. Not Scotland, but far enough away from Makepeace Farm to offer us some comfort.

Neesh's health food business is the front for their operation. The money they make subsidises their safe houses. Five of us share the top-floor flat above the shop. Neesh lives in the flat downstairs, and Jo and the others from the bunker are in other safe houses, elsewhere in the city. We work when we can, and we do what we can to help – but our faces are on the news, and on Wanted posters across the country, so we're mostly stuck in the loading bay and the flat. The hoodies are useful, but we can only use them in the service road, out of sight of the street.

So we learn to live together, in each other's pockets. We learn to do what Neesh and Caroline ask us to do. And we try to ignore the locks on the door, and the handguns in the kitchen. I don't want to think about what happens if we're traced here. I think the nightmares will seem tame if we have to fight, trapped in our tiny safe house. And I don't want to lose anyone else.

*****

"You know what we need?" Dan pushes away his empty cup, and stands up.

Amy laughs. "You think you're the king of this kitchen, don't you?"

"I am!" Dan puffs out his chest in mock offence.

We're crowded round the small table – two chairs, a kitchen stool and a couple of packing crates to sit on. Charlie's come back to drink her tea, and Jake snuck in while no one was watching.

Dan walks to the fridge and throws open the door, and looks upset when we drown out his announcement by shouting over him.

"Sandwiches!"

"Breakfast sandwiches," he corrects us. "Bacon and sausages and eggs and … what else do we have?"

He peers into the fridge, and starts pulling out packets and boxes, passing them behind him without looking. Amy and I jump up and ferry the ingredients to the worksurface, and then we're all helping. Opening, chopping, mixing, frying, while Dan stands behind us, slicing bread at the table.

I find I'm blinking back tears. I don't know what I'd do without these people. They're holding me together, after the camp and the bunker. After Ketty and Jackson and Bracken. They're reminding me that I haven't lost everyone. That I can still get up in the morning, eat sandwiches with Dan, be useful to the group, laugh, watch the sunrise.

That this didn't end with Saunders. That we're still walking.

Chapter 2: Promotion

Ketty

Early meeting this morning, so I'm up and out of the tiny rooftop flat by seven, checking my khaki Service Uniform in the mirror by the door before I leave. After a week in the job, I still can't resist a smile at the Corporal stripes – Brigadier Lee might want to leave me as an RTS Senior Recruit, but someone else in the Home Forces wants me and Bracken in London. No argument from me – I'm out of the Recruit Training Service, I'm out of Camp Bishop, and I'm not going to waste this promotion. I just need to keep *Colonel* Bracken sober enough to do his job.

Down five flights of stairs, painkillers and the elastic support bandage on my knee controlling the limp in my stride, and out onto the street. It's a short walk to the office at the Home Forces Building, and I want to be at my desk before Bracken gets in, ready with coffee and this morning's briefing. There's a chill in the air as I walk, and the thin slice of sky between the buildings is striped with orange clouds. It takes getting used to after life at camp, this feeling of being hemmed in by buildings. No training fields and woodland here. No one to train, and no one to discipline, either. No Lead Recruit job. I'm at the bottom of the ladder in London, and so is Bracken, but if we work together we can climb our way up.

At the end of the street I wait for a bus to drive past, then cross the road to the HQ building. I flash my pass at the door, walk through the scanner, and wait while the guard checks my gun and searches my bag. The document case is hardly large enough to smuggle anything into the building, but it gives the guards something to do every morning. I push the gun back into the holster on my belt and pick up the bag.

Past the lifts and up three flights of stairs, pushing my knee and building the strength back up. I will not be limping forever, and the more I use the muscles, the stronger they get. I push the pain to the back of my mind and keep climbing, one step after another.

Bracken's outer office has space for a desk, a chair and a filing cabinet on one side, and a leather-upholstered bench on the other. There's a map hanging over the bench – strategic locations across England, Wales, and Northern Ireland; Scottish border posts; ports, roads, and rail links. Major towns are marked, and there's a grey shaded area where Leominster used to be. Behind the chair, there's a window that looks out onto a narrow light well, and a view of other office windows. Everything in here is old – the worn dark green carpet, the dark wood furniture, the vertical blinds at the window – and there's a dusty smell that never goes away.

But it's better than a hut in a field, and a flat of my own is better than the Senior Dorm and the Medical Centre. Doctor Webb isn't here to hand me crutches every time I stand up, and I don't need Woods' permission to talk to Bracken. I'm Bracken's assistant now, and I get to decide who comes in, and who gets sent away. It's also up to me to keep him sober, brief him with what he needs to know, and get him to meetings on time.

I drop the document case on the desk, and head out down the corridor to the coffee machine. I put two cups of coffee on a tray, and stop at the document drop on the way back to the office. The Private on duty hands me Bracken's briefing folder, and I carry everything back to my desk.

Before I check the documents, I pick up the phone and dial a number I know by heart.

"Nevill Hall Hospital, High Dependency Ward."

"Corporal Ketty Smith, calling about Liam Jackson. Do you have an update for me?"

There's a pause while the nurse rustles some papers.

Come on, Jackson. Pull out of this. Don't let the terrorists beat you.

"Sorry Corporal – no change. He's stable, but there's no improvement."

"You'll call me if he wakes up?"

"It's on his file, Corporal. We'll let you know." She sounds impatient, like the nurses every morning.

"Thank you," I say, and hang up, as I do every morning.

*****

When Bracken arrives, the paperwork is ready and I've finished my coffee. Not long to go before his first meeting of the day, so I need to make sure he's briefed and alert. I give him a few minutes to hide his whisky bottle in the filing cabinet, then let myself in and put his coffee down in front of him.

"Thank you, Ketty. Have a seat. What's waiting for us today?"

He looks exhausted. With one elbow on the desk and his forehead resting on the fingers of his hand, he looks as if he's shading his eyes from the light in the office.

"Coffee, Sir," I say, jokingly, indicating the cup with my pen. "And then a meeting with the big boss."

Sober up, Sir. I need you to do your job.

He takes a sip of coffee and makes a face. "That's today, is it?"

I make a show of checking my watch. "In about ten minutes, Sir."

He sits upright in his chair. "Right. Right. So what do I need to know?"

"The agenda says you're talking about tracking the terrorists. Specifically Ellman and her friends from the bunker." He nods, and drinks more coffee. "And then there's the prisoners. Questioning of William Richards and some of his co-conspirators. And there's still the mystery of the women from Makepeace Farm." I look up. "Apparently they haven't responded to interrogation yet."

He raises an eyebrow. "Tough women," he says, with a note of respect in his voice.

Very.

I remember the prisoner at Camp Bishop. How she sat in silence and looked right through me, even after Jackson and I had used our fists to persuade her to talk. If her friend is anything like as tolerant of persuasion, it could be a while before we learn who they are, and what they know.

"What's the latest on the bunker group?"

"Still missing, Sir. No trace of them after we tracked them through Skipton." I flick through the papers. "Some rumoured sightings of Ellman and Pearce, but none near their last known position, and none together. Ellman's been reported in Kendal, Durham, and …" I look again at the report. "… Margate."

"That seems unlikely. They were heading north from Makepeace."

"Yes, Sir. And there are reported sightings of Pearce in Birmingham, and from agents in Edinburgh."

Bracken shrugs. "So we haven't found them yet."

"No, Sir. But we've got units on alert all over the country. It's only a matter of time."

He drinks the last of his coffee. "Anything else I need to know?"

"It says here that the interrogation of William Richards is scheduled for this week." He nods. "Can I assume that we'll have access to the recordings?"

"I'm going to push for access to the interrogation, live. I want to see what he's hiding."

"Very good, Sir." I can't keep the smile from my face. "That would be useful to know."

Bracken pulls a notepad from his desk drawer and pushes a pen into his breast pocket. He looks up at me again.

"And Jackson?"

I shake my head. "No change, Sir. Thank you for asking."

*****

We make it to the meeting on time. Major General Franks' meeting room has a large table, and a view of the London Eye across the Thames. It's a reminder of her place at the head of the Home Forces, and ours as new arrivals. I send Bracken in with his paperwork, and take a seat in the corridor outside. As the assistant of the lowest-ranking officer present, I'm the runner for this meeting. Runner, guard, message carrier. Whatever they need.

I'm making myself comfortable when Franks marches out of the room. I jump to my feet and salute.

"Corporal Smith. At ease."

"Sir."

She holds out her hand for me to shake. Her grip is firm and confident, and she's smiling. She's an older woman, slim and athletic, with short-cropped silver hair and an air of relaxed authority.

"Welcome to London," she says. "We're very pleased to have you and the Colonel working for us. I've pushed to bring you here – I think you can offer us some unique insights into our missing terrorists. Help us track them down. I gather you knew some of them personally, at Camp Bishop?"

"Yes, Sir. I was the Lead Recruit."

She raises an eyebrow. "So you taught them everything they know?" She laughs. "I'm sure your insights will be invaluable to our investigation. You've briefed Colonel Bracken?"

I nod. "I have, Sir."

She lowers his voice to a stage whisper. "And does he need coffee this morning, Corporal?"

I keep my face neutral. "Another cup wouldn't hurt, Sir."

She smiles again, and winks at me. "Keep him on his feet for us, Corporal Smith. We're going to need you both if we're going to find your missing recruits. There's a place on the Terrorism Committee for him if he can show some progress."

And she turns and walks back into the meeting room.

So that's my job here. Keep Bracken sober, and give you profiles of the kids we lost.

Consider it done.

The Battle Ground series

The Battle Ground series is set in a dystopian near-future UK, after Brexit and Scottish independence.

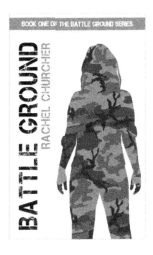

Book 1: Battle Ground

Sixteen-year-old Bex Ellman has been drafted into an army she doesn't support and a cause she doesn't believe in. Her plan is to keep her head down, and keep herself and her friends safe – until she witnesses an atrocity that she can't ignore, and a government conspiracy that threatens lives all over the UK. With her loyalties challenged, Bex must decide who to fight for – and who to leave behind.

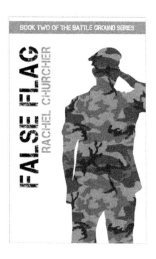

Book 2: False Flag

Ketty Smith is an instructor with the Recruit Training Service, turning sixteen-year-old conscripts into government fighters. She's determined to win the job of lead instructor at Camp Bishop, but the arrival of Bex and her friends brings challenges she's not ready to handle. Running from her own traumatic past, Ketty faces a choice: to make a stand, and expose a government conspiracy, or keep herself safe, and hope she's working for the winning side.

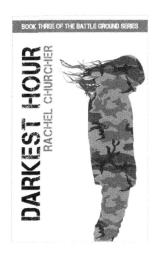

Book 3: Darkest Hour

Bex Ellman and Ketty Smith are fighting on opposite sides in a British civil war. Bex and her friends are in hiding, but when Ketty threatens her family, Bex learns that her safety is more fragile than she thought.

Book 4: Fighting Back

Bex Ellman and her friends are in hiding, sheltered by the resistance. With her family threatened and her friendships challenged, she's looking for a way to fight back. Ketty Smith is in London, supporting a government she no longer trusts. With her support network crumbling, Ketty must decide who she is fighting for – and what she is willing risk to uncover the truth.

Book 5: Victory Day

Bex Ellman and Ketty Smith meet in London. As the war heats up around them, Bex and Ketty must learn to trust each other. With her friends and family in danger, Bex needs Ketty to help rescue them. For Ketty, working with Bex is a matter of survival. When Victory is declared, both will be held accountable for their decisions.

Book 6: Balancing Act

Corporal David Conrad has life figured out. His job gives him power, control, and access to Top Secret operations. His looks have tempted plenty of women into his bed, and he has no intention of committing to a relationship.

When Ketty Smith joins the Home Forces, Conrad sets his sights on the new girl – but pursuing Ketty will be more dangerous than he realises. Is Conrad about to meet his match? And will the temptations of his job distract him from his target?

Balancing Act revisits the events of *Darkest Hour*, *Fighting Back*, and *Victory Day*. **The story is suitable for older teens.**

Book 7: Finding Fire and Other Stories

What happened between Margie and Dan at Make-peace Farm? How did Jackson really feel about Ketty? What happens next to the survivors of the Battle Ground Series?

Step behind the scenes of the series with six new short stories and five new narrators – Margie, Jackson, Maz, Dan, and Charlie – plus bonus blogs and insights from the author.

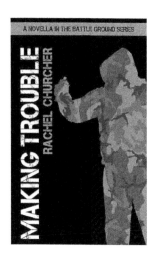

Novella: Making Trouble

Fifteen-year-old Topher Mackenzie has a complicated life. His Mum is in Australia, his Dad is struggling to look after him, and Auntie Charlie is the only person who understands. When his girlfriend is forced to leave the UK after a racist attack, Topher faces a choice: accept the government's lies, or find a way to fight back.

Download FREE from freebook.tallerbooks.com

Acknowledgements

The Battle Ground series represents two years of hard work – not just for me, but for the people who have supported me and helped to make it happen.

A huge thank you is due to my amazing proofreaders, who have given up their time to read every book and send me helpful and insightful feedback. Thank you to Alan Platt, Holly Platt Wells, Reba Sigler, Joe Silber, and Reynard Spiess.

Thank you to my *False Flag* beta readers, Jasmine Bruce, Diana Churcher, James Keen, and Karen MacLaughlin, for encouragement and insightful comments.

Thank you to all the people who have given me advice on the road to publication: Tim Dedopulos, Salomé Jones, Rob Manser, John Pettigrew, Danielle Zigner, and Jericho Writers.

Thank you to everyone at NaNoWriMo, for giving me the opportunity and the tools to start writing, and to everyone at YALC for inspiration and advice.

Thank you to my amazing designer, Medina Karic, for deciphering my sketches and notes and turning them into beautiful book covers. If you ever need a designer, find her at www.fiverr.com/milandra.

Thank you to Alan Platt, for learning the hard way how to live with a writer, and for bringing your start-up expertise to the creation of Taller Books.

Thank you to Alex Bate, Janina Ander, and Helen Lynn, for encouraging me to write *Battle Ground* when I suddenly had time on my hands, and for introducing me to Prosecco Fridays. Cheers!

Thank you to Hannah Pollard and the Book Club Galz for sharing so many wonderful YA books with me – and for understanding that the book is *always* better than the film.

Special mention goes to the Peatbog Faeries, whose album *Faerie Stories* is the ultimate cure for writer's block. The soundtrack to *The Greatest Showman*, and Lady Antebellum's *Need You Now*, are my go-to albums for waking up and feeling energised to write, even on the hardest days.

This book is dedicated to Alan, who has lived with me for more than 20 years, and understands 'write what you know'.

About the Author

Rachel Churcher was born between the last manned moon landing, and the first orbital Space Shuttle mission. She remembers watching the launch of STS-1, and falling in love with space flight, at the age of five. She fell in love with science fiction shortly after that, and in her teens she discovered dystopian fiction. In an effort to find out what she wanted to do with her life, she collected degrees and other qualifications in Geography, Science Fiction Studies, Architectural Technology, Childminding, and Writing for Radio.

She has worked as an editor on national and in-house magazines; as an IT trainer; and as a freelance writer and artist. She has renovated several properties, and has plenty of horror stories to tell about dangerous electrics and nightmare plumbers. She enjoys reading, travelling, stargazing, and eating good food with good friends – but nothing makes her as happy as writing fiction.

Her first published short story appeared in an anthology in 2014, and the Battle Ground series is her first long-form work. Rachel lives in East Anglia, in a house with a large library and a conservatory full of house plants. She would love to live on Mars, but only if she's allowed to bring her books.

Follow **RachelChurcherWriting** on Instagram and GoodReads.

DOWNLOAD A FREE BOOK IN THE BATTLE GROUND SERIES!

Fifteen-year-old Topher Mackenzie has a complicated life.
His Mum is in Australia, his Dad is struggling to look after him,
and Auntie Charlie is the only person who understands.
When his girlfriend is forced to leave the UK after a racist attack,
Topher faces a choice: accept the government's lies,
or find a way to fight back.

Making Trouble takes place before the events of *Battle Ground*,
and can be read at any point in the series.

FREEBOOK.TALLERBOOKS.COM

Printed in Great Britain
by Amazon